LOVE & VIRTUE

LOVE &

VIRTUE

DIANA REID

First published in Great Britain in 2022 by Trapeze,
an imprint of The Orion Publishing Group Ltd
Carmelite House, 50 Victoria Embankment,
London EC4Y 0DZ

An Hachette UK company

1 3 5 7 9 10 8 6 4 2

First published in the Australia in 2021 by Ultimo Press
an imprint of Hardie Grant Publishing

A CIP catalogue record for this book is
available from the British Library.

ISBN (Hardback) 978 1 3987 0642 2
ISBN (Export Trade Paperback) 978 1 3987 0643 9
ISBN (eBook) 978 1 3987 0645 3
ISBN (Audio) 978 1 3987 0646 0

Typeset by Born Group

Printed and bound in Great Britain by Clays Ltd, Elcograf S.p.A.

www.orionbooks.co.uk

For my parents

There is no creature whose inward being is so strong that it is not greatly determined by what lies outside of it.

— GEORGE ELIOT

Middlemarch

Many wish not so much to be, as to seem to be, endowed with real virtue.

— MARCUS TULLIUS CICERO

Laelius de Amicitia

PROLOGUE

IN A BASEMENT bar on a university campus, a boy and a girl hold each other, their limbs loose with alcohol.

The dance floor hums and throbs around them. But the laughter and the phone camera flashes and the hands that reach around to clap his back are elsewhere—far away from their tongue-fumbling embrace. His hands cup her bottom, which feels pert and perfect, and his rising erection bumps her where their hips meet.

For a moment they pull apart. The boy is wearing a cap, which the girl removes. She puts it on her head backwards, because she thinks that this is a flirty, endearing thing to do. Except when she puts it on, the rim licks her forehead—wet with sweat—and she feels for the first time that the music is oppressive, and the air is choked with smoke. She puts the cap back on his head and smiles. She yells—her voice distant and empty—that she wants to go outside.

He can't hear her. He turns his ear towards her mouth and she yells again. She can almost feel the force of it reverberate, brushing back up against her lips. He nods.

They make their way through the dance floor, emerging in the courtyard, where the noise is no longer poured directly into their ears but is somehow louder. The air is clean and liberating. They feel weightless. The girl sways more. She says she wants to leave together.

They walk hand in hand to the boy's room. She takes the stairs with a wild, loping gait, and when she leans on him, he leans against the wall, because he too can barely stand.

In his room they pull at each other's clothes with an urgency they've learned from television. A few drinks ago, either one of them would have been just as happy to make out for a bit, or smoke in the courtyard, or go to 7-Eleven for a sausage roll. But now there is tugging and even sighing.

Abandon floats like debris in their drunken minds, and their world takes on a liquid reckless colour, where actions are impulsive, and tongues are down throats, and clothes are on the floor.

When the drink dissipates, the girl's senses return to her one by one.

The sight of a roof with a slow-revolving ceiling fan.

The ashen, mint-tangy taste of menthol cigarettes. She is not sure whether it's coming from his mouth or hers.

A smell both animal and chemical: the alcohol in heavy breaths sticking to unfamiliar sweat.

The slippery touch of his back, clammy beneath her hands. And pain, not sharp but steady, where he thrusts inside her.

Sound joins much later, when the heaving, sticky vacuum of the room is punctuated by a too-loud voice—her voice—that says, in an almost business-like fashion: 'I think I'm going to vomit.'

In one movement, the boy pulls out and, one knee on the bed and one foot on the floor, reaches under his desk for his metal bin. It smells like a pile of coins, and the vomit makes a clanging splash where it hits the sides.

The boy cloaks her bent and bare body in an academic gown, which hangs on the back of his door underneath a permanently damp towel. She folds into it, and he retreats under the covers, asking if she is okay.

She does not remain in his room for long. She limps out, leaning on another girl, who appears, faceless and timely like a paramedic, in her hour of need. He stays, and makes an unpopular decision to leave his bin in the hall.

The whole evening seems suspended in a giddy, consequenceless haze: a night projected on a screen, and reduced to darkness when they tumble into sleep. The clutch of their bodies, the immediacy of it all—for now—fades to black.

1

———

ALTHOUGH IT HAS been years since Eve and I were friends, I despair that I will ever shake her. This is because she has been selfish enough to take up a place, however minor, in public life. No matter how exhaustively I block her on social media, and distance myself from her friends, and avoid talking about her with mine, she refuses to live malleably in my memory. Instead, she crops up: in bookshop windows; on the Explore function on my Instagram; profiled for the weekend paper.

In photos she looks radiantly intelligent. It's her cheekbones, as I always told her. High, prominent cheekbones that assert themselves like convictions. In these photos, the kinds of photos that also appear on the jackets of her books, her face is engaged and alert, but basically passive. Like the photographer caught her when she was not quite thinking—just letting clever ideas rest in her brain.

Whenever I say I was at university with Eve, people ask me what she was like, sceptical perhaps that she could have always been as whole and self-assured as she now appears. To which I say something like: 'People are infinitely complex.' But I say it in such a way—so pregnant with misanthropy—that it's obvious I hate her.

It's a big claim, I know. To hate a person. What would Eve say? She'd be methodical, as always, starting with the universal and then moving to the particular. She'd ask: *What does it mean to hate?*

I hear her voice in my head, bouncing the idea around. I can't hate someone unless I know them intimately, she tells me. Hate is very personal. It requires care.

A thought experiment: Eve, angular face and pliant hair, crosses a road. I choose a place I know to make it as vivid as possible. The road is King Street, Newtown. Eve crosses where there is no intersection, talking to me over her shoulder as she goes. Looking at me, she doesn't see the oncoming traffic. With a thud so flat it sounds fake, she rolls up onto a car's windscreen. To my surprise, the windscreen doesn't shatter. The car, braking on impact, swerves, and the passenger side hits a streetlamp. Eve rolls, limp, back onto the bitumen. I imagine this taking place in summer, so the bitumen is hot and the smoke from the car feels like it emanates from the earth. There's crunchy glass everywhere, and, as I approach, I see it smattered across her pale chest like breadcrumbs.

How do I feel? When I see her face—that equilateral triangle of nose and chin and cheekbones—blood-specked and ravaged. *How does that make me feel?* Amid the heat and the rubbery smoke and the sirens, I'd be lying if I said that I didn't feel the tiniest flash of glee.

That I still feel so much—that her suffering thrills me, and her success cruels me; that I cannot just *get over it*, but insist instead on resenting her—it all suggests to me that, in spite of everything, I'm still a little bit in love with her.

—

EVE AND I lived on campus in our first year at university, in a residential college. Our rooms were adjacent. I was eighteen and she was twenty, which meant I was a teenager and she was not. At the time, this seemed a significant distinction.

There were several colleges on campus, but Fairfax was the only all-female one, and proudly so. A century ago, it had housed some eminent suffragettes, and it had been resting on those political laurels ever since. Its feminism operated on the level of 'Women in Medicine' and 'Women in Finance' discussion panels, always conducted in a tone of revolutionary awe, as if any combination of *women* and *profession* were still subversive.

Our rooms were on the first floor of the First Year ('Fresher') Wing: a brick octagonal structure from the seventies, which jutted out from the original Victorian building with thrusting, unapologetic ugliness. The rooms were exactly what you would expect from an institution that housed hundreds of young adults: single beds and little desks that looked like they had been stapled to the wall, and carpet brave enough to withstand whatever we might throw at it.

I heard Eve before I saw her.

My room was small, with a window that overlooked a tree and, through its leaves, the car park.

'It's very light,' I said.

My mother looked around. The glossy pamphlet that lay on the bed showed thin white women rowing, and laughing in groups, and seated at high-backed chairs in front of white tablecloths. That was the kind of sumptuous living she'd imagined for me when I'd been awarded a scholarship to Fairfax College. This room with its flimsy carpentry and bare bed—the mattress thin and inauspicious—seemed like a scene from another institution.

'Yes, well, it's typical dorm living, isn't it?' she said.

I wondered where in pop culture this *type* was situated.

She opened the wardrobe to reveal five plastic hangers. On one of them she hung my navy Fairfax College jumper. A straight-haired girl with bulbous pearl earrings had sold it to us on the lawns before we entered the building. It cost eighty dollars.

'Is it mandatory?' my mother had asked.

The girl twirled a strand of platinum hair around her finger, and I noticed she was wearing the same navy jumper draped over her shoulders like a cape. 'It's not like a uniform. But you're expected to wear it when you're representing the college.'

'Like a uniform,' my mother said.

'What?'

When my mother handed over the money, I thanked her loudly, so the girl didn't think I was the kind of adult who still expected her mum to buy her clothes.

'Of course.' She looked at me with that classic maternal half-smile, which was infuriating in how much it professed to understand. 'Of course I'll pay for your jumper.'

Now the jumper swayed on the hanger, and my mother turned back towards me. 'Listen.' She tilted her head towards the wall, her little smile the kind that usually preceded a bitchy comment.

I listened. Someone next door was playing guitar: up and down scratches of chords and a pleasant voice drizzled on top.

'You should go and introduce yourself.'

'Mum, she's playing guitar.'

'It's not the Sydney Symphony.' The smile was back. 'You can interrupt her.'

'I don't want to interrupt her.'

'Why not?'

'Everyone else is unpacking; she's having a jam. It doesn't bode well.'

'You don't know how early she got here. She might have finished her unpacking.'

I didn't know this at the time, but most people would have arrived earlier than me. Most of the college residents, including the guitarist next door, were from Sydney. This surprised me, because I would have thought that they all had places to live already, and probably with much larger bedrooms. But Fairfax wasn't 'typical dorm living': it was a community, as the glossy pamphlet would tell you.

My mother and I, on the other hand, had driven up from Canberra, leaving just after eight that morning. This was effectively a two-day affair, because the previous day had been spent packing and fighting. My mother wanted me to be prepared for any eventuality and to pack accordingly. I wanted to appear nonchalant and easygoing, which meant packing as little as possible so I might appear to be above possessions—like materialism was just something that happened to other people. Everything from thermal socks to a zany patterned shower cap was held up by my mother and dismissed by me as 'patently ridiculous' with a vitriol that shamed me. Then we sat at dinner, just the two of us, both trying to inject the scene with a sense of finality. All I felt was a heavy, schoolgirl depression—the Sunday sense of early-to-bed and waking to responsibilities.

My mother started to unpack the first of my two wheelie bags (the second being her prize in a hard-won negotiation). She pulled out *Middlemarch* (900 pages of concessions to me) and placed it on the desk. I moved it to a different spot, as if to prove she wasn't being helpful.

'What is it?' she asked.

'Nothing.'

'What?'

'I don't want to live next door to the kind of person who plays guitar by themselves.'

'It's not that loud. And you're a deep sleeper.'

'I'm not worried about the sound. I'm worried about what that says about her.'

'God, Michaela, you're so judgemental. You've got to give people a chance.'

I must have looked hurt, because her face softened. 'Are you worried about introducing yourself while your mum is hanging around? Because I'm about to leave.'

'Don't go yet,' I said, in a voice that would have been a whine if it had only been louder. Instead it was a whisper.

My mother stepped over the open wheelie bag and hugged me. 'You'll be fine,' she said, and kissed the top of my head, which made me want to cry. 'You'll make friends. Everybody always loves you.'

'That's not true,' I said. '*You* love me.'

'You'll be fine. People always surprise us.'

The singing from next door was clearer now. The guitar had been abandoned, and 'Mercedes Benz' by Janis Joplin rang unaccompanied through the wall.

My mother laughed, her shoulders shaking under my chin, where I was still enfolded in her hug. 'She does sound fucking lame,' she said.

—

THE FIRST TIME I remember actually seeing Eve, she was on stage, and I was in the audience. Of course, I probably saw her before that. I'm sure we would have swapped unremarkable remarks in the corridors.

'So you went out last night?'

'Yeah. You?'

'Yeah. Good night?'

'I think so.'

'How did you pull up?'

'A bit dusty.'

These kinds of conversations were repeated many times a day, the participants interchangeable. So, despite living in adjacent rooms, by the end of that first week I knew Eve as well as anybody else at college—that is, not at all.

Part of the Fairfax offering—the *community* it so proudly fostered—was the opportunity to define ourselves in competition with the other residential colleges. So there were tournaments for sport and amorphous 'culture' prizes, which meant the full gamut of attention-seeking disguised as self-expression: debating, drama, public speaking, singing, dance, art.

Eve signed up to represent Fairfax in drama, with a piece promisingly titled: 'What Women Want'. Self-proclaimed feminist content usually fared well with the judges, who were looking for 'diverse voices' and, being former college residents themselves, usually looked no further than recent Sydney private school graduates.

So, a week after we'd all moved in, we assembled in our navy Fairfax jumpers in the Main Hall to watch a line-up of excessively accented monologues—almost all the male ones seemed to be Cockney (*Oi, you wot?*) and all of the female ones were broadly reminiscent of *Kath and Kim* (*noice, un-youse-you-elle*). At least, until Eve ascended the stage. Like a star rising, or a comet in reverse.

She began by subverting form: a monologue without words.

She stared at the audience, unbroken.

She sighed.

She started to cry. (Real tears, which elicited reluctant respect.)

She wiped her eyes, and wiped her hands on her pants. They left little blue-jean tearstains.

She unbuttoned her jeans.

Surely not?

Her hand descended.

The audience sat in tortured attention. One half of us were boys, mostly private school-educated, who grew up following Victoria's Secret models on Instagram and infecting their parents' family desktop with every virus that has ever washed up on the semen-stiff shores of Pornhub. Several of them had lost their innocence in boarding house dormitories, but they maintained a strict, locker-room secrecy about this. Nonetheless, it didn't take much imagination: beds stacked heads against the wall; penises stacked parallel and upright; synchronous wanking under the blue light of the same shared laptop. (Laptop rather than iPod Touch, because, if there is one thing that is crucial to a contemporary man's sense of his own virility, it is the size of his screen.)

The other half of us were women. Sure, we were all abreast of the politics of female masturbation. As celebrities had reliably informed us, the new boyfriend was the hand. One of my new-found college friends, Portia, even told me that in her last year of school the counsellor had recommended the year twelves practise frequent masturbation to relieve stress. The school Portia had attended was an expensive secular inner-city establishment: the kind where advertising executives or wealthy music managers sent their children. There was a lot of cocaine in the bathrooms at the senior school musical, and on the weekends, families took their labradors to climate protests. So perhaps Portia's story was a high watermark of tolerance, but the point remains: it was all very healthy and throbbing and modern.

But up to a point. A point, which wasn't apparent until it took the crystalline, pointy-faced shape of Eve Herbert Shaw on stage, one hand white-knuckled against the seat of her chair, the other writhing in her crotch.

A moaning exhale from Eve. An anxious inhale from the audience.

'Oh god,' she shrieked, shaking her head with pleasure.

'Oh god,' the audience tittered behind their hands, which had risen to cover their open mouths.

Then silence.

'I just came,' Eve announced, to more titters.

'Do you think that's funny?' Audience interaction: the experimentation with form continued. She was addressing a boy in the front row. His hair was long and scraggly and he was pitiably afflicted with hormonal acne.

'Do you think female pleasure is funny?' she asked, her eyes wide.

It might have been funny, if she had adopted a confessional, Phoebe Waller-Bridge style: raw, but also self-deprecating. This was raw and proud. I imagine a large part of the discomfort was the stiffening in many male pants in spite of themselves. This was not laughter-as-amusement, but laughter-as-coping.

'I don't care what you think.' Eve knocked over her chair and exited.

The stage was a flimsy wooden platform, not an actual stage, so to properly exit Eve had to climb down wooden stairs and slam the door. A breeze tickled our ankles.

More tittering mingled with cautious applause.

The breeze returned as the door swung open.

Eve launched herself on stage, two stairs at a time, and yelled, eyes scrunched, fists tight: 'I SAID, I DON'T CARE.'

Masterstroke.

The judges thought so too, and she was awarded second place.

The girl who won performed a Shakespeare monologue about a woman who, for reasons that were unclear, was forced to choose between saving her brother's life, and saving her own chastity. The judges congratulated both the winner (she chose chastity) and the runner-up for capturing 'the raw female experience', and said that Eve's use of audience interaction had been 'very Brechtian'.

Eve, of course, thought she should have placed first, and would describe the event later as that time that she was robbed. But the main objective had been achieved: everybody knew her. Even people who weren't there, who'd only seen clips filmed on phones. Eve became a name that was attached to a story. She was both a person and an idea of a person, which—I would come to learn—was very important to her.

—

THAT NIGHT I saw Eve in the corridor, coming back from her shower. She was wearing a towel, her wet hair running rivulets down her shoulders. Her collarbones glistened.

'Well done tonight,' I said.

'Thanks.' She smiled, and opened the door to her room. Before it closed behind her, she turned back to me, stopping it with her foot. 'You don't think it was too . . . too much?'

'No, I thought it was cool. It was very, um, experimental.'

She nodded on the word *experimental*, like we were talking about an abstract proposition and she was in complete agreement. 'That's definitely what I was going for.'

I tried to think of an experimental playwright. When the silence stretched to awkwardness, I grasped at: 'It was very Sarah Kane.'

'You think so?' Eve stepped forward, propping the door open with her shoulder and adjusting her towel. Her face was dewy from the shower, and water stroked her sloping shoulders.

I looked away.

'You like Sarah Kane?' she asked.

I looked back. The towel seemed secure.

'I guess so,' I said. 'Is she the kind of person people like, though? Aren't her plays very hard to watch?'

'I love her.' She pronounced *love* with venom. 'This is so weird, standing in the corridor. Do you want to come in?'

Her room was the same as mine, but the desk and bed were on the opposite wall: a mirror image. And hers was a mess. Clothes spilled out of drawers, wire hangers sprung beneath my feet, empty shopping bags lay under textbooks on the floor. A laundry basket at the base of the bed was empty, but for a banana peel and a set of car keys.

She sat on the bed and pulled her wet hair behind her shoulders. She picked a brush up off the floor and raked it through her hair with such decisive strokes that water droplets flew onto the wall. 'I'm so glad you liked the monologue. I don't know why it was so daunting. I usually don't care what people think. I probably should care more, to be honest.'

'I wish I didn't care what people think.'

'I can be incredibly antagonistic,' Eve continued, as if I hadn't said anything. 'My mother always tells me I'm antagonistic. But she's an alcoholic, so as I always tell her, it's just learned behaviour.'

'That must be tough.'

'She's right, though. At school I was always mouthing off at everyone. I thought I was so smart. I, like, really believed I was the cleverest person in the room, including the teachers. But that was only because they were all morons.'

I laughed and leaned back. I was wearing a thin pyjama singlet, and the windowpane was cool against my bare shoulders. She apologised for the mess.

'No worries. Your photos are cool.' Her walls were covered in polaroid photos, each with a date written in black marker at the bottom. From where I stood at the window, I could see how evenly they were spaced across the wall above her bed. They seemed to cast judgement on the messy floor.

'Aren't they great?' Eve looked up at the photos. 'Do you have a film camera?'

'I usually just use my phone. Isn't film expensive?'

'Have you read *On Photography* by Susan Sontag?'

'No.'

'I just don't want to mediate my whole identity through social media.' Eve resumed the vigorous hair brushing. 'I think photos should be a stolen moment in time. Not this thing on your phone: this way of constantly curating your life even while you're experiencing it. Otherwise the likeability of our experiences when photographed—like, travels or social events or whatever—becomes the main metric by which our lives are valued. And that's so arbitrary and depressing, don't you think?'

It wasn't something I'd thought about, except to think that it didn't warrant much analysis. Now I wondered whether that was vapid. 'Is that what Susan Sontag is about?' I said.

'No, not really. It's just my musings.' She tossed the hairbrush into the tangled sheets. 'But I usually scan the polaroids and post them anyway, so take my musings with a grain of salt.'

I laughed, but I wasn't sure at what point she had started joking. Her cultivated self-awareness insisted she did not take herself too seriously. The problem with Eve was that I was never sure how seriously *I* was expected to take her.

She shivered. It was a violent motion, and she clutched the towel to hold it in place. 'God, I'm freezing.'

'Someone's walking over your grave,' I said.

'What?'

'It's something my dad used to say. When you get a random shiver.'

'Are you close to your father?'

This didn't seem relevant. 'I think it's just an expression,' I said. 'I should probably put some clothes on.'

I left her with a final, 'Well done again tonight.'

She didn't respond.

I lay in my bed, listening to her move through her room, humming. She seemed fully formed, like the final draft of herself. I must try to have more opinions, I thought, before I fell asleep to the sound of her soft, illegible songs.

2

THE BOY NEXT to me was preparing a bong, and I was trying not to look alarmed. After snipping the weed with paper scissors, he pushed it gently into the funnel with such meticulous devotion that I found myself quite moved. It was Saturday night, the weekend after Orientation Week. Since the moment I had said goodbye to my mother to the tune of Eve's guitar, I had been either blind drunk or cripplingly hungover.

The alcohol was useful for making friends. In my case it had been a literal instrument of friendship. I met Emily in the line to the St Thomas' College bar on our first night. St Thomas' College was the all-boys college next door to ours, so the line was long, and Emily was using the time to sip Smirnoff from a plastic water bottle. As we neared the entrance to the bar, I offered to hide the bottle under my shirt. Emily accepted gratefully, and I followed her and her two friends, Claudia and Portia, for the rest of the night, never using their names. We lost each other on the dance floor, and reconnected the following day in the dining hall, where we tried to establish at what point we separated, and how we got home, with detached, narrative interest. As if we were solving a mystery, or co-writing a screenplay. 'Where did you end up last night?' they'd ask.

'I don't know, I just don't know,' I'd say.

'Look at us, we're messes already.' On account of mutual social climbing—the kind of climb that leaves blood under the fingernails—our acquaintanceship solidified into a clique: *us*.

I didn't question whether these were really 'my people'. That suggests too critical a stance. I was conscious only of surviving the week with a secure reputation, and it felt not so much that I'd chosen these friends as that chance and circumstance had thrust them upon me.

And now I was thrust, with my three new friends, along with six or seven boys, into a bedroom at St Thomas'. It was larger than any of the bedrooms at Fairfax, complete with a double bed and a working fireplace. The others sat on the bed and the desk, and I was next to our host on a flesh-coloured couch. 'That couch looks like a vagina,' I had commented on entering, which all the boys seemed to find very funny. The open windows on the other side of the room brought no relief from the heat. The backs of my legs stuck to the light pink leather like a sweaty handshake.

'Where did you get it?' I asked, pointing to the weed our host was fondling so lovingly.

'You looking for a dealer?' He was wearing a grey shirt, spotted with sweat across his broad back, and a St Thomas' College cap placed backwards, so a cloud of blond curls poked through the front. His hair was fluffy, like lamb's wool, which belied his muscly frame.

'Yeah,' I lied. I had never done drugs. It was only now, watching this boy gently grind and arrange the grass, that I realised how complex the doing of drugs was. It was about so much more than consumption. It had all the features palaeontologists try to identify from the fossils of early hominids: equipment; ritual; language.

'There's a girl in Uni Village called Jenny. We call her Jenny Four-Twenny.'

I looked at him blankly.

'Four twenty? Four twenty blaze it?'

'Oh, right.' I laughed, to be included, and wondered how much weed I would have to smoke before I had the confidence to make those kinds of references: to drug-talk fluently.

He didn't look at me. He was busy drawing a long drag from the bong. The water at the base bubbled, and I laughed, like it was a personal joke that nobody else in the room understood.

He exhaled, holding the bong in his lap, and offered it to me. I took it without thanks, and sucked, thinking how satisfying the bubbling was.

I returned it to him, and he passed it on to the boy on his other side.

'So, do you like girls?' he asked me.

'What?' I wondered whether I was already feeling the effects of the weed. I remembered my personal development and health class in school, where we'd learned about a man who was schizophrenic and didn't know it until he ate one pot brownie and murdered his entire family. How disappointed my mother would be, I thought, if I murdered all my new friends.

'Apparently you're a lesbian,' he said.

'What?'

'You've got short hair.'

I ran my hand across the nape of my neck, where it was shortest. 'So I must sleep with girls?' I was feeling a keen, prickly irritation now, which was consonant with neither a murderous rampage nor Bob Marley songs. Perhaps I wasn't high yet.

'Yeah.'

'You're entitled to your fantasies,' I said.

'All right, turn it up.' He said this loudly, in the same voice that he had used for 'four twenty blaze it', so I intuited that it was meant to be funny.

I looked at him through narrow, stinging eyes. 'Where do you get off?'

He laughed at this, a head-back roar, and clapped me on the back so hard it tingled. 'Hey, Claudia!' he shouted across the room, like it was a football field.

Claudia, sitting on the bed less than a metre away, shouted back. 'What?'

'Where do you get off?'

'Fuck off, Jack.'

He nudged me and laughed, as if we'd executed a successful prank.

Portia was sitting between Claudia and Emily, and she shouted over the laughter: 'Wait. What?'

Portia's fashionably noodly legs were looped over Emily's. Seeing as Emily had a broken ankle, encased in an orthopaedic boot that stretched up to her knee, this did not look very comfortable. But alcohol made Portia liquid-limbed. Indeed, her predominant personality traits were being drunk, and being filmed being drunk, which meant she was one of the most popular girls in college.

Owing to her particular combination of beauty and stupidity, Portia was, in the eyes of the boys at St Thomas' College, the ideal woman. Her contributions to conversation would often be to simply state: 'Wait. What?' This was never said apologetically, rather offered like a catchphrase, with a stunning smile that erupted across her face. It was said with such charm and frequency that it was easy to forget she studied biomedical engineering and was, by every metric other than her own behaviour, extremely intelligent. Or at the very least, intelligent enough to realise that nothing is sexier to a young and fragile man than not understanding what he is saying.

'Hey, Emily,' I called, ignoring Portia. 'Why don't you tell them how you broke your foot?'

Emily insisted that she did not want to tell the story, until she was certain her protestations had captured the room's attention. Then she began: 'So last night for some reason I forgot to eat dinner, and it got to like one in the morning and I was out of my mind, and I realised that I was so ravenous that I was like: I'll die if I don't get Macca's. And Nick wasn't drinking, because of soccer trials, so he was like: Oh, I'll drive you.'

The boy with the bong made a suggestive whooping sound, as if Nick had offered not to drive her to McDonald's, but to make passionate love to her. Nick was a tall skinny boy with quiet eyes and curly dark hair that matched his Italian surname. He raised a beer in silent acknowledgement. The room snickered.

'Anyway.' Emily's tone was castigating, as if she were a teacher. She only continued when she had silence. 'So Nick drives me to Macca's, he parks his motorbike, and I'm so drunk I don't even think to go order at the counter. Instead I walk through the drive-through.'

Nick nods at this, laughing over the top of his beer. 'I was in there at the counter like: oh my god, how have I lost her already?'

The boy next to me on the couch was laughing so hard he was wheezing. He kept repeating in a slow deliberate way, 'Walking through a drive-through.' He held his hands out in front of him and swiped them, as if across a screen.

'Wait. What?' Portia said.

I leaned back against the leather, sitting so low that I was almost lying flat. My arms were folded, and I felt them rise and fall as I laughed—hard artificial laughs, like stomach crunches.

'So Nick finds me and pulls me out of the drive-through,' Emily continued, 'and we start driving back, except when the motorbike stops at the lights, for some reason I fall off.'

Portia, Claudia and I had already heard this story several times that day. But we gasped at this part anyway, and said things like, 'Oh no!'

'Anyway, conveniently the bike is right outside RPA Hospital, so Nick dismounts and literally carries me into emergency.'

'What, drop and run?' someone asks, and we riffed on this for a bit.

'Package delivered.'

'No signature required.'

Nick reddened.

Emily had to shout to get to the end. 'No, he stayed. He stayed for ages until I got a bed.' The word *bed* was enough to provoke laughter. One of the boys got up from the desk and mimed how he imagined Nick and Emily might have used the hospital bed.

'So I just lay in bed with the chicken nuggets on my lap, waiting for an X-ray. When I woke up I was in hospital; I was in so much pain, and I had this big chunk, like, half a chicken nugget, just festering in my mouth. So I was like: well, the only way out is through.'

'You didn't,' Claudia prompted.

'I just swallowed it.'

I laughed at that, not noticing how much I was laughing until I had to wipe my eyes. The boy sitting next to me kept bending over to wheeze. Every now and then he'd slap his leg, and sometimes he slapped mine.

'That is rare,' he kept saying. Then he pointed to Emily, 'You,' he said, using his finger for emphasis, 'you are one cooked unit.'

For the next few weeks, any time one of the boys saw Emily wobbling on crutches through campus, they would give her a high five and say something like, 'Winner winner chicken dinner.' If I was there, they'd high-five me too, because they knew I understood the reference. This gave me the comfortable sensation that we were all people who actually knew each other. Friends even. The high five was difficult for Emily, because it meant holding two crutches in one hand, but she always executed the manoeuvre with grace. Even on one leg, she bent herself into convenient shapes.

Emily Teo was the prettiest and least-brilliant daughter of a prolific Sydney barrister. Her elder sister had duxed her school and was studying law and commerce. Emily, to her shame, had come second and was studying law and arts. She had three younger sisters, making her the second of five daughters.

'Like the Bennets,' I said.

'Except half-Chinese and not in want of a husband,' she replied.

When I laughed she apologised immediately: 'We had to study *Pride and Prejudice* in year twelve. I've been making that joke for ages.'

—

'SACKERS SEEMED TO like you.'

I was sitting with Claudia on the oval behind Fairfax, sipping coffee. It was about midday, and the coffee was inducing a swelling nausea.

'Who's Sackers?' I asked.

'You *know* Sackers. You always do this.'

I didn't know how to convey to Claudia that the St Thomas' boys were, to me, genuinely interchangeable. I wondered whether I had one of those conditions where I couldn't distinguish human faces. Their haircuts certainly didn't help: short on the sides and long on the top, but not so short as to be Hitler Youth nor so long as to be a bit gay. A masculine cut that dripped good taste and fiscal security, although I was starting to think they were the same thing.

'Sackers? We were in his room last night. The one with the weed.'

I thought back to last night, to Emily's chicken nugget story and the skin-coloured couch. 'The one with the fluffy blond hair?'

'Yes.'

'I thought he said his name was Jack.'

'Jack *Sackville*.'

'How am I supposed to know that Jack is called Sackers? This is like a Russian novel.'

Claudia scoffed and picked at the grass, putting it in her coffee cup like it was a bin. 'I think he might want to get with you.'

'As if.'

'You don't think so?'

'No.'

'Why not?'

'He thinks I'm a lesbian.'

She looked at her coffee cup thoughtfully, and placed the plastic lid back on. 'He's probably just flirting,' she said.

'It seems a circuitous way to flirt, but okay.'

We were silent for a moment, and looked out across the oval. A man wearing high-vis was riding a lawnmower on the other side, zigzagging slowly towards us. The cut grass smelled dry in the heat.

'You know, someone was murdered on this oval,' Claudia said, like she was commenting on the weather.

'What?'

'Yeah, like decades ago.'

'A student?'

Claudia nodded. 'She was visiting a St Thomas' boy. They found her in the morning all beaten up. And dead, obviously.'

'Do they know who did it?'

'No. They never caught him.'

'Was it another student?'

'Surely not, right? Surely St Thomas' is the first place they would've looked.'

'You'd think.'

I went back to my room and read about the murder online. My head throbbed and my stomach was suggesting the possibility of being sick, without making any commitments one way or the other. I read that around thirty years ago a girl had been raped and murdered on the St Thomas' oval. I wasn't shocked to read that she had been raped as well as murdered, even though Claudia hadn't mentioned that part. It was depressingly implicit. What shocked me was her age. Like me, she was eighteen.

—

I KOWTOWED TO my mother's advice. Like most parental advice, it was as sound as it was unsolicited.

My mother believed in the age-old adage that if you want to make friends, you have to be a joiner-inner. I found this a contempt-ible, fascistic sentiment, but I did want friends and I did like singing. I thought, amid the drinking and the drugs, it couldn't hurt to meet some people on more familiar turf. So I auditioned for the St Thomas' Chapel Choir and, because I could read sheet music and there were very few altos that year, I got in. We rehearsed every Monday and Thursday evening, and performed on Sunday evenings in the little chapel at St Thomas'.

The chapel, which would have been a free-standing structure at one point in time, had been subsumed into a wing of first year rooms. The bricks were pale yellow, and the windows were covered with a copper grille, which shed tears of green rust onto the exposed bricks every time it rained. This gave the building, which often smelled of a sweet, acidic cocktail of pot and vomit, a weepy appearance.

Inside, the chapel was small and filled with music stands and empty pews. It was in this room that I auditioned before the choir-master, and it was there that we gathered after our first rehearsal, late one Sunday evening. An alarmingly thin boy—thinner than Jesus on the crucifix above our heads—with a flop of thick black hair and negligently long fingernails had brought beers to rehearsal.

'And what do you study?' I asked Nicola the soprano, another first year in the choir. I still felt ill from the night before, and was stroking the label on a beer bottle in soothing regular motions. The label was wet with condensation and peeled off under my thumb.

'Music,' she said. 'At the Conservatorium.'

'That's cool,' I said. 'Is your instrument singing? Or voice, I suppose. Do they call it voice?'

'They call it vocal and opera studies.' She had eyes like plates, round and white, and a very flexible mouth. Underlining it all was a weak little chin, which she dropped when she spoke. Every utterance was apologetic.

'Right. So are you opera or just vocal?'

'I play the cello.' She tilted her head down, like she was very sorry for burdening me with this tiny piece of biography. I decided to spare her and turned my head to the other side of the room, trying to pick up a loose thread of conversation.

Eve was holding court, talking about how she'd spent her gap year. Her particular focus was how reductive it is that people associate tourism in Colombia with cocaine, while also hinting that she had, of course, partaken. I laughed like the thought of cocaine didn't send a shiver of the illicit up my spine and Nicola, sitting at the edge of her pew, made a noise that I can only describe as a squeak.

Eve had a way of steering conversations around to her experiences and interests. As a result, she often appeared the most informed and interesting person in the room.

The boy who had brought the beer was on my other side and he turned to me, seemingly as tired of Eve as I was of Nicola.

'I don't think we've met.'

'I'm Michaela,' I said. 'Thanks for the beer.' I took a sip.

'Not a problem. It's disgusting, isn't it?'

I pulled the bottle from my lips and laughed, which caused me to cough into the back of my hand. He patted my back so vigorously that other people stared.

'Nothing to see here! Nothing to see here!' he said, still hitting my back and waving with his other hand. 'Just a cool girl trying to down a big delicious beer.'

'So, Michaela,' he said, when my coughing had subsided. 'We've never met before, so I'm obliged to ask (in order of importance): What school did you go to? What ATAR did you get? What degree are you doing?' He ticked the questions off on his fingers, jiggling his head as he did so.

I laughed again. He was funny—without the simpering insecurity that often suggests humour is a crutch. I didn't feel, even, that he was trying particularly hard to impress me. He seemed most intent on amusing himself.

'I went to school in Canberra. A random Catholic school.'

At this, he stood up so quickly the whole pew pushed back with a scrape and started to walk out.

'I'm kidding, of course,' he said, sitting back down. 'We Catholics have to stick together.'

'I'm only nominally Catholic. Like, I don't practise.'

'Michaela'—he put a hand on my shoulder—'this is a safe space.' Looking at his pale face, his eyebrows knotted in faux concern,

I suddenly found him ugly. He seemed a sweaty, slippery, beanpole of a person. I wasn't sure how he'd slid away from making fun of himself to making fun of me, or the exact point at which the line had been crossed.

'I don't think safe spaces are for the benefit of white Catholics,' I said humourlessly, taking an imperious sip of the beer he'd bought me.

'No safe space jokes,' he said, miming taking notes, and because of his commitment to the bit, the way he straightened his back and widened his eyes, mime-writing with prim strokes, I gave him a laugh.

Eve, apparently tiring of the other side of the room, had approached the pew where we were sitting and stood in the aisle.

'Eve, we meet again.' He stood and kissed her on the cheek, which was not a way I had seen a boy greet a girl before.

'We did musicals together in high school,' Eve said, pointing to him.

'Michaela was just telling me she's from our nation's capital!'

'Oh yeah? Do your parents work for the government?' Eve asked. She sat down at the edge of the opposite pew, her feet spread in the aisle, and leaned forward, resting her beer on her knee.

I swallowed. 'No. Well, sort of. My mum's a teacher.'

'I think teaching is such an important job,' Eve said, like it was very insightful.

'That's lovely, Eve. What about doctors? Are they important too?' the skinny boy asked.

I laughed, then wished it hadn't been quite so loud, because Eve sat up, crossing her legs, and I wondered if she was offended.

'It's different. It's not a traditionally female job, and therefore undervalued by society. Nurses, however . . .'

'Ugh, don't get me started!' he interjected, throwing up his hands.

'You don't like nurses?' Eve smiled, and I sensed that they were playing a game.

'I adore nurses,' he said. 'I worship nurses.' He paused as Eve took a sip of her beer, then said in a quick burst, 'I'm downright priapic at the thought of a nurse.'

Eve snorted, but managed not to choke on her beer. 'You almost got me,' she said with a finger-wave of admonishment.

'What does priapic mean?' I asked.

'It's a medical condition where you have a constant erection,' Eve said, without a whiff of condescension, which made me glad I'd asked.

'Why are you laughing?' the boy asked, his voice shrill with mock indignation. 'It's a very serious medical condition. It's very sad. Can you imagine going through life with a *constant* erection?'

'I can't imagine that, no,' I said.

'Well it's not *beyond* imagination, unless you've got very limited empathy. You *could* imagine it if you tried. You're not trying hard enough. Think about it. You get up in the morning, you have an erection. You go buy a coffee and everyone in the cafe is like: oh my god, is that an erection? It's so early in the morning!'

'We get the gist, Balthazar,' Eve said.

I assumed I'd heard incorrectly. 'Balthazar?'

'Oh, sorry, we haven't been properly introduced.' He turned to me and held out his hand.

'Your name is Balthazar?'

'My parents are sadists, that's correct.'

I laughed. A hard, cackling laugh that was much louder and more fluent than any of my other laughs that evening. 'That's the bougiest thing I've ever heard.'

'Everybody calls me Balth.'

'That's not better.'

'I was going to change my name when I came here—you know, start fresh. But I went to a Sydney private school, so you're basically the first person I've met who I didn't already know. My past *haunts* me.'

'And how did Balth go down at . . .' I raised my eyebrows expectantly.

'Grammar.'

'Ah. How was Balth received at Grammar?'

'With much ridicule, until I joined the debating team. You see, debating is to Sydney Grammar what First XV rugby is to other schools.'

'That sounds fake.'

Eve leaned forward and said, with enough force to reassert herself as the centre of the conversation, 'That *is* fake.' She reached across the aisle to jab Balth in the arm, but the distance was wide, and the stretch awkward, so she only landed with a soft prod.

'It's true! It's true!' he said.

'Just because I'm from Canberra doesn't mean I'll believe all your bullshit stories about being cool in high school.'

He turned to me, blocking out Eve. 'I like you, Michaela. You know what day it is.'

'She knows you're full of shit,' Eve said. 'You know Michaela and I have rooms next to each other?'

'No, I did not know that, because I'm not obsessed with you.'

'Good for you. I'm going to try to meet some new people. Good to see you again, Balth.' Eve said this last part with so little conviction that it was almost intimate, like she was only pretending to dislike him for the fun of it.

'So . . .' Balth turned back to me. 'You two are very close?'

'We have rooms next to each other, like she said.'

He brought his beer up to his lips, and raised his eyebrows.

'What?'

'Nothing,' he said.

'Are you going to tell me I'm obviously a lesbian because of my haircut?'

'What? No. What a bizarre thing to say.'

'Oh, sorry. You wouldn't be the first.'

'Well I'm not so reductive. And your sandals gave you away.'

'Ha.'

'I'm kidding. I just think it's funny you're friends with Eve, that's all.'

'Why?'

'It's just . . . I've never known her to sustain very functional friendships.'

'Right.' I didn't know why I was so defensive. Eve and I really weren't friends at all. In fact, I hadn't spoken to her since the night after her drama performance.

I must have seemed prickly, because Balth excused himself. I sat alone for a moment, eyeing the room. I detected a slight pain behind my left eye, and told myself it was probably a headache. With that, I felt it expand, feeling less like a twitching pain and more like a throb, taking up half my head. Making friends, the hovering, the awkward entry point, answering their questions with another follow-up question—it all seemed too hard.

—

BACK IN MY room, I lay on my bed and, with an energy that shocked me, I cried.

Those early days at Fairfax exhausted me. Sleeping and waking in that room, with its paper-thin single mattress and plastic orange curtains, I heard my thoughts echo and expand, and watched the surfaces around me faded to unreality. The snatches of remembered conversations, like foul-tasting shots, accumulated, until I awoke each morning with a throbbing head and tender stomach, unable to say whether I'd found a single person I could really talk to.

The people—Eve, Emily, Claudia, Portia, Sackers, Nick, Balthazar—paraded through my mind like I was flicking through their Instagram Stories. The conversations we shared had no significance or resonance. We all overlapped without touching. I could chat to any of them: I could quip or question until they liked me, superficially at least. But what I wanted most was to talk *about* them. To clarify whether I was laughing with or at Balthazar; was in awe or scared of Eve. I wanted to talk about all of the things that had happened to me in that first week—some of which I could only remember in snatches, and some of which I wished I could forget. I needed someone who could confirm that the world as I perceived it was real to someone other than myself.

Several hours later, while I was fending off sleep with my laptop on my chest, I heard muffled talking and the thud of Eve's door swinging against the wall as it opened. Two voices fell into the room, like the volume had been turned up. I could make out stray sounds—the rumble of Balthazar's words, and the tumble of Eve's giggles—before there was silence, which I could only assume contained a kiss.

Forgetting I had nobody to tell, I felt a gossipy thrill.

A moan emerged, and I felt, in addition to the tingling anticipation in my heartbeat, a stirring in my groin. Not quite arousal, but a call to attention: a pricking of the ears.

The moaning formed words. It was a high-pitched baby voice. I cringed, but leaned closer, until my ear brushed the cold wall. I couldn't quite squeeze meaning from the words. The voice, whiny and cartoonish, was speaking French.

I lay down and resumed my TV show, keeping the volume on three bars so the sound through the wall would only travel one way. In the background, Eve's baby-voiced French sex talk continued, cloying, into the night.

3

THAT FIRST SEMESTER I had lectures in the Quadrangle twice a week. I was lucky to have classes there, in the university's most iconic spot. It's where tourist buses unload, and where people pose for graduation and wedding photos. Inside the Quad, there is no view of the rest of campus or the Sydney skyline. There is a great belltower, which chimes in the early evening, and just beneath it an archway covered in ivy. Sometimes the carillon play modern tunes, ringing out anachronisms, like the *Game of Thrones* theme song, in a gentle church-like tone.

Whenever I stood in the Quad, particularly at golden hour, when the bricks were honey and the shadows were long and thin, I couldn't help but take myself—my ambitions and my pursuits—a little bit seriously. The building impressed upon me a sense of narrative and character. This was university as it appeared in films and books. It looked exactly how it was meant to, and I, uprooted and settling here, must therefore be exactly where I was meant to be.

The first year subject I was taking was a crash course in moral theory. Its title was glibly alliterative: Morals and Mores. I had never studied philosophy before. I chose it because it sounded similar to

English literature, and I figured I could read novels in my spare time—not that I did much of that in my first year.

The lecture hall was stuffy. The windows were slits of glass carved into the sandstone, and they opened only a sliver. There were steep wooden benches with clunky fold-out tables where students could rest their Macs or Moleskins or etch graffiti with an empty pen. When I stood to leave, I would touch the back of my thighs, trying to work out whether the gaps between the slats had left a striped imprint on my flesh.

Our lecturer was Professor ('call me Paul') Rosen. In all physical respects, 'Paul' was unremarkable. He dressed like he was in denial of both his age and size. He wore the jeans and boots of boys I knew around the colleges, and his button-up shirts attempted (not quite successfully) to disguise his stubborn beer belly. He always lectured with a bottle of Diet Coke. When he took a sip in between sentences, he'd wipe his mouth with the back of his hand.

Somehow, in between the beer belly and the Diet Coke, he dripped charisma. His was a masculine, unapologetic charm: an imperviousness to being liked which was, ironically, immensely likeable.

I arrived late to our first lecture. I sat at the back and looked down on the rest of the class. I saw Eve in the front row.

Professor Rosen took a sip of Diet Coke and, setting it back on the lectern, attempted to impress upon us that there were many different fields of study within morality, and that what we would learn in this course would scarcely make a dent. 'By the time I'm finished with you, you will know less than when you started,' he insisted with pride. It was as if knowledge were a trap, and he was here to rescue us.

He then explained that when we thought about morality, we were probably thinking about what philosophers called 'normative ethics', or 'practical ethics', but what we would look at in his course would also include 'metaethics'. I typed all of these terms, feeling my chest constrict. In the front row, I could see that Eve wasn't taking notes. Sometimes she nodded or murmured as if to say 'go on', like she and Professor Rosen were engaged in private conversation. For me, the little sips of Diet Coke were sweet relief: essential pauses where I could sprint to the end of his sentence and try to chase his thoughts.

'What do I mean by metaethics? What does *meta* mean?' he asked the room.

Eve raised her hand. 'I only know what it means in a literary sense.' She said this in a self-deprecating way but also very loudly, so that the whole lecture theatre would be in no doubt as to her literary credentials. 'It's when a text is self-referential, like, it's aware that it's a text. Like when the narrator of a book acknowledges that they're narrating it subjectively.'

'That's correct, but unfortunately not very helpful.' He said this with a laugh that seemed to include her, even as he put her down. I leaned forward and felt the flimsy bench creak beneath me.

'*Meta*, for our purposes, just means *beyond*. So, beyond ethics. It will be easiest to explain by way of example. Give me an example of an immoral action. Whatever pops into your head.'

Silence. Even Eve was momentarily subdued.

'I'll wait.' He sauntered to the lectern, took a sip of Diet Coke, and exhaled with a loud 'ah'.

I laughed, then covered my mouth.

'You.' He pointed to me. 'At the back. What's an immoral act?'

'Murder?'

'You don't sound so sure.'

A few people laughed, but it felt like the whole room.

'Murder,' I said, my voice just as soft as the first time. 'Definitely,' I added.

'Definitely?'

Panic must have squirmed across my face, because he released me. 'I'm just kidding. That's a good starting point. In fact, it's the classic starting point. Murder is wrong. What else is wrong?'

'Cheating.'

'Stealing.'

'Ruining the environment.'

'Offshore detention.' This last was from the boy seated next to Eve in the front row. I saw her smile and touch his arm.

'Political. Nice. Okay, let's stop there. What we're interested in for the moment—for the next few weeks, at least—is not *what* is good or bad, but how we claim to know. Our friend at the back says murder is definitely bad. Most of us would agree. But how do we know? The answer for much of history was derived from religion. We know because God says so, and God has moral authority. Even our suggestions today—murder, cheating, stealing—those first few all derive from the Ten Commandments. But in a secular world, where do we derive moral authority? Are morals just socially constructed, or are there universal standards that exist independently of social mores? We're going to take a step back from debates *within* morality and instead try to understand what we mean *by* morality.'

The boy sitting next to Eve raised his hand with an assertive little cough.

'Yes. Please interrupt me. Interruptions are great. They're helpful for everyone.' I found his earnestness less engaging than his sarcasm. I opened Facebook in front of my notes and looked at my unread messages.

'What's your name?' Professor Rosen asked.

'Luke.' His voice was very deep and assured. He had fine features adorned with delicate wire-framed glasses and glowing skin, all of which made him look too young for that voice.

'What's your question, Luke?'

Luke did not ask a question. Instead, he said, 'It's unclear to me how can we can "step back" from substantive debates within morality, because the methodology by which we conduct metaethical studies requires certain ethical commitments. For example, you could argue that when you philosophise via reasoned argument, you are making a normative judgement as to the value of reason. Even methodological commitments are normative. They're not a dichotomy.'

I didn't know what *normative* meant. I was au fait with dichotomies, but basically everything else this sure-worded boy had said was as nonsensical as it was multi-syllabic.

Paul smiled: a sarcastic curling of his lips, totally devoid of warmth. I found it strangely comforting, like he was letting me in on a private joke. I closed Facebook and returned to my notes. 'What does *normative* mean, Luke?' was all he said in response.

'Evaluative, basically. A normative claim is one that takes a stance as to desirability or permissibility.'

I still didn't know what *normative* meant. I looked at Eve. She was nodding vigorously. My throat felt tight, like it was twisted in a spiral. I looked at the clock. We had over an hour to go. I typed '*normative:*' and my fingers hovered, waiting for Paul to respond.

'Yep, so, I don't really like to get too lost in terminology, because that tends to lead to useless arguments about semantics.' I enjoyed the hypocritically casual way he said *semantics*, like that wasn't also terminology. He went on, 'But normative means, "to do with norms". Like, social norms. So a normative proposition is essentially a claim about whether something is good or bad. "It's wrong to murder," is a normative idea, for example. That's a controversial one, actually.' He laughed and caught my gaze. I looked away. 'We'll get into that later.'

I watched Professor Rosen for the rest of the lecture, in a state of almost manic attention. My fingers transcribed independently of my mind, and my typing was soft and persistent, like rain. I fixed my eyes on his face—his sardonic smile and hunting stare. He looked around that lecture theatre like it was full of possibilities.

When it was over, Eve found me walking across the Quadrangle back to college. 'He's great, isn't he?' she said.

'Yeah,' I said. 'He's fast, though. I couldn't get everything.'

'You took notes?'

'Yeah.'

'Oh.' She fished sunglasses out of her bag. They were tortoiseshell frames, with a cat-eye shape, and they sat atop her cheekbones like arches. 'The first lecture never means anything. It's all just introduction crap. Nothing substantive.'

———

LIKE AT PRISONS and nursing homes, dinner at college was always early.

On the night of the Scholarship Dinner, I was one of the last students in the dining hall when I arrived at five fifteen, my academic gown rustling behind me. It looked borrowed and ill-fitting. I let it fall from my shoulders and yanked it back conspicuously, trying to display a sense of irony.

We were in the last cicada-humming days of February. Emily, Claudia, and Portia were not on scholarships, so I arrived at the dinner alone and slipped into a chair near the door. As my eyes adjusted to the hall's wood-panelled darkness, I saw I was sitting next to Nicola, the cellist. She acknowledged me with a mortified sort of smile.

'Did I miss anything?' I asked. 'I didn't realise I was late.'

'I was playing at five,' she said.

'Ah.'

She pointed to the front of the room. A screen hung down from the ceiling. Projected on it was an 'order'—a mix between a program and a menu. There were musical interludes between each course, and matching wines with absurdly detailed descriptions. Words like *woody* and *chalk* that, to my mind, had nothing to do with taste.

In the middle of the table, a bottle of white was sweating. I offered Nicola a glass before I poured my own.

'I don't drink,' she said.

I turned and looked towards High Table, hoping the proceedings might start and relieve me from the equal burdens of making conversation or enduring silence. As I did, Eve slid into the seat beside me.

'God, get me a wine.'

'Did you want white or red?' I said.

'There's both?'

'What did you expect? It's a formal dinner.' I pointed to the screen.

Eve laughed and said in a posh voice, '*Formal* dinner indeed.' Then, switching to her normal voice, she added, 'It's fucked, isn't it.'

'I know. No rosé.' I said this in mock outrage, which made Eve snort. I poured her a red.

'Seriously! This whole thing! It's fucked.' Her hands flapped as she tore into the bread roll that sat neatly on her side plate. 'They have matching wine, and linen napkins, and these fluffy little bread rolls.'

Eve turned to Nicola. 'Don't you think it's fucked?' she asked, through a mouthful of bread.

Nicola looked from us to the napkin in her lap and back again, eyes wide.

A hiss of white noise saved her. The college master was standing at the lectern, smiling in an expectant, school principal way. Attending a Catholic school had taught me a bit about religion, and a lot about authority, so I was instinctively suspicious of the master, starting with the fact that she was called 'master'.

'God, I hate this woman,' Eve whispered. Her breath tickled my eardrum.

'She's not very charming, is she?'

'None of the older girls like her. They were telling me about it.'

'Really?'

'Yeah. They say she never involves the Student Club in decisions, and doesn't listen to complaints or anything. She runs this place like a school.'

With what (I can only imagine) was enormous courage, mustered over the course of our whispered conversation, Nicola shushed us. It was short but firm. You could almost see the spit flecks flying. When we turned to look at her, her little chin was resting in her hands and her enormous eyes were fixated on the master, as if nothing had happened.

I looked at Eve like a co-conspirator, and we tried not to giggle.

When the master's speech was over, Eve turned back to me. 'So you got a scholarship to study . . .'

'Just arts.'

'Oh, me too.' Eve sipped her wine, eyeing me over her glass. 'I thought most people here would do medicine or something with maths.'

'Nicola is at the Conservatorium,' I offered, turning to her.

She wilted and looked at her dinner plate.

'Or at the Con,' Eve said, with a dismissive flick of her hand. 'So is that why you chose Fairfax? Because of the scholarship?'

She held my gaze tightly. Her genuine curiosity, the fact that the answer to this question wasn't self-evident, suggested that for Eve the scholarship was more flattery than necessity. I could have deduced this from her appearance: she wore several delicate gold necklaces, the clutter probably intended to look casual. Her skin—make-up free—glowed nonetheless with product.

I tried to remind her, gently, that the money Fairfax bestowed was more than placement advertising for her intellect.

'It's a pretty good offer. It's not like you'd say no.'

'You didn't get a scholarship to any of the other colleges?' She looked at me intently. She seemed to emit sparks.

'Not really, no.' I hated bragging. This was not because I was embarrassed by my achievements—on the contrary, I would have worn them on a t-shirt if I didn't think it would be socially alienating—it was just that my instinct for self-preservation usually prevailed. Eve, however, thought humility was socialised by the patriarchy, and that women should cultivate a masculine frankness about their success. It was always *frankness* in herself, but *arrogance* in men. I think she just liked people thinking she was smart.

'Did you get ninety-nine point nine five too?' she asked.

When I answered, 'Yes,' Eve shifted in her chair and adjusted her robe.

'I had some weird interviews at other colleges,' I offered.

She looked at me expectantly.

As I told her, I pictured the master who had interviewed me at Rumwold College—his bald patch and beard, the way I sat in an armchair next to his fireplace rather than across a desk like I had in my Fairfax interview. He didn't take notes. He held my gaze while I answered, nodding thoughtfully, his chubby thumbs touching.

For his final question, he asked me how I would respond to an imagined situation. He painted it gently: a landscape in watercolour, figures blurry and distant.

You're at the college bar. A man is interested in you. He's been talking to you for several minutes. You've both had a bit to drink. You want to stop talking to him. Unprompted, he tries a move on you. What do you do?

I contemplated his question: leaning back in the armchair, prodding the hypothetical with the long stick of reason and acuity—a stick which is never on hand when an eighteen-year-old has 'had a bit to drink'. By the time I was recounting the interview for Eve, I already felt that the person who had sat and pondered in the armchair was not me at all but a very young girl.

'Depending on the move,' I said, 'I would probably slap him.'

'You know, I'm so happy you said that,' he said, 'because so many women come in here and they say things like'—here he made bunny ears with his hands—derogatory little quote marks—'*I'd tell the college*, or, *I'd go straight to the master*. Of course, we can't hear about it every time.'

By the time the email arrived with an offer for a scholarship, I had told my mother about the interview. If shrill insistence counts as encouragement, then she encouraged me to decline.

I omitted this last detail about the scholarship offer when I told the story to Eve. I was glad I did, because whatever chill had passed between us before had vanished. There was a warm spark now: the sputtering of a friendship. She asked me to repeat parts of it, her hand on my arm in comfort and in shock.

'I can't believe that. You should have slapped *him*. Sitting there picturing someone coming on to you. What a creep.'

'Oh no, he wasn't creepy.' I recalled his warmth, his humour, the way his laughter felt like praise.

'No, that's really creepy. It's hard to tell sometimes. As a rule of thumb, if you're asking yourself whether a man was being seedy, clearly he was. They behave as if they're not doing anything wrong, so you internalise it.'

I remember she used that word. *Internalise.* It was the first time I'd heard it.

As we filed out of dinner, Nicola rushed ahead of us, palpably relieved at her release. The black gowns converged in the doorway, and I could feel their hems rustling at my ankles. Eve slipped her arm through mine. She looked at me and smiled—a brilliant, neat-teethed smile: 'You're the first cool person I've met here.'

———

IN ONE OF our early lectures, Professor Rosen suggested to us that morality is just a matter of abiding by social convention. He suggested this by means of an allegory. He never used images on his lecture slides, so the slide for most of the class just read 'Ring of Gyges', which meant nothing to anyone. Later, I would tease him about never using images, or even dot points, and he would tell me he hated pandering.

'A professor with disdain for his students?'

'Sometimes you have to give people the cliché they want.'

The story was from Plato, and Paul told it like this: 'A shepherd stumbles upon a tomb marked with a large bronze horse head. Inside the tomb, he finds a corpse. The corpse wears a ring, which grants the shepherd the power to become invisible at will. The shepherd returns home. Wearing the ring, he seduces the king's wife. Together, they murder the king, and the shepherd assumes his throne. For the rest of his life, the shepherd rules as king.'

'What would you do with the Ring of Gyges?' Paul asked. 'Would it still matter to you that you do the right thing, even if there were no risk of being caught?'

To a good person, we were expected to deduct, possession of the ring would make no difference. Virtue was not the same as fear of punishment.

I wondered whether I knew any good people. My mother came to mind.

Luke—who, I intuited, was almost certainly not a good person—continued to sprinkle the lectures with his comments. As the semester progressed, Paul took longer to call on him. By the fourth week of classes, he would point to Luke's raised hand and say, 'I'll get to you,' like he was telling a dog to sit.

'That's Luke Thompson,' Eve told me. 'He's a genius. He topped English in the HSC.'

Since Eve had declared me 'cool' we attended lectures together, which was how I'd come to learn that Eve always spoke about other people's intellect in hyperbolic terms. Short of geniuses, there were also people who were 'brilliant' and 'talented' and 'gifted'. There was a boy called Kirk, for example, who was only fifteen; he'd been accelerated twice in primary school. I speculated that he might be one of the 'gifted' ones. Eve didn't agree. She just thought his parents must have been pushy. 'Girls got accelerated at my school. They weren't smarter than the other smart girls. Being accelerated just means your parents wanted you in a different year. Like, you could read and you were being bullied.'

Luke, however, was a 'genius'. Apparently.

I rarely understood his interjections. He spoke in a quick, clipped voice that was aggressively articulate. He sat like he spoke: imposing his self-confidence on the people around him—at the centre of the his row, his legs spread wide and his arm lounging on the back of the bench, a pen dangling idle in his hand.

Today he began, 'I've actually read some of Plato's other works . . .'

'Epic.' Professor Rosen was leaning on the lectern, arms folded, looking down at Luke. Eve poked me in the leg.

'Well, I was just wondering how you can reconcile this reading and—'

'We're not here to discuss his other works. There's a philosophy undergraduate Facebook page if you're interested in setting up a reading group.'

'Oh, he's such a cunt,' Eve whispered.

'I know. It's awesome.'

'Apparently he's slept with his students before.'

I wasn't surprised. 'A girl can dream.'

'Would you actually?' She glanced at me. She almost looked impressed.

'Yeah, why not?' I wanted to speak with Eve's audacity. 'I reckon he's hot.'

'The last girl he slept with is doing a doctorate at Oxford now. Apparently.'

I took this as a challenge. My desirability, in Professor Rosen's eyes, would hinge on my academic robustness. I started doing the readings before class and highlighting in yellow anything I didn't understand in the PDFs. As each lecture progressed, I would un-highlight as concepts were clarified, distilled in Paul's words.

I googled Professor Paul Rosen many times. I looked at his old headshots on the university website, right above his bibliography. They were very serious, and suggested to me a vanity that I found all the more endearing because it implied vulnerability.

I read his bibliography and texted Eve immediately:

> Guess what Paul's 'area of interest' is
>
> *Omg I know. It's too good to be true!*
>
> LOVE
>
> *You can't make that shit up*
>
> Wtf is Philosophy of Love?
>
> *Idk, ask him*
>
> I'm going to read some of his papers
>
> *Oh god, you're obsessed*
>
> I'm a slave to my education

I downloaded several papers, which all had long and charmless titles like: 'Love as an Affective State' or 'Love and Perception: Mutual Recognition and the Empathetic Imagination'.

I scoured these papers for salacious personal insights. I wanted to find a lost relationship or an estranged lover contained in a metaphor. But there were no metaphors, only mathematically precise paragraphs that circled a seemingly unanswerable question: what is love? The very act of writing a paper, with justified margins and academic font, and a précis at the top in smaller, italicised font, seemed to suffocate the question—to choke it on the way out. I had never been in love. And I never had the sense, while reading those papers, that I was learning anything about it.

I kept Paul's papers saved on my desktop. I could have moved them to a file or even deleted them, knowing they were easily available online. Yet I kept them. I expected that an older, wiser, more philosophically sophisticated version of myself might find them useful, perhaps before the semester was out. My personal growth was on an ambitious schedule.

4

CLUTCHING CHEAP WHITE wine in a damp paper bag, I entered the Thai restaurant just behind Claudia and Portia. The air was sticky-sweet, and the woman at the cash register eyed our paper bags suspiciously. 'BYO?'

We nodded, and she sent us upstairs with a quick jab of her hand.

Empty tables filled the upstairs room, which made Claudia pull out her phone and start typing furiously. 'The boys will be here in ten. Of course. They are *hopeless.*'

She put her phone away with an air of resolution, only to pull it out again a moment later and read aloud: 'Sackers is asking if we want anything from the bottle shop. Why are they at the bottle shop? They should be coming straight here. It's like herding cats.'

'Wait. What? Isn't it herding sheep?' Portia said.

We ignored her.

'Why did we invite the boys?' Claudia sat in the nearest chair and put her phone in her bag, clipped the bag closed, and dropped it on the floor, like she was throwing it in a bin.

We hadn't invited the boys. Claudia had. It was her idea to throw a surprise party for Emily's birthday, and she was the one who had been texting furiously about the operation all week.

I think we should invite the boys

          Maybe not? Will make it harder to organise

But Emily would want Nick there I reckon

          Why?

Because they've been seeing each other

          Well maybe just invite Nick?

But then it'll look like Emily and Nick are a thing

          They're not a thing?

No. They're just seeing each other
But it's not like it's a Thing

I ended this circular conversation by confirming that Claudia's starting proposition was correct.

          Right. Then I think we should invite the boys

Now the boys entered to cries from Claudia about how they were only just in time. Claudia had texted Emily to ask how far away she was and, as she always did, Emily said 'two minutes' when she meant ten.

'Get under the tables,' Claudia ordered with militant urgency.

Ten minutes is too long to spend under a table as a child playing hide-and-seek, let alone at a nineteenth-birthday party. Portia filmed the whole thing on her phone, which reminded me of a movie about a man who was buried alive, filmed from inside his coffin. Critics had praised its Hitchcockian suspense. I doubted Portia's iPhone was producing the same effect.

My knees started to ache like an old lady kneeling too long in prayer, but I fought the urge to give up on the surprise and get out from under the table. I sensed that this would be not only deeply antisocial but some kind of moral failing.

When Emily finally entered and we all emerged, to the sound of scraping chairs, it was an anticlimax.

Claudia manoeuvred Emily into a seat next to her, so she could explain the mechanics of the surprise. I sat next to Nick. He shifted in his seat. At first I thought it was to make room for me, but he did not shift back. He did not acknowledge me either: he was turned towards the other end of the table. We sat in silence, watching the people around us make conversation. Feeling increasingly uncomfortable, I strained to hear.

Emily was saying that this was her first outing without her moon boot and joking that she missed it.

I remembered then how Emily had broken her ankle in the first place and I said to Nick: 'So, you ride a motorbike. That's pretty cool.'

He turned to me, his thick brows furrowed, like I'd said something offensive. 'What?'

I doubled down and repeated myself, louder. 'I said it's pretty cool that you ride a motorbike.'

He laughed, a loud hoot that seemed propelled by relief. He had very white teeth. 'I'm a delivery boy, so fuck you.'

'Like, food delivery?'

'Yeah. Motorbike is heaps faster than cycling.'

'I bet you're the only delivery boy who lives at St Thomas'.'

He took a heaped forkful of noodles and spoke through his food. 'Definitely the only boy at St Thomas' with a real job. Not, like, an internship with a parent's friend.'

'I had a real job at home,' I said. 'It was the worst.'

'Oh yeah?' He pulled his beer towards him, a little smile-in-training on his lips. Previously, I had always seen Nick from across a crowded room, eyes humourless and blank beneath thick brows, even while he smiled and laughed. Now those eyes were focused on me intelligently, like I was open to interpretation.

I told him about working in a juice bar in Canberra over summer: a little kiosk whose tropical-coloured trimmings couldn't mask its essential drabness, where customers ordered anything cool and sweet to deal with the dry January heat, and I spent a lot of time sitting on a crate in the back lane inspecting the pulp under my fingernails.

'So you're from Canberra?' Nick asked.

'Yeah.'

'I didn't know that.' His surprise struck me as odd, but only because it seemed so genuine. This was the longest conversation we'd ever had, so I didn't know when or why he would have given any thought to where I came from. 'I just assumed—'

'Yeah, well I assumed you were an arsehole because you ride a motorbike, so we're even.'

'People are surprising.' He opened a new can of beer.

I lifted my glass, full of yellow-tasting wine, in a kind of toast. 'Surprisingly so.'

Nick laughed, but in the same non-expressive way he usually did—like taking a breath, or blinking. I wondered whether I sounded like a wanker. We each sipped our drinks, silent for a moment.

Nick pushed the conversation. 'This must all seem a bit . . . a bit much, then? Like, all this Sydney private school bullshit where everybody already knows each other.'

'It's fucked,' I said. 'Like, if you don't think about it too much, then it's so fun. All the parties and being surrounded by friends all the time. But that's the problem, right?'

He nodded. 'Nobody thinks about it.'

'Exactly. And I just worry that these boys will grow up to work in banks, and then cheat on their wives with their secretaries, and have a panic attack when they realise they don't have an inner life.'

'Savage.' He tilted his plate towards him, scraping it clean. 'I dunno, I guess it's easy for me to say. I grew up with a lot of them. But I think they're good guys, when you get to know them.' He spoke so quietly that I had to lean forward to catch each word.

'Maybe,' was all I said.

He looked up, his smile returned. 'Do you study arts or something?'

'Yeah. Why?'

'Inner life.'

'Is that something only arts students have?'

'Surely that's what your HECS debt is paying for. Your inner life.'

'Can't be bought. Can't be taught. And what do you study? Science or engineering or something useful?'

'Finance.'

'Sick one. Enjoy having sex with your secretary.'

The same breathy laugh, which—although probably intended to be polite and inclusive—only pushed me away. Then Nick looked around the room, seemingly searching for a new conversation. I turned as well, to make it look less like I had just been dismissed.

Further down the table, the boys were throwing prawn crackers. Sackers threw a fistful at Nick. People laughed like he'd thrown confetti. He rubbed his hands together, brushing off the pink prawn dust, and it fell like dandruff on the tablecloth.

At the other end of the room, Claudia took Portia's phone and picked a new song to play through the portable speakers. Drums clattered like dropped cutlery.

'I know this song,' I said.

Nick looked at me. 'Do you? They're local.'

'Yeah.' I laughed, surprised at myself. 'I've met the band.'

'Really?'

'I—' Remembering how abruptly Nick had turned away when I joked about his middle-aged self having sex with an imagined secretary, I paused. 'I went to their concert last night.' For some reason, I didn't feel he would appreciate the whole story.

—

THE DAY BEFORE, Eve had texted me and said we *needed* to go out. She had just bought tickets to a gig off a friend. I envied the easy seriousness with which she could use the word *gig*.

The only event I had ever been to that could generously be described as a 'concert', was the year eight school dance, where all the girls from our school and all the boys from our 'brother school' (although we didn't treat them like brothers) stood with their backs against opposite walls, as if waiting for a firing squad. In the last twenty minutes of the evening, when the lights were mercifully turned off and 'Low' by Flo Rida started to play, everybody had tentatively pooled in the middle of the hall and some of the braver boys started bumping against the girls. I had one such dance partner, who emailed me that night saying he thought I was 'hot and cute' and asking would I like to see him again. His Hotmail profile picture was a sports car, and his email was a combination of his name and favourite sport (rugby, I think). I deleted the email immediately and cried, and didn't tell another soul, because, for reasons I didn't fully understand, being 'hot and cute' seemed a very shameful way to present to the world.

This *gig*, because it was a proper gig, didn't start until after nine. At about seven, when the sun still had a little warmth in it, we walked to a bottle shop on King Street and spent several minutes giggling in the coolroom, saying that we wanted to be the kind of women who drank beer.

'Let's start now,' Eve suggested, and pulled out a sixpack of Young Henrys Newtowners.

'Newtowners?' I queried. 'Is there something cheaper?'

'When in Rome.' She smiled.

'I don't know if we should start with craft beer. It seems a bit zero to hero,' I said, but she had already left the coolroom, leaving me clutching my bare arms in a weak attempt to smooth the goosebumps.

We bought the Newtowners and I transferred her exactly half, down to the cent, and for several minutes after couldn't shake my resentment that it was more money than I had spent all week.

'I need to get a job,' I said.

'Don't you have the scholarship?'

'I feel like I should save it.'

'Nah. Enjoy it. You have your whole life to be subsumed by capitalism.'

Eve was the first person I'd met who invoked political theories to justify her personal choices. She was also, more so than anyone I'd ever met, perfectly sure of those choices. I found it hard to imagine her as a product of a larger system, her actions originating from anywhere but herself.

'Do you have a job?' I asked.

'Sort of. I do a lot of tutoring.'

It was only later that I realised what a racket tutoring was. It required three things: a car, a high ATAR, and (relatedly to both) a private school education. Armed with each of these, Eve would zip around houses from the Eastern Suburbs to the North Shore, helping students from her school, or friends of her family, or friends of either of those, by essentially doing their homework for them. All for sixty dollars an hour, or 'a dollar a minute', as Eve proudly told me. And all cash in hand, which might have been difficult to reconcile with her passion for high-income-tax welfare states, but the inconsistency never occurred to me at the time.

We went to Camperdown Park, sat by a graffitied wall, and drank our beer while the trees dripped gold and the sky turned from peach to navy.

At nine thirty we went to the gig, which was upstairs at a pub. I knew none of the words, so I couldn't sing along, but I could jump and smile and feel the push of bodies against mine. The lead singer had a scratchy voice, and seemed to shout-sing. The band sounded loud and erratic, with a constant rumble from the drums to which I timed my uncoordinated bopping.

Twice, Eve disappeared after yelling something indistinct in my ear, and came back minutes later with vodka cranberries. The second time, I yelled 'water' at the back of her head as she disappeared, but she returned again with a sickly pink drink that made my tongue feel like a dried-up fruit peel.

The jumper that I had tied around my waist fell off in all my bopping, and when the gig was over we waited for everyone to clear out, before finding it sodden and smoke-smelling in a corner. We decided to leave it where it was. The band was packing up and one of them, with a nose ring and a bowl cut, asked if we were okay.

'I was just looking for my jumper,' I explained.

'Do you need help?'

'No, I've found it, thanks. But now I've found it, I don't want it.' I picked it up between two fingers, and he wrinkled his nose.

'That's life, I guess.'

'Very true. It's about the journey not the destination.' I was drunk. I dropped the jumper back on the floor, where it made an uncomfortably wet slap against the boards.

He laughed and wiped his nose with his finger. With his bowl cut slicing straight across his forehead, and his finger moving left to right across his nose, his face looked very square. He was wearing high-waisted corduroys, which must have been very hot to perform in.

'I loved your show,' I said.

'Oh yeah? Thanks so much.'

Eve was at my side. 'You were amazing on the drums,' she said. I didn't know he had played the drums. They all looked the same to me.

'Thanks.'

'I used to play drums,' she offered, and I looked at her, surprised. 'I played in the school orchestra, because I thought if I played percussion I would look the coolest.'

'You would look the coolest.' He turned around and called to the stage, where the other three band members were packing up their gear. 'Aren't people always telling me I look the coolest?'

A murmur and a raised middle finger was all that came from the stage.

'Except the first concert we did, they put me on the triangle,' Eve continued. 'I was so mortified, I held the triangle up so it covered my face like a mask. And I only hit it about three times in the whole piece, so I was holding it there for a long time.'

'It sounds like they really needed you.' He was fanning his baggy white shirt for airflow.

'What can I say? I was a big value-add.'

'Well, I'd better pack up. Glad you guys enjoyed it.'

He walked off towards the stage, but halfway there he turned back and said, 'Hey, Triangle Girl, do you guys want to come for a drink? Meet me downstairs?'

We waited downstairs, while Eve talked very fast about how great this was, how much she loved the band, and whether the drummer wanted to sleep with her.

'I don't know, he called you Triangle Girl.'

'You think that's a good sign?'

'Oh, absolutely. It's very explicit.'

She laughed, and tossed back the last of her drink. I tried to count how many I'd had. Maybe seven.

'I'm going to sleep with him.'

I frowned at her matter-of-fact tone. 'So we're confident he'll sleep with you?'

'Of course.'

She said this without irony, and I laughed to cushion my discomfort. I shook my head and took another sip of my drink.

'When I was in high school, I used to attach so much social capital to sex.' Eve said this like a thesis statement, and I felt our conversation shift, holding me at arm's length.

'Well, you wouldn't have had much time for me,' I said. 'I was a flaming virgin.' I talked about it like it was a lifetime ago, although it was really only a few months. Still, sitting in that bar, the cranberry taste swirling around my mouth, chewing a black plastic straw, I was the oldest I had ever been up until that point.

'Oh, me too. But I used to think sex was such a *cool* thing.'

'I think we all did.'

'But it's really not. People *love* sex, Michaela.'

I took another sip. The glass was almost empty, so I traced the straw around the bottom. I wanted Eve to think I knew, from experience, exactly what she was talking about. 'These are great insights.'

She deliberately ignored my sarcasm. 'Like, if you want it, it's there. I never realised how *active* I could be. It's like buying bread.

If you want a loaf of bread, just go to the supermarket and get some. If you want to have sex, just—'

'Go to the sex supermarket.'

'You know what I mean.'

'I think this whole conversation needs to be couched in terms of you being a very attractive, white, thin, privileged woman.'

She ignored me. 'Before a night out, I just decide: I'm going to have sex tonight. And that's what happens.'

As if on cue, the drummer appeared, and slapped the table with both hands. There was another band member behind him and the drummer introduced us with a thumb over his shoulder. The other guy smiled and waved, and I forgot his name immediately.

We went to an Irish pub on King Street which Eve suggested, perhaps so she could make the following observation: 'Isn't it funny how, all over the world, from Berlin to Tokyo, Irish pubs are places where Australians go to get pissed?'

'I thought there were lots of Irish convicts in Sydney,' I said.

'Sure, but I don't think it's a cultural institution. It's all commercial. Like, how many Irish people do you think endured the siege of Dubrovnik?'

'I've never been to Dubrovnik.'

'It's beautiful,' said the drummer.

'You have to go. Great Irish pubs,' Eve said, and the drummer put his arm around her shoulder, like he was proud of her for being so hilarious. This endeared me to him. I felt at last that we had something in common.

We sat on couches at the back and talked for several hours, until Eve put her hand on the drummer's knee, and they started to kiss. Anxious that I not just sit and watch Eve, but keep pace, I turned to the man I was sitting next to—he was either the guitarist or the bass guitarist, I couldn't remember which—and made a face as if to say: well, we're here now.

We kissed too.

I saw myself from the other side of the crowded room, planting sticky sweet kisses on a musician with a septum piercing, and I tried to make a mental note, so I might remember it in the morning. I had a mounting sense, which had been festering all night, that I was living an anecdote, and I wanted to be sure of the structure when I awoke the next day, my head foggy with hindsight, and reconstructed it with Eve.

Soon the four of us were out on the street.

I made them walk to Istanbul on King Street, the late-night kebab shop, where I ordered hot chips and ate them like an animal, putting three or four in my mouth at a time, while we waited for the Uber.

It turned out the two musicians lived together, and we ended up at their house. I don't remember having a conversation about whether we would stay, but I went to the guitarist's room, which was strung with those little coloured prayer flags that you see in pictures of the Himalayas.

'Are you Buddhist?' I asked him.

He just laughed and kissed me.

———

I WOKE UP wearing my jeans, my mouth chicken-salt-and-chemical-flavoured, the morning light making playful shadows with his stupid little flags.

The room was musty and I found it difficult to breathe.

He stirred and said, 'Hey,' in an awkward way that made me wonder whether he knew my name.

He rolled over to lie on his side, his bare back towards me. I thought about Eve. *I just decide: I'm going to have sex tonight.* I had decided, when I kissed him, to prove to Eve that she wasn't exceptional, or, if she was, that I was too. So I said, 'Hey,' and when he turned around, I leaned in. His mouth tasted stale.

We had sex then, slowly, with me on top, and with a lot of fumbling around on the floor for the condom. Once he was inside me, he seemed to lose all urgency. My mind wandered, and I tried to look elsewhere—at the walls, or up at the little flags—rather than down into his face, so I might prevent myself from checking whether his mind wandered too. Too self-conscious to commit to any noise, I tried tossing my head, then scrunching my eyes, to disguise my avoidance of eye contact as rapture. I wondered that this bumping and tossing could so captivate Eve, let alone all people, for all time. When he finished, the relief I felt was that of hearing a school bell chiming the end of class.

'Do you want breakfast?' he asked, after we had lain quietly for several minutes. Minutes that were probably longer than the sex, but trickled by more fluidly. I said I should find Eve.

She was downstairs, an egg roll dripping yolk onto a brown plastic bag that was splayed like a plate on the kitchen table.

'He didn't want one,' she said, motioning to the drummer. 'He's vegan.' She mouthed *vegan* as if it were an insult, and I laughed. Eve was a vegetarian and had already given me a dog-eared copy of *Eating Animals*, and peppered my inbox with Peter Singer think pieces about speciesism. So what she was mocking when she mouthed *vegan* was the kind of people who mock vegans.

Meanwhile, my hangover was catching up with me, and I couldn't move my mind to words.

'We should go,' Eve said, and I nodded gratefully.

'You don't want breakfast?' Eve's drummer was sitting at the kitchen table with a coffee.

'No, I think I need to sleep,' I said.

'Well, see you,' said my guitarist.

We left, picking our way through the front room, which was full of vinyl records and haggard-looking plants. Out on the street, Eve started to laugh, squinting against the morning sun.

'That whole night was ridiculous,' she said.

I put my hands on my knees and leaned forward. My black jeans felt much hotter and thicker in the morning than they had last night. 'I'm not having a good time,' I said.

'Let's get you something to eat.'

She took me to the cafe she had already been to, and the barista smiled when he saw her. 'Back again?'

She ordered me a bacon-and-egg roll with barbecue sauce and aioli, and a long black.

'I don't drink long blacks,' I said.

'It'll help you shit later,' she said.

'I don't want to shit later.' I was conscious our conversation was loud, and taking place right next to the coffee machine. On the other side of it, I could hear the barista snort with amusement.

I was sure Eve raised her voice, playing up to him. 'Trust me, you'll feel so much better after you've shat. Post-grog bog.'

I sipped the coffee tentatively at the bus stop. It was bitter and adult-tasting. The bacon-and-egg roll, however, felt like it was absorbed into me by osmosis, rather than chewed and swallowed and digested.

On the bus, which was dotted with four or five other passengers, we sat next to each other in one of the high seats second from the back. We rumbled down Parramatta Road from Leichhardt in a straight line back to the university.

'This is so convenient,' Eve remarked.

'We know how to pick 'em.'

She asked me about my night, and whether I had slept with him, and I told her (with a little pride) that I had.

'You slept with him this morning? Why?'

'It seemed like the surest way to get out of his bed.'

'I think just getting out of his bed would've done the trick.'

'Whatever. Now I can always say I slept with someone from . . . what band did we see last night?'

She cackled at that, slapping the seat in front of us, so that other passengers turned to stare.

'I'm obsessed with you,' she said, and for a moment I felt less nauseous. I let my head vibrate against the window.

'Is every shop on Parramatta Road a wedding dress shop?' I asked when we passed three in a row.

'I know! I've been thinking that.'

'Should we count them?'

We stopped when, in the distance between two bus stops, we had already passed ten.

'When do you think you'll get married?' Eve asked, looking over her shoulder out the window on the other side of the bus.

'Never.'

She turned to me. 'You want to be single forever?'

'No, I don't mind the idea of a partner, but I don't want to get married.'

'Why?'

'I just don't like the institution.'

'Michaela'—she said my name in a heavy, patronising tone—'as a child of divorced parents, I can tell you, it's not very sophisticated or original to rag on the institution.'

'I don't care if other people get married. It's just not for me. I don't want to wear a white dress and pretend I'm a virgin being palmed off for a dowry.'

'So don't wear a white dress. Get married in a red pantsuit or something.'

'It's not just the virginity. I just fundamentally don't think you should contract love.'

She looked at her hands, her eyebrows pulled together. 'Have you been in love?'

'No.'

'I don't think a contract is such a bad thing. I think love is a kind of ownership. That's what monogamy is.'

I was too tired to have this debate, and sensed that the tide was pulling out, the bus leaving the station, and that I had neither the capacity nor inclination to catch up. I let go, and let it drift beyond my grasp.

Now, whenever I hear one of those scratchy-sounding, voluptuously vowelled, yawling songs, I always say, in an offhand way, that I slept with the guitarist. I don't say bass or otherwise. And while that might be the anecdote, it's the full-bellied bus ride that is the memory: the sense of being hugged, and also stretched, as we bumped down the road to bed.

5

WHEN I HANDED over my student card, the woman at the help desk looked at me with contempt. Wordlessly, she returned my essay and waved me along. There was a feedback grid stapled to the front.

I had worked slavishly on this philosophy essay: taking notes that were longer than the prescribed text; drawing out those notes as diagrams, which I would add to and redraw as new ideas were squeezed into smaller and smaller spaces on the page—all the while wondering how Eve was progressing with the assignment. Wondering, but never asking, in case curiosity was read as weakness.

The feedback grid had criteria like *addresses the question*, *spelling and grammar*, and *originality of thought*. There were five rows of boxes, where the marker could place ticks corresponding to the criteria. My ticks ran down the grid in a jagged line. A handwritten number on the top right-hand corner indicated the grade: 63. I looked from the name in the top left to the number and back again. There was no mistake.

On my walk back across campus to college, I threw out the essay. I tried to scrunch it into a ball, but it was nine pages long, so it unfurled when I tried to bend it into shape. Instead I folded the thick pages, bright white in the sun, like a letter, and slotted it into a silver-lidded bin. Before I did, I wondered whether I should go to the library and put it in the recycling. Then, annoyed that my tantrum had unravelled so quickly into order, I released the essay, and the garbage bag sagged to accommodate it.

Later that day, Eve knocked on my door and opened it in one continuous motion. Her essay was in her hand, evidently not at the bottom of a bin.

'Have you got yours back yet?' she asked.

I contemplated lying. 'Yeah, I got it as soon as I saw the email.'

'How'd you go?' She was seated on the edge of my bed, legs crossed.

'You first.'

She hardly needed the prompt. 'I got ninety.'

'Oh wow, did anyone else get a high distinction?'

'Not that I know of. I've asked a few people.' She pulled out her phone. 'Luke got eighty-four; he said Kirk only got seventy-nine.'

'Sounds like you topped.'

'Yeah, I think I probably did.'

'She's a genius!' I was sitting at my desk in a swivel chair, and I swung away from Eve as I said this.

Like someone who, upon leaving a room, remembers why they entered in the first place, Eve looked up from her essay, which she was flicking through admiringly. 'So how'd you go?'

'Not good.'

'I'm sorry.' Whatever empathetic pang Eve might have felt was buried beneath a wave of personal triumph, which crested even as she spoke the word, *sorry*. It was as if she had taken my disappointment, fashioned it into a trophy, and was now brandishing it in front of me. I wanted her out of my room.

'Yeah, it's annoying,' I said, 'but it's not a big deal in the grand scheme of things.'

'In the scheme of the course, you mean?'

'Yeah, well it's worth thirty per cent of the course. And in the scheme of life it's worth even less. Maybe, like, five per cent?'

She didn't laugh. 'Are you going to tell me the mark?'

'No.'

In a singsong whine, she said, 'Please.'

'Why, so you can feel good about yourself?'

'No.' She laughed. 'I already feel great about myself.'

With her laughter—the flat line of her top lip revealing her perfect teeth, and her delicate shoulders shaking slightly—a bubble of tension burst. I was comforted to think of myself as Eve's opponent. This game could spin out forever. Wrestling together, in mutual admiration, the hope that I might beat her next time, and she might beat me the time after clarifying us, pushing us to greater heights.

'Fine. I got sixty-three.'

Eve raised a hand to her face. 'Oh.' I shrivelled under her gaze. 'But you tried really hard.'

My throat was taut and sore. '*C'est la vie*,' I said.

'Did he give you much feedback?'

'No,' I lied. The feedback (in the form of sentences that were question-marked or underlined with 'No!' written next to them) was at the bottom of a bin.

'You should email Professor Rosen. Apparently you can dispute your mark. He might have made a mistake.'

'I can't be bothered, to be honest. It's not worth getting worked up over.' I hoped that my resignation to academic mediocrity made me seem mature. I thought that if I engaged in some kind of dispute, it would only be to validate her—to confirm that this essay was a really important event in my life, and therefore a really important achievement in hers.

When she left my room, I read all the headlines on the *Guardian* homepage to remind myself that my failures were unimportant.

Then I looked up on the university website every person who had won a prize for philosophy in the last five years and tried to find them on LinkedIn. Feeling neither better nor worse, but bored and with itchy eyes, I went to sleep.

In the morning, before I got out of bed, I emailed Professor Rosen and asked for feedback. My email was very formal and full of apologies, especially for being an imposition on his time, which was ironic, because, as he would later point out to me, 'the real imposition was the time it took to read all those apologies'.

> *Dear Professor Rosen,*
> *I am sorry for contacting you out of the blue, but I am a first year philosophy student in your First Year Morality class.*
> *I am emailing regarding the mid-semester essay. I can only imagine how long they took to mark, and I am grateful for the feedback, and I apologise if I missed some of it, but I would like to discuss it further with you.*
> *I would really appreciate some more feedback so I can try to improve by the end of the course.*
> *If you do not have the time, or do not give individualised feedback as a rule, then I totally understand, and my apologies for wasting your time.*
> *If you are able to give feedback, do let me know what time would suit. I'm free whenever.*
>
> *Kind regards,*
> *Michaela*

His reply, which came half an hour later, was curt. He wrote emails like texts, which made him look very efficient, and made me feel silly for starting mine with 'dear'.

> *Michaela, no problem, always happy to give feedback. How's 4 pm this Thursday after class?*

I thought it would be foolish to abandon form at the first hurdle. I composed my response like a letter.

> Dear Professor Rosen,
> 4 pm Thursday is perfect. I can't thank you enough for making the time.
>
> Best wishes,
> Michaela

This was not how I had imagined it. In the private, innermost corners of my mind, reserved for my most foolish and clichéd fantasies—the kind that only floated to the surface when I was easing gently into sleep—I had thought a lot about my first conversation with *Paul*. It began with him congratulating me on a comment I'd made in class. I would look him in the eye, as an equal, and ask him some incisive question, which he would flounder at first to answer. He would watch me leave, impressed, and I would linger like a challenge in his mind.

Instead, I was arriving docile at his feet. In hindsight, I can see how well that suited him.

—

ON WEDNESDAYS AFTER dinner, Balth and I went to student night at the movies. During the day, I usually texted him a list of all the films I'd be happy to watch. These were long lists.

'You're a low-hanging cinematic fruit,' Balth observed. 'Did you honestly want to see that Turkish film about child abduction?'

'It was billed as a comedy.'

'What is wrong with you? It's got subtitles!'

'I'll watch anything, as long as it's a picture on a screen.'

'Does the picture have to move, or would you be happy with a slideshow?'

'Honestly, I'm not fussy.'

We were walking down King Street; people on dates held hands and eye contact as they thronged past. Balth insisted we stop at the IGA for snacks. I was conscious that the aisles were narrow. I made sure he walked in front of me, so we wouldn't have to stand side by side, shoulders touching.

'I have a question for you,' Balth said.

'Definitely Scotch Fingers.' We were in the biscuit section.

'That wasn't the question. And that wasn't the answer either.' He pulled out a packet of Tim Tams, and I made a face.

'Do you want to come to the ball with me?'

'What?'

The annual St Thomas' College ball was a subject of universal interest at Fairfax, not because it was an event that everyone would actually attend, rather because everyone would experience it, even if the experience was only one of rejection and exclusion.

For girls with St Thomas' boyfriends, their invitations had been secured when their relationships began. Cynical minds like mine might even have assumed that it was this event they pictured when they first bit their lips and fastened their courage and said, 'Maybe we should be exclusive.'

The single girls, however, sat somewhere on a scale from performative indifference to performative (at least, I hope for their sake it was performative) despair. Eve and I sat resolutely in the indifferent camp, outposts of a revolution that never gained any traction, insisting smugly that this wasn't high school, and balls were trivial. We thereby constructed our confidence on the foundation of how much we didn't care.

I was looking at Balth while he scanned the aisles for any specials. I wasn't sure if his invitation was serious. Without waiting for me to respond, he looked at his watch and said with a little jump, 'Oh god! We'll miss the trailers!' He brushed past me. Under the fluorescent lights, his body looked elongated, like an afternoon shadow.

'What did you say?'

'Oh god, we'll miss the trailers?'

'No, before that.'

'I asked if you wanted to come to the ball with me.'

'What do you mean?'

'Sorry. It's very dense. I should've explained. There's this thing at St Thomas' called a "ball", which is another word for "party", which is when a whole group of people get together and manufacture a good time.'

'Bag?' The man at the checkout was immune to Balthazar's charms. He looked at him with dead eyes, like his soul had long since fled.

'No, thank you.' Balth picked up the Tim Tams and turned to me. 'So do you want to come?'

'Don't you want to ask Eve?'

'Eve? Why?'

'I thought you were . . .'

He opened the packet while we walked and offered me a Tim Tam. He made a sound like, 'Aha,' but more garbled, cushioned by the soggy biscuit in his mouth. 'I forgot you had rooms next to each other.'

'I wish *I* could forget.'

'God, I'm so sorry. That was a one-time thing. I hope you didn't hear anything'—he ran a hand through his hair. It flopped back over his forehead—'anything too mortifying?'

'Just *un petit peu.*'

'What?'

'Only on her end.'

'That's a relief.' He pulled out a second biscuit and ate it in one bite. He swallowed then said, 'Well, that's settled. You'll be my hot date.'

'It's not like a date, though, is it?'

He laughed, wide and loud, and there was chocolate stuck to his teeth. 'No, not like a date. Only ironically.'

'Then I'd ironically love to come. Thanks, Balth.'

By the time the movie started, Balth had finished half the packet of Tim Tams. He threw what remained on my lap, saying: 'Save me from myself.'

The movie was a remake of an old Hollywood franchise, but recast with women in all the lead roles. Balth made me laugh so loudly that I was shushed, by turning to me every ten minutes or so, and asking, 'Do you feel empowered yet?'

—

ON THURSDAY I wore my favourite red miniskirt to class, with a cropped white blouse. The blouse floated just past my waist, where the skirt began. The skirt was short, and in the lecture theatre I used my laptop case as a cushion to make sure the thin wooden slats didn't imprint on my thighs. I wore Converse high tops, with the laces wrapped around the ankles. I always wore these with skirts. I thought they made me look accidentally attractive. Like I wore the same shoes every day, without even thinking, and had no idea how long my legs looked rising up out of them.

I wasn't wearing make-up, but in the time it took to arrange my hair in a delicate sweep across my forehead, I could have contoured myself a new face.

When class finished, Eve sidled to the end of the row and waited for me on the stairs. I put my laptop in my bag and headed to her.

'I'm staying back, sorry.'

'Why?'

'I asked Professor Rosen for feedback.'

Her eyes widened. 'Oh.' She looked down at Professor Rosen, who was standing at the lectern, hand over the microphone, talking to a student. 'That's a good idea. I'm sure it'll be really helpful.' She touched me on the shoulder before she turned to leave. I think it was intended to be patronising, but she was standing on the step below me, so it had more of a comforting effect.

I followed her down the stairs, and waited for Professor Rosen to finish. When he did, I approached slowly.

He smiled at me. 'Michaela? Let's go to my office.'

—

UNTIL PROFESSOR ROSEN shut the door behind me, I had never been in an academic's office. His overlooked the Quad, and was as monastic and book-lined as I'd imagined—though on the wall next to the door there was a charcoal drawing of a nude woman. The figure was not facing the artist, so only her back, a coil of dark hair, and a ballooning bottom that rested on the floor were visible. The drawing was almost life-size. I wondered if it was a gift from a friend, or if he had drawn it himself. I scanned it quickly for a signature. There was none. I sensed that if Professor Rosen could draw, he would always sign his work.

There was a fireplace at one end of the room, with two armchairs and a little coffee table between them. At the other end was his expansive desk, covered in books and papers, arranged with a disorder that frustrated me: books slanting between bits of paper, post-it notes, a drink coaster from a nearby pub. On either side of his desk were wooden chairs. He motioned me into one.

'Sorry, it's chaos in here,' he said.

I had seen some article on my Facebook feed about the correlation between high intellect and messy workspaces. Einstein, apparently, had a very messy desk.

I laughed and said something meek and witless like, 'All good.'

'So, you want to discuss your essay?'

'Yes, thank you for making the time.'

He sat with his elbows resting on his desk. 'Where is it?'

I felt the creeping heat of shame: the sinking into myself. I was a schoolgirl unable to produce her homework. 'I'm sorry, I didn't bring it. Sorry.'

He sighed, and turned to his computer. 'I'll print it.'

I looked out the window. It was long, thin and church-like— leadlight, with a diamond pattern across the glass. It was ajar, and the light from the Quad sliced through it theatrically.

'Student number?'

'I—sorry—I've got it here.'

He watched me as I fumbled in my bag for my student card, hands still on the keyboard. When I read him the number, he typed forcefully and quickly, as if to make up for lost time.

'Ah, yes. I remember this one.' He had pulled up the essay and was scrolling through it. He printed it. His deliberate clicks through the menu, rather than a swift Ctrl + P, betrayed his age.

The printer was on the other side of the room. He didn't look at me as he stood to get the essay. When he returned, the essay on his lap, he propped himself on the edge of the desk, at a diagonal to my chair. He was almost standing.

'So, you think the mark was unfair?'

'No, not at all. I just—I really did try to read the paper and understand it. I want to do better.'

'So you don't want to dispute the mark?'

'No, I just want to understand what a good essay looks like. So I can write one next time.'

He smiled and, as his gaze moved from my essay to my face, I caught it sliding over my body.

I was sitting with just my toes touching the floor, my legs raised above the seat, not slouched on it: so they would look thin and fleshless, like chopsticks. I was glad I wore my red skirt.

He touched his chin, a similar motion to when he wiped his face after a mid-lecture sip of Diet Coke. 'That's very rare.'

'Really? I would've thought that's the whole point of arranging a feedback session.'

'You would think.'

He moved back behind his desk as he spoke, still holding my essay. 'In a nutshell, the problem was that there was too much exegesis and not enough structure. Both of which are fixable, so that's good news.'

'Sorry, what's *exegesis*?'

'It means the bit where you summarise the philosopher's argument.'

'Right.' I remembered his discussion in class about *normative*, how he made fun of Luke for using it. 'So for the bit that's a summary, we say *exegesis*.'

He laughed and scratched at his beard. I dropped my legs, feet flat on the floor, thighs thick and relaxed against the chair.

'Yeah, it's stupid jargon, but that's beside the point. What I mean is that you spent too long trying to show me that you understood the paper I'd assigned. I don't care, to be honest. I expect my students to understand it. I wanted to know what you *thought* about it. Did you disagree with it?'

'Not really. It was pretty well argued. I mean, it's Kant.'

He laughed again. 'Yeah, I know, it seems like a hard task. But you don't have to say he's wrong. You just have to find something—some facet of his reasoning—that doesn't sit right. For example, maybe you disagree with the whole object of his categorical imperative?'

'But I don't disagree. Isn't that, like, the point of morality? That people aspire to be good?'

'Yes, but maybe you don't think that being good can be measured by adherence to prescriptive rules. There are alternative ways of thinking about morality.'

He talked for some time, with almost indulgently long pauses between thoughts, and smooth, firm gestures. What mesmerised me, as in his lectures, was the humility that was embedded in his confidence. He was totally committed to the process of thinking: its structured exercise. His thoughts never roamed; they paced from one side of the room to the other. He could trace the steps and, more importantly, he could retrace them. His every argument was up for challenge, and any objection—so long as it was targeted—produced a spark in his eyes and a slow-dawning smile. Like an archaeologist, who has just discovered another spot to dig.

I nodded where I agreed, and scrunched up my face where I didn't. At one point, he wanted to show me a particular paragraph, which he thought had the 'kernel of a good idea—and that's all you need, one good idea'. He leaned across the desk and offered the page to me, pointing to the sentence. I leaned in too, and when I took the page, our hands almost touched.

Eventually, he sat back in his chair, the essay lying limp in his lap.

'Look, I can tell you understood and engaged with it, even if your approach wasn't as adversarial as is ideal. I'm going to give you a seventy-four.'

'That seems excessive,' I said. 'Don't change it.'

'Don't tell me what to do.' He spoke with surprising force. The whole room seemed to sit upright. My heels lifted back up off the floor, my legs hovering over the chair. I said, 'Sorry,' very quietly, and immediately wished I hadn't.

I stood to leave. 'Um, thank you.' I pulled my red skirt down, smoothing it over my thighs. 'And thank you for making the time, I really appreciate it.'

'No worries, happy to help.' He was still looking at the computer screen while he spoke.

When I reached the door, the charcoal drawing looming over me, he called, 'Michaela?'

'Yes?' I turned to face him.

He had pulled out a glass bottle of Diet Coke. His hand was around the neck, the bottle perched on his knee.

'Good luck with the next essay. You've got a lot of potential.'

—

IT IS STRANGE now to think that, although my *potential* might be my own, its realisation was owed very much to Paul. First, because he declared that I had any, and second, because in that first meeting he showed me, through conversation, what using it might look like.

For the remainder of the semester—and, indeed, all the semesters that followed—comments offered in lectures and disagreements in tutorials took on the shape of a choreographed dance. I realised that intellectual sophistication was measured in conflict. Most of the 'questions' raised were really just objections.

Surely it's problematic to say that . . .

I think what the reading is really getting at . . .

I'm troubled by the suggestion that . . .

So, I added a new colour to my note taking. While I was still typing every word of Paul's lectures diligently, there were some phrases I highlighted green. Green meant: I'm not sure I agree.

6

BECAUSE I AM a coward, I texted Eve to tell her that Balthazar invited me to the ball rather than telling her to her face. That way, I thought, I'd be spared her reaction. When I saw her the following day she didn't mention it—she merely gestured to it, with a string of subtle hostilities.

In Professor Rosen's lectures, Eve and I sat together. During the ten-minute break in the middle, Luke would usually get up on the pretext of stretching his legs or going to the bathroom—whatever it took to walk by us. I deliberately didn't react when he said Eve's name with surprise, as if he hadn't noticed her. Given that Eve always sat in the front row, and the seating was raked, the entire theatre was a vantage point from which to see her.

Today, he said Eve's name like a revelation, nodded to me—which I also didn't acknowledge—and leaned on the lectern in front of us. He talked loudly, like our conversation was a credit to us, and overhearing it a privilege.

Eve, as she always did, made the conversation her own. 'Do you know what Michaela is doing next week?'

'What's Michaela doing next week?'

Talking about me in the third person had the intended effect. I let Eve answer for me.

'She's going to the St Thomas' College ball.'

Luke looked at me. 'You're not.'

'Only ironically,' I said.

'Whenever you hang out with those boys ironically, you're really just flirting with post-irony.' Luke laughed, and Eve turned to him and smiled brilliantly, as if to reward him for his fine sense of humour. 'I was *so* disappointed in her when I found out.' This was not something Eve had expressed to me. I admired how expertly she was manipulating her disappointment—fashioning it into a personal joke, which I would spoil if I treated it seriously, much less defended myself.

'Right, well I promise I'll leave if I feel like I'm starting to actually have a good time.'

'Your carriage will turn into a pumpkin,' Luke said.

'Exactly.'

'So you're at Fairfax with Eve?' Luke sat down, two seats away, and faced us. Eve and I turned our bodies as one towards him.

'Yeah, I'm from Canberra, so, you know, it's somewhere to live.'

'Only ironically though, right?'

'Something like that.'

Eve turned to me. Our faces were very close. 'Do you know what the theme was for last year's ball?' She looked at Luke, as if to allude to a prior conversation.

When I said, 'No,' I was ashamed to hear how sulky I sounded.

'The Silk Road.' Eve emphasised each word.

'Actually?'

'Apparently they had waiters dressed as geishas,' Luke added.

'What? Why?'

'Crazy, right?'

'Was Japan even on the Silk Road?' I asked.

Eve and Luke raced to assert their superior knowledge. Eve's was ethical: 'I think that's beside the point,' and Luke's empirical: 'It definitely was.'

Luke looked at Eve and shuffled in his seat. Her face confirmed he'd missed the mark.

She tossed her head, dismissing him, and turned to me. 'The point is: these privileged white boys are commandeering other cultures for their own amusement.'

Luke nodded vigorously. 'Yeah, it was a massive deal last year, according to my brother. There was an article in the paper about it.'

'The student paper?' Eve turned outwards, allowing him back in.

'This was national news, surely?'

Luke didn't catch my sarcasm. 'Yeah, the uni paper.'

Eve looked at me, a smile in her eyes. 'She was kidding.'

Luke must have felt uncharacteristically unconfident, because he gave up on Eve and turned to me instead, perhaps hoping for a more sympathetic audience. 'You should write an article this year,' he said. 'About the ball.'

'No, I shouldn't.'

'Why not?'

'Eve, you should do it. That kind of confidence is more your brand.'

Eve put a hand on my arm, which was fleeting, and more for Luke's benefit than mine. 'Michaela's kidding. She's perfectly confident. And competent.'

Luke looked from me to Eve, and back again. When his eyes settled on my face, they were freshly curious, as if meeting me for the first time.

I put my hand on Eve's arm, and held it. 'Seriously. You should write about the ball. I could be your source.'

Eve didn't look at Luke, and the broad, cheeky-eyed smile she gave, while my hand still encircled her delicate wrist, was just for me. 'Now that's an idea.'

Professor Rosen reassumed his place at the lectern, signalling the end of the break. Luke returned to his seat.

I opened Facebook and saw a notification: Luke had invited me to a house party. I turned around and tried to meet his eye. But he stared resolutely ahead.

—

EVE TOOK MY role as source seriously. So it was partly to elicit information, and partly for the stated purpose, that I reached out to Claudia and asked whether I might borrow a dress for the ball.

Emily was in Claudia's room when I knocked, and squealed when I tried on the dress. It was a long red silk creation that Claudia had worn to her year twelve valedictory dinner. Later, a quick eBay search confirmed that I couldn't have afforded it, even second-hand. Emily took a photo of me from behind, so I could see how the low back scooped just short of my bum. I was still wearing my anklet socks, but if I only looked from the calves up, I looked slinky and sexy, as if I were the kind of woman who had power over men.

'I think it's a bit loose in the boobs.'

'Yeah, that was always going to be the problem area.' Claudia pointed to her own enormous chest, which was overspilling her sports bra. She shared Portia's thin-limbed good looks, and her dark-blonde hair was so straight and shiny that it would probably never look better than it did in high school: tied up with a ribbon, ponytail swooshing halfway down her back. But Claudia was a rare case, in that her conventional attractiveness had not, so far, made her life any easier. Her boobs were, indeed, the 'problem area'.

They were not quite big enough to medically justify a reduction, but nonetheless so large that they overburdened her skinny frame and haunted her youth.

Once, when Claudia was drunk, she told me what it was like attending the most expensive private boarding school in New South Wales with the largest and earliest-blooming bosom in the country. This was the kind of boarding school that had a representative equestrian team, and the bosom was the kind that made triangle bikini tops look like postage stamps on two large envelopes. It was almost comical to think of someone so abundantly privileged suffering so much, but her stories soon curdled any initial laughter.

When she was about twelve, the half of the class whose company she had always preferred growing up suddenly turned, as a sweating, fist-pumping pack, against her. Whenever the teachers turned their backs, the boys would try to land pens in her cleavage; rumours started about her letting Sam O'Connell titty fuck her behind Cabin D when she was still so young that she had to google what that act entailed. When she was in her final year, her attention was drawn to a group chat titled 'Rack Queen Claudia' which consisted of photos of her taken on boys' phones, usually with her head cropped out and just her breasts in frame. Some of these photos were taken through the girls' dormitory window, while she was changing.

If this had any effect on Claudia's confidence, it was not evident. She seemed to have a robust suspicion of all men, viewing them with narrowed eyes ready to roll in frustration at any moment.

'You can just use Hollywood tape,' she offered, and pulled the sides of the dress back. When I straightened my shoulders, you could see the bones of my chest. I thought it looked very elegant.

'Are you sure I can borrow it? It's so nice.'

'Oh, totally, you have to.'

'You're sure? I could, like, rent it from you.'

'Don't be ridiculous. It's Zimmermann but it's actually from the resort collection, not ready to wear, so it's randomly quite cheap.'

I nodded, annoyed at the flippant way she tossed off these terms, and annoyed that I didn't really understand them. 'Oh, I've been meaning to ask,' I said, in what I hoped was a convincing show of spontaneity, 'do you know what the theme is this year?'

'I think it's something French,' Emily said.

Claudia nodded, 'Apparently there'll be a crêpe stand and poodles and stuff.'

'Wow. Poodles.' I wasn't sure how the poodles would be involved, or even why, but 'wow' seemed the only appropriate response. '*Fantastique.*'

Emily looked up from her phone. 'Oh, you speak French?'

'No, just, you know, ambient French.' I thought for a moment about telling them how particular phrases had ambiently wafted through my open window on the wave of Eve's rippling (and suspiciously frequent) orgasms. A pang of loyalty pulled me back.

'I'm glad it's French-themed though,' I said. 'Not, like, "The Sun Never Sets on the British Empire" or something.'

Neither of them laughed.

'I don't think any of the previous themes have been that bad,' said Claudia.

'Yeah,' I said, 'but you're not the type of person who would be offended, are you?'

'*I'm* not offended.' Emily said. Despite the lightness of her tone, I felt chastened.

When Eve and Luke and I had sat in the front row of the lecture theatre, and discussed cultural appropriation, the people we'd so loudly defended were not part of the conversation. Like the 'moral agents' we discussed in tutorials, their rights, their feelings were hypothetical. Realising this, under Emily's very real gaze, and realising how stupid I was to have not seen it earlier, my cheeks grew hot.

I had taken the dress off and was standing with it clutched in front of me. I dressed quickly, turning to face the wall. I felt silly doing it, like I was accusing them of something, and when I turned back I didn't look either Emily or Claudia in the eye. 'Thanks for the dress,' I said.

As soon as I was on my own, I texted Eve.

I know the theme.

I had just locked my screen and put my phone back in my pocket when I felt it vibrate with a response. Eve's excitement expressed itself in maniacal punctuation.

OMG! Tell me!!

You're going to die

I can't wait!!!

British Raj

NO?!? Your ducking kidding me!
*You're smh

Yeah I am lol

You don't know the theme?

No, I do. The theme is French

French?!

Oui

What kind of French?

I don't know. Poodles apparently

The dots that indicated she was typing a message hovered for a few seconds, then disappeared. I was about to put my phone away when they were back again.

Fucking hell
This is not my week

I replied with a GIF of a poodle looking sad, which did not elicit a response. I let the screen go dark.

—

THE FACEBOOK EVENT description for Luke's house party was not promising.

> And a gentle reminder to all you legends that this house has a 0 Tolerance policy for fuckwittery of any kind: mansplaining, misgendering, general misdeeding. As always, when getting absolutely belted, be guided by John Stuart Mill's party principle: people should be free to party however they wish, up to and until the extent to which their partying causes harm to someone else.

'Sounds like a riot,' I said.

Eve frowned over the phone screen. 'It's amazing how not-fun liberal political philosophy is when applied to social occasions.'

'Amazing.'

'Whatever. We're obviously going.'

What surprised us both was that the evening turned out to be quite a riot after all.

—

AS WITH ALL house parties, the early stages of Luke's was dominated by two kinds of conversation: the lifeless ones, where participants stood facing out to the room, keeping both eyes on better options; and the ones where people clung to each other's attention with desperate excitement.

Eve and I moved between the rooms, performing our conversations for other people. The topics ranged from wantonly contentious

(How is 'privacy' constructed for a generation that has already given up its data?) to contentiously wanton (which slang is correct: *finger-bashing* or *finger-blasting*?). The answers were ones we'd already arrived at in previous discussions ('privacy' in our parents' sense is conceptually redundant; *finger-bashing*, if not incorrect, is definitely worse, because it sounds so maladroit). Our interactions were cheap and single-use, and the other people too unimportant to cause us any next-day anxiety, or *hangxiety* as we called it. Except when Eve used a phrase of mine—something I'd said before—and it got a laugh. Then I'd wonder whether this recycling was a personal joke—a kind of prank on our audience, which only we understood—or whether I didn't matter at all, and Eve would have said the exact same thing had she turned up to the party alone.

When Eve and I had exhausted our bottle of rosé—so sweet and cheap it tasted more like corn syrup than wine—we started skimming beers off the top of laundry tubs filled with ice. Then to the kitchen, in search of a bottle opener.

Next to us, a woman who insisted on calling us 'dude' several times a sentence, offered to open our beers. She took a breadknife from the top drawer and hacked at the bottle like she could decapitate it.

'Is this your house?' I asked.

'Fuck no. Dude, I wasn't even invited.' Giving up on the breadknife, she opened the bottle using her teeth, with a crack that would make a dentist's heart sing.

'Thanks.'

'All good, dude.' She left the kitchen for a 'boogie', but not before looking Eve up and down and commenting: 'Dude. Great threads.'

Eve was morally opposed to fast fashion. In theory, so was I. Except in Eve's case, this stance didn't restrict her to op shops finds—she also had a lot of clothes that were ethically manufactured by Australian designers. It was impossible to tell which was which, because she was so thin, so confident, that her model-proportions perfected any garment. Tonight she was wearing a hot pink linen boilersuit with vegan leather sneakers which I knew for a fact cost several hundred dollars. It must be nice, I thought, to wear your morals so well.

'Fun party, dude,' I said.

A quick eyeroll acknowledged my impersonation.

'Hey, you never told me . . .' Eve raised her chin and gave me that calculating stare. I took a quick defensive breath.

'How did your meeting with Professor Rosen go?'

'It was fine.' Eve looked at me with reproach, like I was hiding something.

In a way, I was. Although what I wanted to conceal was not so much *how* the meeting went, but how our relationship had shifted in its aftermath. Now, no interaction with Professor Rosen, however small or fleeting, was insignificant. They all contoured a narrative, which, in my mind, was only in its most nascent stages. An acknowledgement of my presence in a crowded lecture theatre, a smile or a nod across campus—these proved that there was something between us. Not quite a flirtation, nor a friendship. But he saw me: there was something that distinguished us from strangers.

Instead of trying to articulate this (perhaps imagined) subtlety, I said: 'He was really helpful, actually.'

Eve raised her eyebrows suggestively. 'How helpful?'

University debaters flooded the kitchen and started swapping eloquent little speeches about how much they hated each other: *I wouldn't put it as high as a sociopath, but he's manifestly a narcissist.*

Eve and I rolled our eyes in one synchronised movement, and followed our bottle-opening friend in search of a 'boogie'.

The living room of Luke's share house had been converted to a dance floor, which meant the couches were pushed up against the walls and a multi-coloured rotating light revolved on the floor. A smattering of guests danced, and at the periphery, people on caps lay on the couches playing noughts-and-crosses with their limbs.

When he saw us, Luke extracted himself from one such entanglement.

'Eve, so good to see you.' He kissed her on the cheek, obviously finding himself very urbane, but lingering long enough for me to cringe. He leaned towards me. 'You too, Michaela.' He said my name with emphasis, like he was trying to impress me by remembering it. 'You've got drinks?'

'Yeah, a friend of yours was very anxious that we get some,' I said.

'A friend of mine?'

'Not really, she wasn't invited. But you should keep her around. She opened this with her teeth.'

'She's got more to offer than I do.' Luke said, with the faux self-deprecation of someone who has always been offered the world.

Luke danced with us at first. Gradually, more people spilled into the room and we lost him to the throng. But Eve kept taking my hand and leaning forward to shout-whisper in my ear, so the crowd served to push us tighter together.

I wasn't on caps, but on Luke's living room dance floor that night, when the walls were wet with condensation, and Eve was mouthing all the words to every song ever sung, I empathised with the people who were.

After midnight, in the bathroom, which didn't so much spin or rotate on an axis as it did trip over itself, I realised how drunk I was. Eve was sitting on the toilet seat, and as she wiped, I commented that she was totally hairless.

'It's not a male gaze thing.'

'Oh yeah?'

'My mum paid for laser in high school, and by the time I realised it's totally fucked to uphold twelve-year-old girls as the gold standard of beauty, I'd already done the deed.'

'Will it ever grow back?'

'That shit's permanent.'

'Well it looks good.'

'You're socialised to think that.'

'All my thoughts are socialised.'

'Shut up.' She flushed.

'Luke's not so bad,' I said when I sat down, and watched Eve watch herself in the mirror. She flicked her fringe out of her eyes before tossing her head so it fell right back again. I was relieved she was looking at her own reflection and not at me, who fell short of the gold standard—socialised or otherwise.

'He's nice, isn't he? I think he's shy.'

I cackled and she looked at me. I wiped quickly and pulled my pants up. 'He's as shy as you are.'

She smiled at her reflection and messed up her hair. 'Insecure, then.'

I thought about how hard Luke laughed when anyone attempted a joke; about how many people were in his house; how he'd invited me despite only knowing me as Eve's friend. 'Yes, definitely insecure,' I said. 'I think he's hot, though.'

Eve moved aside so I could wash my hands and studied my face in the mirror. 'Do you just think everyone is hot?'

'Kind of. Until you get to know them.'

'How do I look?'

I turned around so I could see her face, instead of her reflection. It was a small bathroom, and her breath tickled my neck.

'Literally perfect.' I delivered this like an insult, as if Eve's beauty were just a matter of taste, not a very important part of who she was as a person.

'Cheers.' She tilted her head and toyed with a smile. I leaned against the basin to steady myself. 'I forgive you.'

'For what?'

'For going to the ball. For organising a Professor Rosen meeting without telling me.'

'Do you want me to tell you everything?'

'Yes.' She tucked her hair behind her ears, as if in preparation, and then, grabbing my face with both hands, she kissed me.

Her lips were soft and ripe, and I bit down on the bottom one and let her scrape it along my teeth. When I pulled back, I laughed, but only because the moment felt so significant, I didn't know what else to do with it.

Still holding my face in two hands, she planted another peck on my lips for good measure, and opened her mouth to speak.

She wrinkled her nose. 'Did you . . .' She looked over her shoulder at the toilet bowl.

I could smell it too. I covered my nose with my hand. 'I think it's coming from outside.'

Opening the bathroom door confirmed my suspicion, because the smell only intensified.

Looking down the corridor, I saw a small crowd of people exclaiming variously through the hands or elbows that covered their mouths and noses.

'That's fucked.'

'Holy shit.'

'Was there a dog in here?'

On the carpet, not a metre from the front door, was a small but pungent poo, presumably human.

I looked at my watch, as if for an explanation. Seeing that it was almost one in the morning, I reflected that there would never have been an appropriate time to use the front entrance as a toilet.

'MDMA is a laxative,' a man wearing a tracksuit said with grim resignation, as if we all should have seen this coming.

'Well that explains it,' I said.

Eve laughed, and I gravitated with her, and the rest of the party, towards fresh air and cigarettes.

'This is more civilised,' Eve declared, pulling up a plastic chair in the courtyard, which was full of smokers and idlers, and over-shadowed by a clothing line.

I sat opposite Eve, and a cheer from inside confirmed that the waste had been dealt with. Luke came out, and from the swagger in his smile, I could tell he was the one who had dealt with it.

Eve propped on the edge of her seat, so I could share it, and waved Luke over. I gave him the free chair, but opted to make him as uncomfortable as possible. 'So, you spent all that time on the Event telling everyone not to misgender each other, but you forgot to remind your guests that it's rude to shit on the floor.'

He didn't laugh.

'Do you know who did it?' Eve asked.

'No idea. I just picked it up with a plastic bag and poured some water on the floor.'

I wrinkled my nose.

'We'll deal with the residue in the morning.'

'Residue.' I tasted the word, recoiling.

'That's a tomorrow-problem.' Eve said. 'Good on you for handling it.'

I was annoyed by her uncharacteristic sincerity, as if he had 'handled' a complex geopolitical dispute, not like he'd just picked a human poo off the carpet.

'Whoever it was, they must have been quick,' I said.

'True.' Eve sat up. 'Surely someone would have seen them pants-down and in the act.'

I put my arm around the back of the chair, seemingly to steady myself, but the effect was to put my arm around Eve. I felt her lean into it. 'Maybe it was a girl,' I said. 'Wearing a very billowy skirt. So she could have just sat down and let rip.'

'And then stood back up and walked straight out the door.' Eve laughed, shaking her fringe from her eyes, and stood up to mime my suggestion.

Luke laughed too, louder than either of us, like it was a joke he had invented and uniquely understood. Eve held the mime a moment too long.

When she sat back down, I nudged her thigh and tried to make a 'let's go' face, but she didn't look at me.

'I might head soon,' I said.

To my dismay, Eve did not treat my statement as an invitation requiring a response.

Luke, however, said, 'See you,' so quickly that he revealed his enthusiasm. He continued, as if to cover his mistake: 'Thanks so much for coming. Sorry about, you know . . .'

'The poo.'

'Well, yes.'

Eve snorted. She took another drag of her cigarette. 'See you tomorrow,' she said, blowing smoke into the night. As she did, she stretched her neck into a long elegant slope.

Looking back over the courtyard from the door, I saw a different scene from the one I'd just lived: Luke, leaning forward, lighting his cigarette off Eve's, a spark flaring where the two white tips touched.

I walked home alone at a furious, defensive pace, Eve's lips still lingering on mine.

7

EVE DID WRITE an article about the ball, although in light of other revelations that night, its significance faded rapidly.

A week before the ball, we were standing in the bathroom at the end of our corridor. She was behind me, pulling back the red straps of my dress while I practised taping my chest. Our voices echoed off the tiles like one.

'Of course, the whole event is still fucked.' Eve had been deploring the theme for several days now.

'Because of the cost?'

'Yeah, and the pageantry of it. All this dressing up.' She motioned to my reflection in the bathroom mirror.

'Thanks.'

'You look great, obviously. I'm just saying: will it be worth it when you rip the bandaids off your nipples in the morning?'

Although that was not something I had ever done, or considered doing, I made a mental note not to try it.

'I think we're making the same point,' I said.

Eve looked at me sceptically in the mirror. Her hands, still holding the dress, were cold against my bare back.

'The pageantry is expensive,' I continued. 'There's a high threshold to entry.'

Under the hum of the fluorescent lights, Eve's face glowed with purpose.

So Eve wrote about a more persistent problem—one that got right to the root not just of the event, but the whole institution. For research, she spoke to the student organising committee. It comprised seven members, but Eve stopped interviewing after five, finding their answers identical. The interviews went pretty much as follows:

Q: What's the budget for this year's ball?

A: One hundred thousand dollars.

Q: Is that normal?

A: It's the same as last year.

Q: And you spend it on . . .

A: It's tight.

Q: ??

A: There's the catering, the design, the DJ, the add-ons. And there's also the competition. You know, you always want to be better than last year's. You want to be the year that's remembered.

This phrase was repeated a lot: *the year that's remembered.*

So these interchangeable boys lost sleep and made phone calls and ran around the grounds at dawn on the day of the ball, screaming at freshmen in cherry pickers that they'd have to work *faster* if they wanted to assemble the Arc de Triomphe in time for the DJ to set up—all with a degree of gracelessness, desperation and attention to detail that they would have mocked in a reality TV star planning her wedding.

And the master, when interviewed, sat back in a plush leather armchair, his fingers delicately steepled, and said to Eve, 'It's a wonderful responsibility for them. A fantastic thing to put on their CVs. I mean, have you ever organised a party for two thousand people, with a one-hundred-thousand-dollar budget, and made a *profit?*'

Eve blinked a few times, her pen hovering over her pad, before she acknowledged that no, indeed she had not.

THE NIGHT BEGAN inauspiciously, with Pre's in a sweaty bedroom.

When I knocked on Balth's door, I felt like a high school girl. It was as if I had somehow recrossed the Rubicon, and was once again a cringing, peer-obsessed creature, deferring authorship of my personality to the imagined gaze of others. Claudia's dress, so delicate and soft, pulled and tugged in painful places where it was fastened with Hollywood tape. And the expensive silk, crisp breeze and absence of bandaids had conspired to expose my nipples, which stood straight and loud: lighthouses for mockery.

Balth opened the door and, in a moment, re-erected my self-esteem. All because when he first saw me, he didn't say anything at all. Instead, he stuttered.

'You look . . . um, I . . .'

'Thanks.'

'No, it's just . . . I don't—I mean, don't take this the wrong way, but you look beautiful.'

'Beautiful?' I said, in what I hoped was a wry tone.

'Well, it's just that, you know . . . I mean, obviously *I* look amazing, so it's a relief to see that you won't be letting me down. I've been fretting about it all day.'

It was not so much the look of him but the *smell* that warranted comment. His hair was gelled into a sticky glob of bottled testosterone; his deodorant was obviously not a subtle bar but a loud, aerosol affair, applied throughout his room like air freshener, and beneath it all was not a hint but an affront of cologne which I imagine was sold as 'musky' but was instead reminiscent of fermented apples. The final touch was a scented candle, which he had inexplicably positioned in the centre of his desk, and which tried to insist—by shouting resolutely over the aromatic din—that we were in an expensive homewares store.

Once I'd crossed the threshold, he popped a bottle of champagne, his hands slipping around the neck so much that I could only assume they were very sweaty. We drank it out of mugs. Mine had brown grime just under the rim, indicating where the water level usually sat. The bubbles of the champagne frothed just beneath it.

People dripped into the room, and the girls took turns complimenting each other on their appearance and being self-deprecating in response.

'Michaela, you look amazing, I love that dress.'

'Oh, it's not mine. I borrowed it.'

'Still, it looks really good on you.'

'Really? It doesn't even fit. It's held together with Hollywood tape.'

'Love that. It works every time.'

My turn: '*You* look amazing. Where's that dress from?'

'Oh I actually had it at home already. I bought it ages ago but wasn't sure if the cut was a bit weird . . .'

'No, it's amazing. Looks really good.'

And so on, until someone declared it was time to get going.

Before we filed into the corridor, Balth asked, 'Are you ready to go?'

'Yes.' I laughed. 'I don't have any other plans.'

Then, before he turned to leave, he touched my arm, in a movement that felt like a leap of faith. I couldn't tell whether he did it so I might catch him, or so that everybody else would see: to mark me as his Date, like marking a map with an X for treasure. For the rest of the evening, every time I saw Balth on the other side of the room or found him in the crowd, I would feel again the soft brush of that touch. It danced through my mind, sidestepping in and out of significance.

—

EVEN MY DEEP and firmly held belief that the event was an indulgence did nothing to alter the experience of it, except perhaps to qualify the memory—to add a caveat that if it was the best night of my life, then it was only because I, being not the best version of myself, had given in to it. If I were invited today, I'd go again, and I would probably perform the same mental tap dance as I did at the time: classifying myself as a spectator; ignoring the reality that, like any party, attendance is participation, and when you're off the sidelines and into the fray, there's no vantage from which to just spectate.

The St Thomas' quadrangle, a beautiful sandstone-framed patch of grass which rolled gently downhill, with a cement path cutting it in half, looked like a film set. On one side an enormous structure had been erected that looked exactly like the Arc de Triomphe, and felt to the enquiring hand like papier-mâché. It was held in place by ropes and sandbags, which, combined with drugs, alcohol and high heels, proved a trip hazard that resulted in at least twenty sprained ankles, five sprained wrists, and one broken nose (a clean face plant). On the other side, at the bottom of the slope, was a row of food stalls, white-tented like a village fair, and through it roamed an array of fire eaters, stilt walkers, and jugglers. There were, indeed, poodles, which were held on leashes by waiters at first, and gradually let off so they could be patted and picked up and pictured on Instagram. To say that my gasps upon entering the quadrangle and taking all this in were of disgust and not delight would be a downright lie.

It was the most extravagant event I'd ever attended and likely ever will, and at no point did the thought that I did not deserve this extravagance—that no one did, that I was greedy and gluttonous for even partaking—cross my mind. This current congregation, plucked and gelled and taped to their physical peak, was very much a pampered, irrelevant minority. But at the time, more exhilarating than a cigarette-thick line of cocaine snorted off a microwaved plate in the junior common room, was the thought that this—this party, this extravaganza—was *the* place to be, and that everyone except us was missing out.

'It's a lot, isn't it?' Nick said, when we met in the line for a crêpe. 'Too much?'

He smiled and gave me that sideways look, as if he were passing a note under the desk in class. 'No such thing. At least, not until after the fireworks.'

'Literal fireworks?'

'Yep, like New Year's Eve.'

I rolled my eyes, but also asked what time they were likely to go off, so I could make sure I was outside to catch them.

'Where's Emily?' I asked.

He shrugged. 'Bathroom, I think. And where's . . .'

'Balthazar.'

'I love that guy. I didn't know you were—'

'We're not.'

He laughed—a big baritone hoot, which filled me like helium when it should have brought me down. It was the way he laughed when he thought he'd got under someone's skin, and it was so Puckish, so pleased with itself, that you had to laugh along. 'I was going to say *friends*.'

'We are friends.'

'So where's your friend?'

'The last I saw he was berating the DJ for not playing more Avril Lavigne.'

'He must be very drunk.'

We lost each other to this blur of heels and blow-dries and dinner suits. Our conversations, like the champagne we drank, popped and fizzed and went nowhere.

—

NICK'S ASSESSMENT WAS correct. Balthazar was very drunk indeed.

I did not see him again that night, but over the following days word spread quickly about how his evening ended. I personally facilitated the rumour, retelling the tale several times in order to eclipse more salacious stories which might have been told about me.

Some time around three in the morning, Balth stumbled back to his room, clutching a kebab from Istanbul on King. Lying in bed, the tender shredded meat overspilling onto his chest and staining his white shirt, he crumpled the wrapping and threw it on his desk, where the scented candle, still valiantly pushing on, set it alight.

A clumsy smothering using the closest thing to hand—his recently removed dinner jacket—was not enough to dull the flames. Indeed, the jacket too caught alight. Soon there were smoke alarms, and fire brigades, and people wandering out of rooms, emerging from sleep, or red-eyed from kick-ons, or awake and aggravated with their date in hand, only moments away from sealing the deal on an evening that up until now had gone exactly to plan.

The fire brigade interviewed the college master and asked many, many times about the fireworks.

'But *why*?' the fireman kept saying. 'It's not some kind of holiday, is it?' (In fact, it was just a Friday night in May.)

So the college was fined thousands of dollars by the local council for neglecting to seek a permit for the fireworks, and for the first time in decades the ball did not make a profit. For this reason, it secured its status as a year that was remembered—and all thanks to a persistent scented candle.

By the time this drama unfolded, I was in bed, my pillow wet with mascara-black tears.

———

AFTERS WERE IN the Jace, which was short for the JCR, which was short for the junior common room. Places, like people, were caught up in the same nicknaming mania that turned Jack to Sackers, and tricked people who knew the code into thinking they had anything in common.

I suspected that Afters would involve everyone sitting on the floor, heels kicked to one side, playing drinking games. I did not anticipate that the games would be so gladiatorial: bared teeth and flared nostrils, sitting up straight to attention.

We started with King's Cup, which Emily lost. To her credit, she drank the whole cup—a mix of beer and vodka and red and white wine—in one go. I gagged watching her.

Sackers was in his element, combining snorting laughs with hand clapping and fist banging on the little wooden coffee table, which flinched in response. The noise was oppressive. I took another sip of wine, swirling the sweetness in my mouth, and tried to focus on swallowing.

Next we played Never Have I Ever. The rules were simple: we went around the room clockwise, taking turns to list something we had never done. If someone else had done it, they had to drink. Innocuous enough. Except the things that had never been done were all graphic and pointed.

Never have I ever had a threesome.

Never have I ever done butt stuff.

And so it went, witless and unrelenting, until Sackers said something I couldn't catch.

Everyone roared. Sackers slapped the table and put his arm around me like we were friends.

'What?' I asked Claudia, who was at my side in a silk slip, not unlike the dress she had lent me, leaning forward, her hand covering her open mouth.

She looked at me and laughed. 'Who is it?'

'What?' I was yelling. 'I couldn't hear. What did he say?'

'He said'—Claudia was yelling too; I turned my ear towards her and felt the pressure of her shout—'never have I ever had sex with Michaela Burns.'

The penny must have visibly dropped, landed even with a clang, because another roar erupted. The room had been watching me, and Sackers shook me harder, laughing and shouting, 'Now she gets it, now she gets it,' with the exact same volume and intonation as if he were a football commentator reporting on a tie-breaking goal.

Slowly, his face red and his dark eyebrows raised slightly, suspended in a self-mocking stance, Nick put his beer to his lips and tipped the can back, finishing it.

The room reverberated.

Watching Nick, snatches of my first night at Fairfax—the day my mother bought me a jumper and held me when I asked her not to go—came back to me.

A slow-revolving ceiling fan.

The splattering sound of vomit hitting the walls of a metal bin.

Pain, not sharp but steady, where he thrust inside me.

I didn't know where we were up to in the game, or why anyone was still laughing, or why Nick, his dark eyebrows raised in blank amusement, wouldn't meet my gaze.

Claudia grabbed my wrist. 'You never told me that.'

It sounded like an accusation.

'It was in O Week. We haven't spoken about it. I didn't know.'

'You didn't know?' Claudia's voice was still loud, but it was no longer a shout. For a moment, I thought she looked concerned.

'No, I was so drunk . . .'

'You couldn't remember having sex?'

Flashes returned to me. Stumbling up the steps. 'I knew I'd got with someone, but I was wasted.' The smell of alcohol on our breath. 'I couldn't have told you his name.' Hands on a clammy back. 'Or picked him out of a line-up.'

What had looked like concern was apparently confusion, which collapsed into a broad smile. 'That's fucked,' Claudia said.

And because the alcohol made my thoughts stumble over each other, or because the laughter was mounting to a throbbing in my ears, or because I felt that every eye was trained on me, and at the same time like I didn't exist—had never existed at all—I laughed with her.

I stayed for another few rounds, until I had sat long enough and laughed enough that nobody could accuse me of being a bad sport. Then, feeling suddenly soul-numbingly sober, I walked back to Fairfax, swiped into my room and, crouching on my bed in darkness, I cried.

More than my vague recollections, Sackers's smile, and the knowing way he looked at me before he posed the question, taunted me. I could bear quite easily—indeed, had borne for several weeks— the hazy clutch of bodies that floated in my memory. But it was the flogging of these bodies for a laugh, for a story, that I couldn't stomach. As I drifted into sleep, I felt the eyes of the room, like a weight, still on me.

—

THE NEXT MORNING, with a heavy head and a sickness that shuffled gracelessly between bowel and stomach, I reached for my phone.

The screen was full of notifications. There were news alerts I dismissed, as well as texts from Claudia.

I showered and brushed my teeth then sat on the edge of my bed, towel wrapped around me and hair wet and dripping down the back of my neck. I opened the texts. There were several from very early in the morning, asking where I was and if I'd left, with spelling mistakes that looked like she'd emptied a bag of Scrabble tiles. Below these barely decipherable missives was a text from nine am:

I think you should talk to Emily. She's upset.

Since the shower, my nausea had faded to an undercurrent. I opened my blinds, registering for the first time what a glorious desktop-background day it was, with fluffy clouds placed against a flat blue sky as if by a graphic designer.

I considered getting a coffee but, still in my towel, with an oppressive tightness in my chest, the thought of clothes and shoes was overwhelming. I lay back on the bed, my wet hair making a pool of the pillow, and replied.

Oh no! Why?

You didn't tell her you used to sleep with Nick

It wasn't an ongoing thing?
It was once!
In O Week!

The staccato pacing of these texts: each self-contained, a little stone thrown in my defence, undermined me.

Ok, well she's really upset. I think you should apologise or something

That was a very Claudia expression. 'Or something' was offered as a sweetener, as if apologising wasn't my only option, although it was so vague and unconstructive it served to underscore that apologising was, really, the only option.

Cringing at how quickly I had switched to defensiveness, scrambling for a flurry of excuses, I decided to get the apology over and done with. I put on running leggings, a sports bra and my Fairfax jumper, as if to convince my body that it was young and healthy, not dehydrated and ill-treated.

I knocked on Emily's door and, hearing nothing, entered. It was dark and a mouldy smell emanated from a pile of unwashed laundry. I felt like I was transgressing, crawling into a very dark and private space. She was lying in her bed and the orange plastic curtains were drawn across the window, which lit them up with a white square, like a film projector. The room had an orange tint, so it was not so much dark and dank like a cave, but dark and plastic, like Tupperware with pasta sauce left at the bottom of a bag.

'Here.' I handed her a bottle of Gatorade, which I had bought the day before and now offered up with an air of self-sacrifice that probably looked to her, in all its earnestness, more like self-importance.

'Thanks.' She sat up in bed and nursed the bright blue drink between her bent knees. 'You didn't have to do that.'

'No worries.'

'Are you sure?'

'Yeah, just have it. It's a gift.'

'Thanks.' She popped the lid, and took a tentative sip.

'How was your night?'

'So fun. I stayed till sunrise. How did you end up?' Her voice was acquiring a clipped formality that I'd heard her use when talking to the master or to her parents on the phone. She hated conflict, perhaps even more than I did, and shared my instinct that it was better not addressed when it could be suffocated with small talk.

It was her smile, however, that made me uncomfortable. It was so conspicuously an effort of will.

I decided to get to the point. 'Claudia told me that you're upset about me and Nick.'

'Claudia said that?'

'Yeah, she told me this morning.'

'Oh, I must have been very drunk last night.' She laughed and shook her head, as if to reprimand her former self. 'It's fine, really. I don't know why Claudia would have said that.'

'I'm sorry. I know you like him . . .'

'I don't like him,' Emily said, so quickly it was unconvincing. 'We've slept together a few times, and obviously we're not exclusive or anything. I wouldn't make any claims to own him. He's not mine.'

'No, I know that. But you'd like to know if one of your friends had slept with him.'

'Well, yeah. I guess that's right.' Emily laughed and sipped her Gatorade.

'I'm sorry.' I pulled out the chair at her desk, then seeing it was covered with clothes, sat on the floor instead.

'Oops,' Emily said, motioning to the chair. 'I'll move my shit.'

'No, no, it's fine—I'm comfortable here,' I said, with the carpet scratching at my leggings and her wardrobe door digging into my back. 'I was just going to say, the reason I didn't tell you—and please believe this isn't just an excuse—is that I didn't know until last night that it was Nick.'

'But you know Nick.'

'Yeah, I know. But we had sex on the first night of O Week, and I remembered having sex, but I was too drunk to remember the guy's name or, like, anything about him.'

'You didn't remember what he looked like?'

'Nope. I remembered that he had thick eyebrows.'

'Nick does have thick eyebrows.'

'I doubt that's how he'd want to be remembered sexually. I'm the guy with the huge . . .'

'Eyebrows,' we said in unison. Emily was laughing now, her shoulders deflated, her head leaning back against the pillow.

'Well, now you know,' I said. 'I didn't realise until Sackers made a joke about it, otherwise, I'd like to think I would've told you.'

'Fucking Sackers.' Emily reserved a special contempt for Sackers because—although he was not the first boy to tell her, 'You're really pretty for an Asian'—he was the most recent. The presence in our conversation of a common enemy drew us closer. She looked at me, eyes rounded with concern. 'God, you must have really totalled yourself.'

'Yeah, I guess so. I don't remember much.'

She fiddled with the Gatorade bottle, flicking the lid on and off. 'But it was . . . you know . . . you're okay and everything?'

'Oh yeah, I'm fine. Like, would I have made the same choices sober? Probably not. Was it different to any other time two people get drunk and have sex? Probably not.'

'We've all been there,' Emily said.

The possibility that I might spend the morning in quiet, comforting conversation, turning past events over and holding them up to new, gentle-toned lights, was extinguished by a knock at the door. I opened it to find Claudia and Portia, looking like shells of their former selves, bearing a problem, which was deemed much larger than my own.

Portia's hair, which had been blow-dried to perfection the night before, now hung limp. Her eyes were glassy and rimmed with black globules of mascara, one of which had fallen and stuck lower down her cheek. She was wearing grey Qantas pyjamas, the type handed out on business-class flights. The flying kangaroo sat flat against her skinny-girl chest.

Emily got up so Portia could take her spot on the bed. 'What's happened?'

'I lost everything,' Portia cried, putting her head in her hands, her bony shoulders shaking with sobs.

'What do you mean?'

'Everything. It's all gone.' She sniffled, and wiped a sleeve on her little ski-jump nose. I wondered what kind of act might look dirty on her, when even wiping her nose on her pyjamas managed to look so expensive and clean. 'I lost my handbag.'

Claudia didn't miss a beat. 'Is that your Lucy Folk one?'

'Yes,' must have been the answer, because the crying started again, harder.

Claudia continued, stroking Portia's back with uncharacteristic tenderness. 'It's okay, I'm sure you'll be able to buy a new one. They're always selling those bags second-hand. What was *in* the bag?'

'My room key, my phone, which had all my pictures on it . . .'

'Surely your pictures will be in the cloud,' I said.

'Not the ones of *last night*, though.' She looked at me the way I imagined I sometimes looked at her: like I was actually stupid.

'I have quite a few of us from last night,' Emily said.

Portia's head straightened. 'Can you send them to me?'

I passed Emily her phone, which was on the floor near my feet.

Claudia started counting off items on the fingers of one hand, still stroking Portia like an animal with the other. 'Okay, so the bag, the phone, the key—we can damage control this. Anything else?'

Her lower lip wobbled. She mumbled something starting with *m*.

'What?'

'My medallion.'

I assumed I'd misheard. '*What?*'

'My medallion. You know: the little gold coins they had at the grazing table last night that said "St Thomas' College ball" and had the date engraved?'

'Yeah?'

'I'll never get that back.'

I inspected her anthropologically, as if through a glass display case. 'What were you going to do with it?'

'It was going to be such a nice memento.'

'But—' I wasn't heard over the sobs, which were even louder now.

Claudia, with a look, suggested I drop it.

'For what?' I said. 'Like to show your children?'

'Exactly.' Her limp hair parted across her beautiful face. For the first time, she was looking at me like I was someone who *really* got it.

8

I WAS TIRED all weekend, and when the Chapel Choir performed on Sunday, the events of the ball still clung to me like a shadow. I stood, as I always did, next to Eve and let her voice overwhelm mine. I sang so softly that, although I could feel the sound in my throat, I couldn't hear anything coming out.

After the service, with 'Make Me a Channel of Your Peace' still sounding in my head, Balth approached the altos.

'Did you two have a magical evening on Friday?' Eve asked, crossing her arms in a performance of irritation.

'Oh, you have no idea. You could've cut the sexual tension with a knife.'

Eve laughed and, by laughing, forgave him.

I walked behind Eve and Balth as we left the chapel and stood on the grass outside. The sun had just set, and the sky was almost purple—the stars not ready yet.

'I have a problem,' Balth said.

'Just one?'

He ignored Eve. 'I hosted Pre's for the ball, because, you know, I'm a social guy. And I have three bottles of half-drunk champagne in my mini fridge getting flatter by the minute.'

'I think it'd be rude to throw it all out,' Eve said.

'Unforgivably rude.'

'Where shall we drink it?' Eve turned to me, her eyebrows raised.

I felt exhausted and sore, like my bones had been wrung dry. But the thought of them having a drink without me made me more tired still. 'Neither of your rooms. They're too messy. And not mine. It's too clean.'

'Oval, then?'

Balth left Eve and me outside the chapel while he ran up to his room to fetch the champagne. I looked at my phone, for no reason really, just for something to do.

'This will be fun,' Eve declared. She was wearing an oversized check blazer over a thin black singlet and jeans. Her hands were in her pockets and her head was turned up to the evening sky. 'We'll sit on the grass, drink flat champagne and talk about the meaning of life.' She said this like she was reading aloud the first sentence in a novel.

So we sat on the grass at the edge of the oval as the night crept in like a rising tide, and we sipped Balth's flat champagne from plastic cups, and we talked about our little lives.

'I heard about the fire alarm,' Eve said, nudging me.

'Don't.' Balth held up a finger.

'Honestly, Balthazar, a scented candle? Who were you trying to impress?'

Balth crushed the plastic cup he was holding, then put his fingers inside to bend it back into shape. He refilled it. We were sitting cross-legged, each with a bottle of champagne in the gap between our legs. Mine was tepid and not entirely flat—the suggestion of bubbles fizzed on my tongue.

'And where did you get to, International Woman of Mystery?' Balth motioned to me with his cup like he was our choirmaster, conducting the conversation.

'I went to Afters.'

'With those "friends" of yours?' Eve made bunny ears around the word *friends*. She was often telling me that my popularity marked me as unprincipled. I never bothered to defend myself when she made claims like this. Instead, I glowed at the thought that she was invested in my moral development.

'Yes,' I said. 'It was predictably awful.'

'Lots of drinking games?' Balth asked.

I nodded.

Eve took a sip and winced, like the champagne tasted foul. 'How facile.'

'Yes,' Balth said, 'we can't all go to intellectual parties where people talk about modern monetary theory and do clever poos on the floor.'

'You told him about that?' Eve asked me.

I smiled. 'I told everyone about that.'

Eve put a hand to her hair and flicked her fringe out of her eyes. It fell over her forehead in two little sweeps, like curtains pulled back to reveal a sunny landscape. 'So, what, you played these drinking games and that was it?'

'Yeah.' I swallowed. 'I left kind of early.'

Eve's eyes narrowed. 'That's not like you.'

'I was really drunk.'

We sat in silence for a moment, and I tried to make out shapes in the black grass. There was a lot of liquid left in my bottle, but I hadn't had dinner, and my head and stomach felt light. 'I was a bit off it, actually,' I heard myself saying, and wondered whether I should stop. 'We played Never Have I Ever, and someone was like: never have I ever had sex with Michaela.'

'What?'

' It was hard to make out their faces in the dark, but I could feel Balth looking at me.

'Yeah, like, I probably overreacted, but I just wasn't vibing it after that.'

Eve put a gentle hand on my wrist. The tips of her fingers were cold, and I flinched. 'Who was it?'

'It doesn't matter,' I said. 'It was just a one-night stand on the first night of O Week. I was so drunk at the time, I actually couldn't remember who the boy was.'

'You couldn't remember?' Eve's hand was on my leg now. I was wearing jeans, so there was no chill of skin on cold skin—just a light, gentle pressure.

'No. Like I said, I was very drunk.'

Her grip tightened. It started to hurt. 'Do you remember anything about that night? Anything at all?'

I shook my head. 'Anyway, mystery solved now.' I laughed and lifted my plastic cup, which was empty, as if to make a toast. I drank from it anyway, to complete the motion.

Balth's voice was almost a whisper. 'Who was it?'

Eve still clutched my leg, just above the knee. I had never seen her sit quite so still. Her gaze, cast out upon the dark grass, seemed to look inwards. If there was a way to tell this story so that Eve—with her love of casual sex and loose, spontaneous indiscretions—might laugh, then the moment had passed. She looked disturbed by what she had just heard.

I thought of Nick, and his sliding, sheepish refusal to look at me while Sackers roared and laughed and clapped my back. For a moment, I entertained the idea that Eve might turn her righteous glare on Nick, and I felt a twist of triumph. But I didn't want to give her a face to colour the story: characters to cast in her mind. The blurrier the picture, the easier it was to bear. Under her tightening grip the story felt sinister and my role in it pathetic.

'It doesn't matter who it was,' I said. 'Let's just talk about somethi—'

'No.' Hearing the quiet forcefulness in his voice, I became suddenly conscious that Balth, like Eve, had been sitting extremely still. He was looking at me with such fierce concern I had to look away. 'Who asked the question?'

'It was Sackers.'

'Of course it was.' Eve removed her hand, and made an exasperated little sound, as if she were about to say something, but Balth cut her off.

'What a detestable waste of skin.'

I would have laughed, but Balth didn't relish the words—he coughed them up, with a sincerity that frightened me.

'He's pretty indefensible,' I said. And then, because the silence was rising, I added, 'He has a very immature sense of humour.'

'Michaela.' Eve said my name like a command, and I met her eyes. 'I don't think there's anything funny about that at all.'

Then, to my horror, she put her arm around me. I sat stiff, looking out onto the dark ocean of grass where, years and years ago, a girl my age was abused and discarded—a mangled lump of flesh and bones to be uncovered in the morning.

—

WHEN OUR BOTTLES were empty, and we'd stood and stretched and bid farewell to Balth, Eve and I walked back to college together.

I had sensed, when I'd told them about Sackers, that Eve had more to say. I had broken our silence—thick with unasked questions—by saying 'Anyway,' in a voice that didn't sound like mine. But having nothing in mind to talk about, it was Balth, who took my *anyway* and turned it into a segue. He told Eve, with rehearsed detail, the full story of how he 'nearly razed' St Thomas'. Now, walking back with matching strides, alone with Eve, the levity receded.

I could still feel the pressure of her arm around me. It had seemed an instructive embrace; one that did not so much comfort me as tell me how to feel.

Eve's hands were in her pockets and she was looking at her feet, careful not to trip in the dark.

'Do you think Balth is gay?'

I paused at the unexpected question. I had been reciting lines in my head: answers to the questions I dreaded, about that first night in O Week.

Instead, I thought back to that night several weeks ago, before Eve and I were friends. My ear pressed to the cold wall; Eve's performed private noises penetrating it. Balthazar had been much harder to make out. I opened my mouth to say, *I don't know, Eve— you're the one who slept with him*, but she cut me off.

'Or maybe he's bi. I could see him with a boy, couldn't you?'

I decided to loosen my grip on the conversation and let Eve pull it where she willed. 'Yeah,' I said. 'I've wondered that. I think he's the kind of person who would come out, though. He's so self-assured.'

'I don't know; all-male private schools are pretty problematic, even now.'

I was silent for a moment. I sensed that Eve was up to her usual trick: opening with a provocation not to solicit my opinion, but to create an environment where she could present her own. These conversations, if I could call them that, always made me feel small, both because I was not really her partner but her audience, and because—despite my resentment—her striking ideas and eloquent face so totally captured my attention.

'Yeah, I guess.'

As I predicted, she continued, needing very little prompting. 'I also think it's confusing, because he's not conventionally masculine, and we're socialised to have such a prescriptive idea for what that looks like.'

'Right, like, maybe he's not gay, just metro.'

'Yeah. Like, if we were in Europe—where the ideal of masculinity is less reductive and all, like, *chicks, footy, beer*—would we be having this conversation?' So this was the topic on which Eve wanted to present: Australian masculinity. It seemed artificial, indulgent even, to discuss it, as if our conversations shaped reality rather than just colouring it for our own amusement.

So all I said was: 'I don't know, Eve; I've never been to Europe.'

—

THERE WAS A cafe on campus, wedged between the medical school and the hospital, where nurses and paramedics and doctors went on their lunch breaks and I went to be alone.

I liked it for several reasons. First, all the antiseptic-handed, uniformed professionals provided a smiling reminder that my struggles were unimportant. Up the road, lives were being lost and saved so frequently that suffering, like a coffee break, was quotidian.

Second, the staff—an Italian family who had owned the cafe for decades—were so incredibly rude that you suspected the experience had to be edifying, like eating vegetables, or receiving a short sharp smack.

Where other cafes might put up obsequious signs . . .

Congratulations! You made it out of bed.
Before coffee ☹ *After coffee* ☺

. . . the signs at Reggio's were forthright, bordering on abusive.

WE WILL NOT SERVE YOU IF YOU'RE ON YOUR PHONE.
Don't disturb the barista. He doesn't want to talk to you.
CASH ONLY. 10% surcharge for complaints about this policy.

I liked the whole Reggio family, from the haggard matriarch, whose sotto-est voce was an ear-ringing shout, to her muscular, singlet-wearing son Luca, who called any non-white female '*bella*' and ignored absolutely everybody else.

The food was overpriced, the coffee dirt-like, and the soy or almond milk chosen to punish you for being so fussy. But I would have paid the ten per cent surcharge and more to spend time in an environment where the customer is always wrong—not just factually, but deeply, spiritually wrong—for thinking that for the price of a coffee or microwaved carbonara you could buy respect.

I was sitting at an outside table—the only one that did not have a little sign on it that read:

NO STUDYING! THIS IS NOT A LIBRARY.

I had forty minutes until my lecture started, and I was trying to finish the assigned reading, which appeared to be thirty pages about a man pumping water, with long sentences, chains of subordinate clauses, and an apparent phobia of full stops that gave me a sense of rhythmic, mind-numbing exhaustion, much like the man with his pump.

I gathered, after reading one paragraph particularly closely about three times, that the man pumping was meant to teach me something about intention. If someone asked him what he was doing, he would reply: 'I'm pumping water,' not, 'I'm contracting these muscles,' or, 'I'm making this sound.' What he *intended* to do was what he described, even though many other possible descriptions of the same action also applied.

A shout from inside dragged me, as if from underwater, back to Reggio's. Luca yelled, 'Soy cap,' and then, without a second's break, his mother echoed furiously at twenty times the volume: 'SOY CAP. WHO ORDERED A SOY CAP?'

I took it from the counter and said, 'Thanks,' like it was an apology. Luca did not look up from the coffee machine.

'You're brave. I stopped ordering soy here ages ago.'

I turned around so quickly that a puddle of chocolate-powdered foam dripped onto my hand. (At Reggio's, coffee was served in takeaway cups without a lid.)

Professor Rosen was standing in the queue behind me, his leather satchel hanging off his shoulder.

'No! You let them win.'

'I caved. I couldn't hack the judgement.' He motioned with his eyes to Luca. It was a childish expression, like we were making faces behind a teacher's back, and I became aware that my heart was beating at a quick, finger-tingling pace.

'He's very intimidating,' I said.

'I can't relate.'

I laughed, and noticed that the glob of chocolatey foam was seeping into the back of my hand. At Reggio's, the napkins were kept with the lids: on the opposite side of the cafe to the counter, so customers had to wobble as far as possible with the risk of a spill. 'Well, see you in class,' I said, and headed across the room.

By the time the lid was firmly on and my hand wiped down, Paul was at my side again, reaching across me for a spoon. He didn't make eye contact, and our silence seemed artificial, when only moments ago we'd spoken so fluidly. 'I was just doing the reading,' I said, perhaps too loudly.

'What? Now?'

'At least I'm doing it before class.'

We walked together out into the sunshine, and I stopped when we arrived at my flimsy silver table.

'True. At least you're doing it at all.' He looked at the table, with my glasses, computer and water bottle spread across it. 'I'm surprised you're allowed to read here.'

'I'm not really. They usually shoo me away, but I like the sense of urgency.'

He laughed. 'And what do you think?'

'Of what?'

'Of the reading.'

'Oh, the reading. It's dense. And granular.'

He looked away, out across the campus, and adopted a distracted tone, which gave me the impression that he was thinking about something else entirely. 'Yes, I don't always set it for first years, but I think it's important.'

I spoke quickly, each word a conspicuous grab for his attention. 'I can see how a lot flows from it. Like, whether our actions are intentional or not, whether we're even capable of conscious, intentional action, then determines whether we can be held morally responsible.'

'Exactly.' He turned back towards me, and looked me up and down. It felt like a reward. 'You don't need to come to the lecture. That's exactly where it's going.'

It was a cold day, but we were standing in direct sunlight, and when I moved my hand to shield my eyes from the glare, I wondered whether there was a sweat patch under my arm. 'But isn't there a whole other field of inquiry that goes to not whether you intended the particular action, but how you know what's right or wrong? We seem to have spent a lot of time on freedom. But I'm still wondering, even if I am free to do what I want, it's not necessarily as if I do so knowing whether my actions are good or bad.'

Paul was watching me closely, punctuating my speech with little nods. I held his gaze like a challenge.

'How does someone know, do you think? I mean, that's sort of the point of the course. Or one of the points. Where do you think you've landed on that so far? What are we? Week ten?'

'Yep.'

He too was squinting in the sun. 'So Michaela, from where are we deriving moral knowledge in week ten, semester one?'

'I want to say "social constructs", but that depresses me.'

'Does it? Why?'

My heart felt suddenly fluttery, and my face was hot. 'Not because I'm looking for a higher power, or anything.' I laughed. It was a shrill, foreign sound that I wished I could take back. 'More like, we inhabit so many different social spaces that to think that morality might be inconsistent across them, it's just . . . depressing.'

'Do we, though? Do we inhabit such different spaces?'

I looked past him, back into Reggio's, where the queue of white-coated, blue-uniformed people had doubled. 'I don't know,' I said. 'I feel like I do.'

When I looked back, there was nothing in his face to suggest he had heard what I'd said. 'I should get going. I can't be late.'

I thought I detected an emphasis on *I*, so—in the faint hope that he might look up at me when I entered, perhaps with a private glimmer of acknowledgement—I sat at Reggio's for several more minutes. I made sure that when I entered Professor Rosen's lecture theatre, I was exactly five minutes late.

—

THAT EVENING I received an email while I was at dinner, and immediately left the dining hall to read it in the privacy of a toilet cubicle. I sat there for several minutes, until the plastic seat became uncomfortable, and I thought it would start to seem odd if I didn't flush soon.

Paul's email was, as always, one single body.

> *I was thinking about what you said today, and I just wanted to say it's a great point, and it's (deservedly) been given a lot of airtime in recent years. You might be interested in some articles (I've attached a few links) on moral ignorance. Obviously, none of this will be assessed, and you won't have time to go beyond the scope of the assigned papers in the exam, but you might enjoy them for your own interest/edification.*

I found his use of the forward slash jaunty and teasing, as if theoretical knowledge were the same as edification, and both were deliverable, by Paul, at the click of a button. Was he, I wondered, intending to flirt? Is that how he would describe his email?

> *Dear Paul,*
> *They do sound interesting/edifying.*
> *I actually had a few questions about the exam. I'm obviously grateful for all the time you've already given me, but I was wondering if I could take you up on your offer in today's lecture, and meet to discuss it?*
>
> *Best,*
> *Michaela*

By the time he replied, I was back in my bedroom, staring blankly at my newsfeed, trying to pretend that my pounding heart wasn't blitzing my thoughts into fragments.

Sure. Friday 2 pm?

After an hour in which I showered, brushed my teeth, texted other people and rearranged the words in my response, I pressed send.

Perfect! Thanks again.

Single-line, Paul-style. Finally, I'd caved.

———

EVE INSISTED WE visit a gallery near uni. 'Apparently, it's amazing. The exhibition ends today.'

'Who said it was amazing? I'm a busy woman, you know.'

'Luke.'

I lay back on my bed, pulling the doona over my head.

'I thought we liked Luke!'

Leaving campus seemed a healthy, normal thing to do, and leaving to go to an art gallery seemed downright sophisticated. But I resented accompanying Eve on what was, apparently, a field trip to research a conversation she would later have with Luke. Maybe that's all art is, I thought, as I pulled on high-waisted jeans and laced my Converse: talking points.

Like a clearing in a forest of derelict terraces, the gallery opened onto a square, which (in a triumph of city planning) was just urban enough for skateboards but too gentrified for drug deals. At its centre was a towering sculpture that was so screamingly optimistic about human potential—to clean cities and civilise parks—that I found it depressing. Around us, grass grew up the sides of buildings and concrete folded in waves over the shells of abandoned breweries. It was midday when we arrived, and the cascading landscape of glass reflected the sun everywhere, inescapably, at once, so it was with relief that my eyes adjusted to the gallery's more subtle fluorescence.

The exhibition was about climate change, and I found myself confronted with the realities of human waste in a totally theoretical way, which was independent of my own choices and behaviour. Like I was witness to a narrative, not a participant in it.

We stood in front of a photograph that covered an entire wall: an overhead shot of a Chinese rubbish tip, probably taken by a drone.

Eve turned to me. The backlit photo—so large it was abstract, with plastic wrappers like splotches in a Pollock painting—illuminated the edges of her silhouette. I could make out individual hairs.

'You know that story you told me about Afters . . .' She spoke in a polite whisper.

'Yes.' I studied the photograph.

'Have you thought about reporting it?'

'Reporting the drinking game?'

'Of course not. I mean, have you thought about reporting what happened in O Week?'

I stood back from the photograph and turned so I was facing her. Her face had a bluish tint. I could make out her eyebrows, furrowed in concern. It irritated me. 'No, I really think it's between me and . . .' I paused. I had detected a thrill—a detached aesthetic appreciation—in the way Eve whispered *what happened in O Week*. Like she had suspended disbelief and sat back to watch the drama unfold. Trying to sit in Eve's position, both appalled and enthralled, I felt my shame paraded before me like some kind of pantomime. To imagine I might 'report' what happened, I assume she pictured me as a victim to it. And where she had a villain, my victimhood could only be embellished.

'It's between me and the boy.' A meek conclusion, which Eve quickly overrode when she leaned closer still.

'You can tell me his name.'

'It doesn't matter.'

I walked towards the next room, which was emitting a hum of white noise. Eve didn't follow me.

I stopped and said, a little louder, 'It was a totally meaningless thing. If Sackers hadn't tried to make a joke out of it, we wouldn't be talking about it now.'

She maintained her whisper—not soft enough to conceal a subtle excitement. 'You can't have consented.'

'What?'

Eve approached me. 'If you were too drunk to remember it, you were definitely too drunk to consent. I don't think it's a stretch to imagine that the college might want to know when its residents are engaging in non-consensual sex.'

'I don't want the college to know.'

She was no longer whispering. Her voice was rich with concern. 'I'm sure they have someone who you could talk to about it.'

Above the white noise, I heard myself swallow. I pointed at the photograph of the rubbish. 'It seems to defeat the purpose, don't you think? It's actually very beautiful.'

Eve didn't turn to look at it. She pushed past me, heading towards the white noise, and I thought I detected a little exasperated shake of her head.

We went through the rest of the exhibition in silence. In the foyer at the end, Eve looked through the gift shop. It sold pointedly useless trinkets, including a few handsomely printed books.

Eve looked up from the architectural book she was leafing through and asked if we should stay for the video installation—an animation about surveillance capitalism—which started on the hour.

'I have to go.'

'Oh, sorry. I thought you didn't have class on Friday?'

I pretended to flick through a zine. It seemed to be about hats. 'I've got a meeting with Professor Rosen.'

I didn't look up from the glossy pages, but I could feel Eve staring at me, and heard her close the book with a thud. 'You're insatiable. You know he has a reputation?' There was a smile in her voice and I looked up to check whether her amusement was genuine. Her joking stance—hands on her hips in half-hearted disapproval—cured my concern that I was an object of pity.

'Honestly, that's part of the charm,' I said. 'I'm not nearly so diligent with any of my other subjects.'

Eve laughed again, and I regretted that I had to leave so soon.

She said, 'Wouldn't it be nice if society evolved to a point where sex could be clean and transactional, where everyone is positively consenting and, like, of the same generation?'

'Wouldn't it.'

'And no complicated power dynamics.'

I thought about our kiss at Luke's—the way she took my face in both hands with such purpose; how intentional, but also inevitable, that act seemed. 'Surely that's what relationships are: power dynamics.'

She dismissed me with a flick of her slender hand. 'Go to your stupid meeting. I hope it's very erotic.'

9

PROFESSOR ROSEN MAINTAINED a strictly professional distance throughout the duration of the course—right up until 'pens down'.

In the week leading up to the final exam, Eve and I went to the Fairfax library every night after dinner. We would sit there in our pyjamas until the early hours of the morning and 'study', which mostly meant: talk. We talked in whispers at first, which crescendoed as Eve's observations hardened into opinions, whereupon she would state her conclusion with the conviction she thought it warranted—loud enough for the whole library to hear. Then a shush from the surrounding students would subdue her. But being so subdued—heads bent, words whispered—only emboldened our friendship. As if we were the only two members of a club in which we answered moral questions with such self-importance, anyone would think we'd conceived them ourselves.

'Did Professor Rosen say anything useful? When you had your academic meeting?'

It was the night before the exam and Eve was returning, in whispers of spit-flecking intensity, to a question she had already asked me several times.

'No, not really. He just went through some examples of how to avoid exegesis.'

I already knew the follow-up question, which she had also asked me every time we studied together. 'He didn't hint at what would be in the exam?'

'Nope.' I sipped the peppermint tea I had brought with me from the dining hall. I found it cold and toothpaste-tasting.

'Were you'—she paused for effect, raising her eyebrows—'busy doing other things?'

'How dare you! As if I wouldn't have told you straight away.'

'Bragged about it, more like.'

The academic meeting, in which I asked Professor Rosen questions I'd concocted for the purpose of having something to say, was nothing to brag about. Unlike our previous meeting, Professor Rosen remained disengaged for the duration. He sat half turned towards his computer, his face oscillating between harried (whenever I was describing the nature of my confusion) and bored (whenever he was responding). I felt like an inconvenience, a waste of his time, and I rearranged myself in the chair—crossing and uncrossing my legs—trying to take up less space. After about half an hour, he said, 'You seem to be on top of it,' in an empty, declaratory tone, which I took to be my dismissal.

'I really can't tell you how unsexy that meeting was,' I told Eve. 'He was almost militant.'

'The military has massive problems with sexual abuse; you might as well say that he was religious about it.'

I laughed, then was silenced by the glare of the adjacent table. 'You know what I mean.'

'Sure.' Eve stood and stretched, her arms raised above her head, soft tendrils of armpit hair on full display. She wasn't wearing a bra, and her nipples were proud beneath her white singlet. While her arms were above her head, she said, loud enough for the whole room to hear: 'I'm going to write a dialogue.'

Loud shushes from the surrounding tables, like sprinklers had been turned on.

Because I didn't respond to Eve—rather, bowed my head under the weight of the shushing—she leaned towards me and repeated herself, in quieter but no less proud tones. 'In the exam. I'm going to write a dialogue.'

'What do you mean?'

'Remember in the lecture when Paul said we don't *have* to write an essay? I think he was hinting that a dialogue would go down well.'

'How original,' I whispered—too weak to convey my sarcasm.

'Hardly.' Eve smiled like she thought it was very original indeed. 'It's very Socratic of me.'

When I sat the exam the following morning, I wrote a dialogue, without being conscious of making a decision to do so. I did not answer the question—rather, a teacher and a student discussed it. Both the teacher and the student spoke in a voice like Luke's: clipped and precise, no florid tokens of respect. The dialogue had a sparring quality. When I finished and looked at the clock, I found there were forty-five seconds to go. Too nervous to reread what I'd written, I looked around at the other students. Then, conscious that I was staring, I looked down at my desk, sitting on my hands, and waited for the invigilator to call 'pens down'. When she did, I jumped.

Outside the exam room, I found Eve. She was standing in a small crowd of people I had never met before. They were discussing the exam animatedly and didn't part when I approached. I had to tap Eve on the shoulder, so she could turn around to face me.

'It was fine. Exactly what I had prepared for. If anything'—here she turned back to the group, to make sure they were listening—'it was a bit easy.'

'Easy?' They laughed. 'All right. Easy for you, maybe.'

I laughed too, and squeezed myself into their circle. When I saw Luke approaching, I moved to make space for him.

'How'd we go?' he said, looking only at Eve.

Everyone in the circle watched.

'Just happy it's over,' she said, with affected modesty.

We went to the pub, our conversation bouncing happily on a pleasant cocktail of adrenaline and relief. It was our last exam for the semester, the sun was shining and the sky was a brilliant winter blue. We sat in the courtyard, and our beers looked golden.

Eve told everyone that she had written a dialogue. I grabbed a beer coaster and started folding it into quarters, then gently ripped it along the seam, trying to get the line as straight as possible.

Eve did not ask me how I found the exam or what I had written, but I was sure that if she did, I wouldn't have said anything about a dialogue.

—

AFTER EXAMS, EVE suggested that we attend the philosophy department's Women in Philosophy mixer. The event was designed to make the discipline seem less masculine, or threatening, or whatever.

'It sounds lame,' I said.

'It's about creating safe spaces for women who study philosophy. What about that is lame?'

'I don't know, it sounds tokenistic. I get my "women in philosophy" quota every time I talk to you.'

Eve rolled her eyes. 'Just come. We'll meet some cool people.'

Upon arrival at the mixer, it only took one glance around the room to see that Eve was right. Eve headed straight for a woman who looked to be in her sixties standing towards the back. She was wearing slim cigarette-leg pants and a white shirt. Her hair was short and curled across her forehead. 'That's Eileen Murphy,' Eve whispered to me as we approached. 'She's head of department.' At Eileen's side, talking animatedly, was a very short, very thin woman closer to our age, with a brown bob that looked both exquisitely sleek and also like it was never touched—like it just fell casually into symmetrical, face-defining shape.

The two women paused their conversation, and Eve opened, as always, boldly. 'I'm surprised at the turnout. Not what you'd expect from a *Women* in Philosophy function.'

I followed quickly. 'We only came because we thought it would be a quiet place to hang out just the two of us.'

They both laughed. The brown-haired woman looked to Eileen, waiting for her to respond first.

'It's atrocious, isn't it?' said Eileen. 'You know, every year, female undergraduates are in the majority, but by the postgraduate level they've all been weeded out.'

Eve straightened. 'Weeded out?'

'By the men. Talking over them; undermining their contribution; telling them that subjects like literature are less important than good old-fashioned pragmatism.' She listed each of these on her fingers, with a little wave at the end, as if to say: *I could go on.* She faded into an arms-crossed silence.

'I'm Violet, by the way.' The brown-haired woman extended an elegant hand, tipped with shellac-painted nails in a red so dark it was almost black.

I took her hand greedily, and Eve and I introduced ourselves.

Eve asked Violet and Eileen about their work. Pointed, interesting questions with little asides and exclamations that suggested she knew what they were talking about. Eve never admitted to not knowing a philosopher. She would qualify her ignorance: 'I haven't read any of his stuff, but I've *heard* of him.'

When Violet asked politely whether I'd read anything by the philosopher she worked on, I said, 'No.' I blinked a few times in the silence that followed. 'I haven't heard of him either.'

Eileen laughed, which Violet took as a cue. 'Haven't heard of him,' she said.

I noticed Violet often repeated people in conversation, especially when they said something to make her laugh. When she did, she appropriated the joke. Her sexy, smoky laugh, combined with that tight brown bob, was so deeply affirming, it was as though the joke was hers in the first place and you, through conversation, had merely returned it to her.

Violet invited Eve and me to the pub with some other master's students. When she asked Eileen if she would come, the older woman just shook her head. 'You know me.'

Violet said to us, by way of explanation, 'Eileen has a no-socialising-with-students policy.' Then, to Eileen, she added: 'Come on. It will be fun.'

Eileen raised a hand, brushing her off. It was an authoritative gesture that would have made me shrink. 'Trust me, Violet,' she said, 'if going to the pub with students is *that* much fun, then you shouldn't be there.'

———

WHEN WE ARRIVED at the pub, the only person I recognised was Professor Rosen. The postgraduate students and several faculty members sat at a long wooden table in a dark corner at the back. Professor Rosen was looking blankly at the table, rotating his beer glass slowly with his thumb and forefinger.

Eve and I sat with Violet at the opposite end. I got us a jug of cider, and Eve ordered a bowl of chips.

'So, did you two meet in Paul's class?' Violet was so poised that a shoestring fry, in her hands, could have passed for a cigarette.

'Sort of,' Eve said.

'We actually met at Fairfax. Our rooms are next to each other.'

'You live at college?' She nibbled the end of her chip. 'Do you hate it?'

Several minutes passed in which Eve criticised the residential college system in general. I was called upon to provide anecdotes, the telling of which Eve mostly did herself, such as the time I was interviewed at Rumwold College and told that the college wasn't interested in hearing about unwanted sexual advances 'every time'. For a moment, as Eve settled into the jug, and her gestures became as fluid as her conversation, I worried I would be called upon to recount how personal and humiliating drinking games like Never Have I Ever could be.

'Do you mind if I join you?' Professor Rosen was standing behind Violet, one hand on the back of her chair—or on her back; from where I sat opposite her, I couldn't tell. I looked to where he had been sitting and saw several empty chairs.

Paul smiled at Eve and me, with a nod of recognition. 'Violet,' he said, 'these girls were in my first year class this semester.'

She raised her eyebrows—two manicured parentheses. '*Girls?*'

'Fine.' Professor Rosen held up both hands in surrender. 'Not girls. Pupils, colleagues, learned friends.'

'I'll take learned friends.' Eve smiled.

'I dunno. I prefer tiny little lady-person,' I said.

They all laughed at that, nobody louder than Paul. I looked over at him and found his eyes ready to meet mine. I looked away first.

I'd expected Violet to be rude, but she approached him like a friend, making no attempt to subdue her charm. She looked up at Paul with a wide smile and, with a neat swoosh of her bob, motioned him into the chair at her side. Her only signs of hostility seemed performed—she disagreed with almost everything he said, but in a tone I interpreted as playful, like his opinions were objectionable, but totally unrelated to his person.

Whenever I said something funny, Paul would look at me, even after the conversation had moved on, a smile playing in his eyes. I found him so different from the person in our last meeting who sat on the other side of his desk and wouldn't look at me, except with irritation. He must be drunk, I thought.

When he left to get another beer, Eve did not wait for him to leave our sight before leaning forward and gazing intently at Violet. 'What's the deal?'

'With Paul?' Violet turned to watch him leave. Another swoosh of smooth hair. 'Oh. He's brilliant, obviously. Knows it, infuriatingly.'

Eve pressed on. 'I've heard that rumour . . .' she said. 'The girl who's at Oxford now?'

'Oh yeah. That was ages ago.' Violet took one of the remaining chips and wiped it along the bottom of the bowl, gathering up flecks of salt. 'Like, in his first year of teaching'—Eve exhaled, a little burst of disapproval, and Violet shrugged—'which makes it all the more astonishing, of course. Just, why would you do it, you know? Surely it's not worth risking your career when you're just starting out. I suppose he thought he could get away with it.'

Eve took a sip of cider. 'It sounds like he has.'

'That's the sad thing. He's, like, brilliant and good-looking, so he's probably just super entitled. Which makes him dangerous.'

'Do you think he's good-looking? Michaela does too.'

Violet looked at me, as if expecting some comment on Paul's appearance. Feeling suddenly jittery, and conscious of my heart rate, I announced: 'I need to pee.' A fact I had been sitting on since we arrived.

As always, it was the tiled loneliness of the cubicle that confirmed what I had been sensing for a while. I was drunk. Sitting on the toilet, I pored over my phone until I became aware of the queue forming outside.

As I headed back to the table, Professor Rosen, still waiting in line for his drink, called out to me from the bar.

'Michaela.' His smile, big and toothy, made him look much younger. 'I'm going outside for a smoke.'

'Fair,' I said.

'Do you want to come?'

I looked back towards the table, where Eve's hands were coming down firmly, emphasising a point I could only imagine she was making very articulately. Violet was nodding vigorously.

'It looks like my best offer.'

He laughed, and stood to the side so I could pass in front of him. He followed close behind me and, as we approached the door, he leaned around me to hold it open, one hand on the door, the other resting, ever so lightly—perhaps just the brush of three or four finger pads—on the base of my spine.

Out on the street, the rumble of the pub like white noise behind us, he pulled out a pack of cigarettes and shook it in my direction. 'Want one?'

'My dad died of lung cancer.'

'Jesus.' He put the pack back in his pocket. 'That's good, because I don't smoke.'

'I never said I don't smoke.'

'*Jesus.*' He laughed and pulled the pack out again, drawing two cigarettes from it. He looked at me, shaking his head a little, and laughed. 'Fuck you.' His laugh flowed out of him, loud and relaxed, unlike in his lectures, when it was a huffy, breathy burst, punctuating a joke, signalling permission for the rest of us to join.

'I wasn't saying that just to fuck with you,' I said. 'He did. Die, I mean.'

'I'm so sorry.'

People my age never assaulted me with sympathy. At this point they would get uncomfortable and mumble or look around, as if searching for an exit. The way Paul looked at me felt like I was being hugged.

'But I still smoke.'

He laughed again, a sardonic, dark-hearted little laugh. 'And you still said it to fuck with me.'

'A little bit.'

I accepted the cigarette, and leaned forward as he held out the lighter.

'So, what's the plan then?'

'What plan?' I took a drag. My limbs felt light. I leaned against the brick wall at my back, one hand pressed against its cold surface.

'The life plan.' He exhaled to the side, careful not to get smoke in my face. 'Do you think you'll stick with philosophy? I'm sure you could do very well.'

'I'm not sure. I don't really know what I'm doing.'

'Just take the compliment.'

Feeling chastised, I looked at the ground, exhaling and watching the smoke fade.

'Well, I really like it,' I said. 'I don't really know what I want to do yet, though.'

'That's fair enough. You're only, what? Twenty? Twenty-one?'

'Eighteen.'

He coughed a bit on the drag he was taking. 'Wow. You're very . . .'

'I've been told I'm mature.' I tilted my chin up as I said this. A proud little inflection.

'Yeah, I would not have guessed eighteen. I think it's the haircut.'

My hand shot up to my hair, close cropped, pixie-like, and shaved across the base of my neck.

'I stopped getting ID'd the day I cut it all off.'

'*ID'd*. Haven't thought about that in a long time.' He paused for a drag of his cigarette. 'Why did you do it?'

'I have really thick hair. It was annoying.'

'And you were sick of looking like other girls.' This was a statement.

Resenting his perceptiveness, I pushed the conversation back onto him. 'And you?'

'Yeah, I was also sick of looking like a girl.'

'No, how old are you?'

He looked up, like he was counting in his head. 'Double you, actually. Thirty-six.'

'Right.' I exhaled in a long, steady sigh. 'How long have you worked here?'

'Ages. I was at Oxford for a while.'

'Oxford. What was that like?'

'Very grand. But very grey. I got seasonal depression.'

I laughed, exhilarated by this personal detail. 'At least that's easy to cure. Like, did you buy a sun lamp?'

'No. I just came home.'

'See? What a quick fix.'

Paul dropped his cigarette on the ground. There was a thin film of rain, and the ground sounded sleek crunching under his boot. As he crushed the stub his weight shifted slightly, halving the already small space between us.

'We should go back inside,' he said.

He was standing very close. Slowly, gently, he put one hand on the brick wall just behind my head.

The bubbling fullness inside my stomach from all the cider, the humming of the pub behind us, the pounding of my heart—all were silenced when I grabbed Paul's face with two hands and pulled it towards mine. I did not think about the action, except, I suppose, I had been thinking about it for months. At the time, with one of his hands behind my head, the heat of his body flush against mine, his bearded soft smile so close to my face, I wasn't conscious of doing anything at all.

He responded slowly, first with one hand still on the wall, the other limp at his side, his mouth wet on mine. Then he eased his free hand behind my back and bit gently on my bottom lip as he pulled me closer.

When we broke away we both smiled. Every pore was tingling, but at the same time I felt relaxed, like I could put my head on his chest and sleep.

'Okay,' he said, his hands cupping my face. I don't think he meant anything by it—he sort of breathed the word, just for something to say.

Before I could respond, he dropped his hands, picked up one of mine, gently squeezed it, and then turned to walk back inside.

I followed him. The inside of the pub felt hot and musty, and I drew breaths of sticky air. My jumper prickled, and my limbs were light and empty.

Back at the table with Eve and Violet, Professor Rosen did not look at me, except in passing. His leg did not touch mine under the table. His hand, when it reached across for a chip, did not brush mine in the bowl. Nothing—not a look or a touch, or even a whispered aside—passed between us.

When he stood to leave, he said goodbye to the table as a collective, not making eye contact with anyone. As he passed my side of the table, which was closer to the door, he clapped me on the shoulder.

So convincing was his performance that, when I was walking home with Eve, she did not ask about Professor Rosen. I had imagined for a long time what it would be like to tell her about this moment, how I might relish the look on her face, how the mood between us would twist and contort. Now, however, the kiss seemed fragile: a crystalline moment which would shatter upon retelling.

I crossed my arms against the cold, which wasn't really cold, except I hadn't dressed for it. I felt the wind at my ankles, and the taste of cider hovered in my throat.

'I think I'm actually a bit drunk.'

'Totally.' Eve shoved a hand in her jacket pocket. 'Fang a dart?'

When we arrived at Fairfax, we walked through the car park up to the oval and sat together smoking, unsure whether the grass was wet or cold until we'd been sitting for a few minutes, and could feel the damp creeping across our bottoms.

'Violet is cool,' I said, tapping my cigarette to let the ash drop. I tapped it too often, much more often than Eve. She let the little spark drag right back with each puff, and the grey accumulate until it fell. I would drag and tap, drag and tap.

'We should become friends with her.'

I looked at Eve, to check she wasn't joking. Her eyes were narrowed as she took a slow deliberate drag.

'She's a lot older than us,' I pointed out.

'Who gives a fuck? She's cool.'

Eve pushed her cigarette stub into the dirt, stood, stomped on it a few times, and then offered me her arms.

I took them, like a child with a monkey grip, one hand around each of her slender wrists, and let her drag me up.

10

MY MOTHER WAS thrilled to have me home for the five-week winter break. We spoke about it on the phone, and she suggested that I might want to stay in Sydney with my new friends. She said this in the smallest possible voice, like she was afraid that if she made the suggestion too forcefully, it would materialise as reality.

'No, I'll come home.'

Louder now: 'Are you sure?'

'Yeah. All my college friends are going to Europe.'

'*All* of them?'

'Don't sound so upset.'

She laughed. 'I'm happy for them. I hear Ibiza is lovely this time of year.'

The people who were most comfortable at Fairfax—if comfort could be measured by social participation—were those who left the quickest. The morning after exams ended, Portia, Emily, and Claudia headed to the airport, looking forward to intersecting itineraries with intersecting friends of friends.

Eve followed a few days later. I walked with her to the train station, because she had refused a lift from her mother. She would be backpacking through Eastern Europe—a trip she'd planned with schoolfriends. She emphasised *Eastern,* so I assumed I was meant to find that more adventurous.

When I returned to college from the station, it was to empty corridors: cleaner and quieter without the daily trudge of students. And when I swiped out of Fairfax for Canberra the next day, it was with a thrill of relief. The Sydney winter air was like a splash of cool water—not cold enough to frost my breath or even chill my fingertips, but just enough to brace me for the day.

The bus rolled out of Central Station through a light drizzle and slow traffic, which made Sydney seem never-ending. Finding that each time I looked up, we were not yet near the freeway, I abandoned the window and fixed my gaze on my phone. I drafted messages to Paul in Notes, and didn't send them.

For days I had been waiting for some correspondence. Of course, because I fancied myself an independent woman—independent, especially, of male approval—I did not admit the waiting to myself. It was post-exam adrenaline that accounted for my blood-fizzing energy, and it was exhaustion that accounted for my new-found purposelessness. If I spent a day alone in my room, reading my phone, cycling through the first twenty minutes of TV shows, if my body felt like a ticking bomb—one that had ticked too long and had lost all sound of suspense—then that was only normal.

At first I thought the only means of contacting Paul was his university email, and I was hardly going to email him about conduct which would almost certainly see him fired. The looming threat of unemployment wasn't very sexy. Any conversations we conducted would have to be in private, away from the shadow of university administration.

It wasn't until I was cleaning out my desk as I packed for Canberra that I realised his mobile number had been in front of me for months, on the title page of my Morals and Mores course reader, along with his office location and consultation hours.

When my head started to fuzz and ache with motion sickness, I put my phone in my jacket pocket and let my body sag against the window. I imagined telling Eve about the kiss.

'I told you so,' she would say, without a trace of triumph.

I smiled to myself at her imagined incredulity.

'How did it happen? You kissed *him*?' Her face suspended in shock, her fringe unmoving.

Upon my arrival in Canberra, my mother's smiling face and the blur of her wave reminded me, with choking tearful certainty, that these conversations were very much imagined.

The story of kissing Paul—the story as I would tell it to Eve—empowered me. But the memory of the kiss, the squeeze of my hand, and the silence that reared up afterwards . . . these were things that happened to a different version of myself. A paper-thin version I wanted to shield from Eve.

—

MY MOTHER WAS making my favourite bolognaise, except I had taken over the cooking. Watching her peel garlic with her fingernails was unbearable. I eased the bulbs from her, my free hand resting on her bony back, and crushed them with the flat side of a knife. In response, she poured me a wine.

She lay her head on the back of the couch, turning it to me slightly, and fired off questions. She was ravenous for details of my new life. I felt, however, as the smell of garlic wafted from the bottom of her largest pot and the wine swilled chill and grown-up in my mouth, that the life I was describing was another person's. This house was real, and I was real in it: the childhood photographs on the fridge; the tattered blanket on the couch; the stacks of my mother's books, dog-eared and doodled with apparent ferocity that, upon closer inspection, actually looked like love.

With dinner on the way, and the news undulating on the TV in the background, we were in our familiar routine. Since my father died when I was seven years old, this was how we closed each day.

When I'd first re-entered the house that day, I could tell she was rationing her excitement. She didn't want me to think she needed me, so she didn't follow me into my room when I unpacked, and she didn't look up when I entered the kitchen to ask her if I could help with dinner. The fridge was full of my favourite foods—food she would never buy for herself—and as her wineglass emptied and she sank lower on the couch, her questions came at a faster pace.

When we sat down to eat, she put a warm hand over mine and squeezed. 'It's good to have you home.'

It was good. It was the most natural thing in the world: to have dinner, just the two of us. I had never found anything but comfort in the smallness of our family unit. As a child, I missed Dad, and I would pore over family photos, asking my mother to tell the same stories many times, to build him up to a character in my mind. But by the time I was a teenager, my appetite for books overtook that for photo albums and family histories. Literature, I quickly learned, was full of absent fathers. Indeed, absent fathers were the stuff protagonists were made of. Then the thought occurred to me that this piece of family tragedy made me not only more worldly—with sorrow-widened eyes—but also more interesting.

My mother, however, whose suffering was always a quiet, swallowed thing, shook me from my solipsism. For literature was full, too, of suffering women. I looked at the grieving, the cheated, the abandoned, the abused, and thought: yes, I understand. I saw my mother in their pain. I'll help you bear it, I used to think, when Fanny Robin, yoked to a dog, dragged herself to death, or when

Gertrude Morel watched her son slip out of her grasp and into love. *I'll help you bear it.*

We have each other, my mother used to say. Which meant that she had me, and which I felt as a unique responsibility to be the best, most glittering me that I could be. All through school I laboured under the weight of her perceived expectations. I was deferential to my teachers, irreverent to my peers, and as popular as a schoolgirl can be without getting into any trouble.

Over dinner, we made plans for the following four weeks.

'You'll want to see your schoolfriends,' my mother said.

'Yeah, but I can see them during the week. We should hang out on the weekend.'

'If you're sure,' she said.

If I wasn't sure, her smile convinced me. It was in my power to make her happy, I thought. And with that thought—that umbilical pull that yoked and shaped me—I knew I was home.

—

AFTER DINNER WE watched an episode of *The Crown*. My mother was a staunch republican, as she reminded me every episode (multiple times, if she were brought to tears). But she 'couldn't get over the humanity'.

'I empathise with every single character at once, even when they're in conflict. Isn't that remarkable? Even when they're in conflict.'

This episode was taking place on a boat, but I lost the heart of the conflict when I saw a notification on Instagram.

@PhilPaul had requested to follow me.

I felt a sudden rush of energy. For something to do—other than punch the air—I stood up, under the pretext of getting a glass of water. At the kitchen counter, I opened Paul's Instagram account, and was dismayed to find he was on private.

My mother was on to me.

'Who's that?'

'Nothing. Just a news alert thing.'

A knowing look made my cheeks burn, so I left my phone charging on the counter, like severing my arm, and sat back down without it.

I couldn't focus on the rest of the show. Their vowels sounded rounded to absurdity, and the acting was so subtle that their faces took on the quality of a blank Word document. I tried to emulate their calm, dignified exteriors, even while my mind surged with the thrill of being Requested.

When the credits rolled I said goodnight and took to my phone like an addict to her next hit. I lay on top of my bed, fully clothed, and accepted the request.

A message appeared almost immediately. It was so quick, in fact, that it led me to suspect he'd already drafted it and had it on hand to copy and paste as soon as my inbox became available. Unlike Paul's emails, this message was meticulously punctuated.

> *Ah, this is embarrassing. But I realised I have no medium other than university email to contact you, which seems a bit formal (for want of a better word). Which is all to say: can I have your number?*

He had asked for my number. More than that, he had used the exact phrase: *can I have your number*, whose irony could only have been employed to disguise basically sinister intentions.

I thought about something witty to say. In the end, I just replied with 'Haha' and my number.

I requested to follow him, and he did not respond. He did, however, text me.

Hi, it's Paul.

Hi Paul, it's Michaela.

Read receipts. Bold.

I like to be held accountable,
otherwise I never reply

That's admirable.

Can you explain something to me?

A long pause. He was probably torn between relief that I was taking the conversation into my own hands and dread about what the 'thing' would be. He was, after all, out on a limb. I suppose that was not only the fun of it, but also the point. Whatever the reason, he replied after a few minutes:

Sure.

So you want my number but you
don't want me to follow you?

The bubble dots indicated that he was already drafting a reply. The pace of the conversation was thrilling. It felt live, passed rapidly from hand to hand. I could picture him, alone and on his phone, thinking about how to respond, and I felt that we were in some ways in the same room, but also tantalisingly apart.

*Aha, I'm sorry. It's not personal,
it's just not a good look.*

What's not a good look?

Following students on Instagram.

And how does having
students' numbers look?

*Less voyeuristic, at the very least.
Thank you for giving it to me.*

> You're very welcome
> Thank you for your lovely manners

I deleted that last part, and then added it back in again. He 'haha' reacted.

> I actually had your number already

This was the second time—I was counting—that I had pushed the conversation along. The first with a direct question, and now with a double text. Perhaps I was too keen, and he was turning away, putting his phone down, becoming absorbed, not with me but with the life outside his phone.

The speed of his response assured me otherwise.

Really? How?

I sent him a photo of my Morals and Mores reader. This reply took longer.

Ah. That's . . . mortifying.

> Hardly. It's a great resource!

I reread that text chain several times over the next few days. I found myself alternatingly funny and hostile.

There was nothing to do, it seemed, but wait for him to text again. I thought about the lessons I'd learned from conversations in the Fairfax dining hall: never double text. If you texted last, he must text next.

It seemed a very passive state for a modern woman, but I assumed my integrity depended on it.

I waited.

—

PAUL DID NOT text.

My days acquired a slow, colourless quality. I dropped my mother at work in the morning, and scrolled on my phone in different rooms of the house, looking at sun-dripping pictures of my friends' holidays. Balthazar called me a few times: always around midday, when it was very late in Europe and he was walking home from a club. If I didn't pick up, he'd send me a voice message instead. These had a rambling, stream-of-consciousness style that I preferred to the phone calls.

I saw some friends from school, most of whom were careful to display a frosty indifference to news about my Sydney life. Our catch-ups consisted of cataloguing mutual friends—whether they had gone to university, where they were working, where they had last been seen—as if we were updating their Wikipedia pages.

In the evenings, my mother and I ate dinner together, and slowly I unspooled the events of my life since departing home. That first semester at university, I realised only now, had been an untethering. Without the anchor of my mother's approval, I had twirled from one relationship to another, in and out of conversations, trying to charm, surprise, delight—not pausing to question whose approval it was I sought, and what that said about me.

Back in Canberra, slowed almost to a stop, under my mother's loving gaze, I was suddenly unworthy. Like a teenager who throws a party when they have an empty house for the weekend, I felt I had trivialised my freedoms.

Framed on the wall of our living room was a photo of my parents when they first met at the ANU decades ago. They were wearing matching campaign shirts, holding hands. In my mother's free hand, she held a megaphone. From where I sat at the kitchen table, they looked over me.

And I? I had gone to parties all semester, where my rich friends found me charming. I gave them my time, my energy, and once— without knowing his name—my body. They love me there, Mum. Believe me.

So it was with an urgent need to reinstate my sense of self that I texted my mother at ten o'clock the morning that our marks were released. She was quick to reply:

> You're a genius! Well done, darling.

Feeling buoyant, I drove to Mount Ainslie and set out on a walk. The wind took a bite out of my cheeks, and although it was a flat, grey day—the distant surface of the lake silver like aluminium foil—it shone with promise.

My hands were in the pockets of my puffer to fend off the cold. My phone vibrated. Opening it, I wanted to throw my head back and cheer to the wind.

An email from Paul:

> Heard good things about your exam. I didn't mark it of course and wouldn't have known if I did (you're all numbers to me). Congratulations.

I concluded on the drive home, rereading it at every red light, that the email was teasingly impersonal. If he had to be appropriate, he would be self-referential about it. The effect was to render his very formality personal: an in-joke.

When I got home, I made myself a peppermint tea, and texted him.

> Thanks for the email.

You're very welcome. Thank you
for your lovely manners.

Ha!

But seriously, you did so well.
You should feel proud.

Well I consider you my mentor, so
you should feel proud too

Honoured.

His congratulations, so formulaic and formal, stifled my elation until, after a few minutes pause, he double texted.

So what are you doing these holidays?

It was as if he had leapt, and our conversation was in freefall.

Paul was teaching winter school on the Philosophy of Happiness. I asked:

What's your philosophy of happiness?

After several hours he replied:

It's overrated.

For days, I was suspended between self-scouring silences and vibrating conversation. At best, the conversation would last a few minutes: a quick burst of back and forth. Mostly, I was meticulous about waiting several hours before I replied to him, relishing the tension—the sense that I held him in suspense.

Winter school ends tomorrow.
My students invited me for a drink
after the last class. Spare me!

> Surely they know it's inappropriate
> to be at the pub with a teacher

Haha. You'd think.

> Also, isn't it the holidays? Don't they
> have anything better to do?

*Again, you'd think. But they're all in
winter school, so apparently not . . .*

> More importantly, don't YOU have
> something better to do?

*Tragically, no. Why? Would you like
to have a drink with me?*

I reread the conversation, my heart pounding. I could not work out which one of us had set the other up. Was that where he intended the conversation to end, right from the beginning? Or was that what I had implied, by asking him what he was doing?

Either way, the offer lay, naked and shivering, before me. I must have hesitated for too long, because Paul texted again:

*I just remembered. You're in
Canberra. Don't worry about it.*

———

I LIED TO my mother so naturally it was as if I had done it before.

'I have to go back to Sydney tomorrow,' I told her over dinner.

'Oh.' She put a forkful of food back on the plate. 'Why?'

'A friend of mine is having a party.'

'A college friend?'

'Yeah. Emily. You'd really like her.'

She held a glass of wine before her face, and didn't drink from it. 'I thought all your college friends were overseas?' She pronounced *overseas* with a stir of parody, like it was a made-up place.

'Not all of them. Emily just texted and she's planning on having this big party, with the boys too.'

My mother exhaled softly, through her nose, on *the boys*, which made me talk faster. 'I don't want to miss it, just because, you know, it's sort of the first time everyone has hung out, like, off campus. I'm probably reading too much into it, but it's still early days, so I worry that every event is . . . an escalation.'

I had spent the afternoon lying to myself: conjuring up Paul-unrelated reasons to go back to Sydney early. I could look for a job. I could see if Balthazar was around. I could go to the library and get a head start on second semester. Canberra was dull anyway.

This mental list was just a thin veneer—architecture that crumbled around a decision I had already made the moment I texted Paul and said:

No no! I was coming back to Sydney anyway

And the facade fell away, leaving only heat, from shame and anticipation, when my mother held up her glass like a stop sign and said, 'I understand. Attendance is mandatory. You're better at these things than I am.'

Then she reached across the table for my hand and, with a squeeze that didn't claim to hold me, she added: 'I'll miss you.'

—

FAIRFAX WAS COLDER and emptier than I'd left it two weeks earlier. I turned the wall heater on and kept holding my hand to it, to check that it was technically emanating some warmth.

At the top of my little black suitcase was a plastic sandwich bag with a post-it note and a packet of contraceptive pills inside.

The note, in my mother's tender hand, read:

You left this in the bathroom. Look after yourself, darling.

My mother's sign-off filled not just my eyes but my whole body with tears. All because it soothed me, and by soothing, rendered me fragile.

I'm proud of you, always.

11

WE WENT TO a wine bar in Bondi, which was almost an hour from Fairfax by bus, and was much more hushed and small-tabled than the pubs I was used to. The two-to-a-table closeness and stack of wine bottles along the wall conjured a sense of intimacy amid the crowd. This persuaded me, if there were any doubt, that we were on a date.

We sat in a corner and Paul ordered, while I read the wine descriptions aloud in a stupid voice to paint him as a snob. He took this admirably.

Our conversation slid between personal details and larger, conceptual discussions: about family; books; the point of studying an arts degree, much less teaching one. I found him as witty and darkly funny as via text, except in person, when he laughed at my jokes, he did so with a little touch of my hand, which was almost self-indulgent, like he was giving me the joke: permitting me to make him laugh.

When the waitress announced that the bar was closing, I was surprised to find that over three hours had passed.

Paul offered to pay, and I accepted in the self-aware way I'd learned from Eve. 'Please. My feminism operates very much within capitalist constraints.'

'Meaning I can pay?'

'Meaning I can't afford to.'

Paul tapped and returned his card to his leather wallet. 'Should we try mine?' He slapped his hands on the table, and raised his eyebrows as he spoke: a picture of spontaneity.

'Are you nearby?'

'I live in Bondi.'

I picked off a complimentary breadstick and broke a piece off with my teeth. 'Of course you do.'

'What makes you say that?'

'You're, like, aggressively cool. I bet you surf.'

'All the time. It's embarrassing, actually, how bad I am, given how often I do it.'

I put the remainder of the breadstick in my mouth and crunched. 'Because surfing is such an embarrassing hobby.'

'You should come with me sometime.'

I laughed. 'Are you addicted to teaching me things?'

I hadn't meant to sound suggestive—to me, the question was genuine. But he gave me a hungry look, which made me suddenly conscious of my skin as a continuous surface against which my body felt strained.

We walked to his house, the sea at our backs and out of sight, with me following a few steps behind.

I thought about what Eve would do if she were here, and imagined that she might make a joke about Paul having a reputation for sleeping with his students. This thought reminded me that she too was one of his students, yet it was me, here, following him to his house. It was this thought that made me speed up until I was level with Paul, and my hand brushed against his.

—

MY FEET WERE up on the seat, and my chin was almost touching my knees. I was hugging my arms, and occasionally slapping them where they were ravaged by mosquitoes. It was a damp, insect-laden night.

Paul's apartment was in a red-brick building, and it boasted a record player and a cupboard full of vinyls, as well as a little balcony—overcrowded with succulents—and water glimpses. These glimpses depended on sticking your torso out over the railing and craning your neck down the side of the building. Paul held my waist while I executed this manoeuvre—to prevent me from falling, I assumed. I saw the water, which was a darker shade of black than the sky.

He poured me a glass of wine, and we smoked. Paul assured me I could use the smaller succulent as an ashtray: 'They can take anything.'

He laughed when I squashed a mosquito on my thigh. 'Isn't that disgusting?' I said, offering my open palm. The mosquito lay, black and oozing, in a little pool of red. 'You always wonder, don't you, whether it's your own blood.'

He took my hand. 'It's probably a mix. Mine and yours.' He wiped the splash of blood with his thumb, then laughed. Another mosquito had landed on my forearm, its thirsty needle extended.

He contemplated it for a moment, before looking at me, his eyebrows raised for permission. I nodded, and he smacked it dead.

'This is untenable,' he said. 'Would you like a jumper?'

'I thought you'd never ask.'

He left me alone on the balcony. I didn't need to crane my neck to glimpse the water. I could hear it: a constant churning that echoed my pulsing blood. I was nervous, but only because everything up until this point had gone so well; it seemed the evening was begging to be ruined.

Paul returned with a jumper. It smelled chemically clean. 'Thanks.'

For a moment, the night was still in our silence. I felt more clear-headed for our pause, and realised I must be about sober by now.

'This is a great place,' I said, just for something to say, although it was a great place, that was true.

'Yes, well, I'm very lucky to have it.'

'This is yours? You *own* it?'

'It was my parents', yeah.'

'Oh, I'm sorry. Have they passed away?' I cringed at the euphemism, which sounded, when I heard myself say it, like a child reading aloud: sounding out words with no meaning.

'Mum lives in Victoria. Dad is in a nursing home.'

'I'm so sorry.'

'It's fine. He's old. It happens.'

Another moment of silence, in which Paul looked at his hands. I felt panicked, like a rope was being pulled, and I did not quite have it in my grasp. 'Actually, I'm not sorry. This is a lovely home.'

'You're right. I'm very privileged. I don't deserve it.'

'Nobody *deserves* anything.'

'I'm basically the poster boy for death taxes.'

He looked at me with an expectant pause, waiting for me to laugh. I wondered how often he'd used that joke before, and how similar the setting.

'I guess that's what the nursing home is for?'

He laughed. My grip on the rope tightened. 'You're not wrong. They're so fucking expensive. That's the cruellest thing. You go, it's sterile, it's heartbreaking, et cetera, and then you leave and all you can think is that you're just haemorrhaging money for the whole ordeal.'

'I must say, that's not a problem I have.'

He laughed. 'Oh, you will.'

I regretted making a joke. I liked how his voice sounded when he said the word *heartbreaking*. It had a little quiver in it, which the *et cetera* only amplified by attempting to disguise. A little quiver that stroked my sense of self and said I was starting to see this man—really see him—in a way that other, less perceptive people wouldn't.

I relaxed into the hug of the jumper and yawned expansively.

Paul watched me. 'Wow.'

I shrugged, the too-long sleeves of his jumper flopping past my hands. 'Sorry.'

'No, no, it's fair enough. I've been boring you.'

'It's one in the morning.'

'So it is.'

'I should go.'

I stood, and brushed down my bottom, which was damp from the seat. I started to pull his jumper off.

'How will you get home?'

'Uber, I guess,' I said, from inside the confines of the jumper. My top rode up with it, and the night was cool on my stomach.

When I pulled the jumper off, he was still seated, and looking up at me.

'You can stay, if you'd like.'

He didn't say it casually. There was no subterfuge to it: no tap dancing around the practicalities—the lateness, the expense of getting home. He just asked me to stay the night.

And I said, 'Okay.'

——

THE LIGHT WAS on in his bedroom, and I stood just beyond its reach in the corridor. I took cautious, trespassing glances around the room. He had a pile of novels on his bedside table, and a larger pile stacked next to it. This one was arranged by colour: black at the bottom, with a crescendo of orange-spined Penguins.

I couldn't help myself. 'I see you're a reader of the classics.'

'I see you've seen that I'm a wanker.'

'A self-aware wanker, then.'

'Isn't that the best kind?' He was folding back the doona, and smiled up at me.

I turned to his desk and pretended to look at the spines. I was willing him to cross the room and touch me from behind, so that I might turn around and fold into an embrace he'd already created.

But he took no such leap. I turned around and found him in the bed.

I resolved that, whatever happened, it would be strange to sleep in jeans, so I took them off. I got into the bed wearing just underwear and a black singlet. Beneath it, the underwire of my bra dug uncomfortably into my chest. I reflected that it was also weird to sleep in a bra, and hoped that men didn't notice that kind of thing, or that, if they did, they added it to their mental list of the unfathomability of womankind and gave it no further thought.

I curled up the way I did every night, when there was no one in the bed beside me: in the foetal position. In my mind, I saw myself from above, waiting for him.

Heart thumping, I lay still and tight, and he moved in exhilarating, excruciating increments.

He rolled onto his side, and I slotted into place.

He slid his arm under my neck.

I knew, with blood-fizzing certainty, that only two things could happen next, although I was uncertain of their order.

Either I could turn my head, and meet his lips with a kiss, or his hand could drift out of the limbo where it lay and commit, suggestively, to an offer, by cupping my breast.

Both of these eventualities were so natural that they were inevitable, like drawing my next breath.

In what felt like a rash motion, but could have only come after an agonisingly unnatural pause, I turned my head and we kissed.

We folded into each other, like a sigh of relief.

I pulled off his shirt and his stomach slumped, vulnerable and exposed, against mine. I dug my fingers into his back and pulled him closer.

He touched me so tentatively, so gently, that I clutched a pillow to my face, and he asked if I was okay. I laughed and said that I was, and he said that he just wanted to make sure. My laugh sounded like someone else's.

When he was inside me, heavy and heaving, it didn't hurt at all, but when he was finished, I felt pleasantly sore, and curled up against him, his exposed tummy flush against my back, and nursed the soreness in my mind as he ran his fingers in gentle trickles up and down my spine.

When I no longer felt quivering and broken, and his hands travelling up and down my back acquired the rhythm of a game, I was able to speak.

'I was worried for a moment that this was going to be a platonic sleepover,' I said.

'You and me both.'

I turned my head and looked at him. 'It did seem ambiguous for a while.'

'I—I'm sorry. You make me nervous.'

I heard that in my heart, which fumbled. I rolled my head back onto the side and closed my eyes. 'Why? Do you think I'm some harassment complaint waiting to happen?'

'God, no. Although'—he stroked his finger down my back, and I tingled—'perhaps I should have thought about that.'

'I think that horse has bolted.'

He laughed, and I shivered.

'You make me nervous too,' I said into the pillow. And then, louder, turning my face towards him, I said, 'I regret choosing the foetal position.'

He laughed. 'It was a bit of a curve ball.'

'Not very sexy of me, I'm sorry.'

He was silent. He rolled me gently towards him and pulled me into a hug. I could feel his stubbly chin on my shoulder. It rested with a pleasant, secure weight. Softly, almost to himself, he said, 'You're actually so beautiful.'

'Actually?'

He laughed, and pressed his finger into my spine, where it found a knot. It hurt and I wriggled a little to absorb it. 'You can't take a compliment, can you?'

'Is that supposed to be a compliment?'

'No, I don't think it is.'

'Okay, I'll take it.'

I fell asleep.

I remember waking in the middle of the night, after what felt like only a few minutes, and regretting that there was one particularly long hair on my nipple. I wondered whether, when Paul had kissed me there, it had bothered him.

—

WHEN I WOKE again, it was still dark. Paul was sitting up in bed, and the light from his phone cast a blue glow. I watched him for a while.

He saw that I was awake.

'What time is it?'

'It's just after six.'

'What are you doing?'

'I never sleep well.'

'How characterful of you.'

'Is that characterful?'

'I have never, ever slept badly in my life. Maybe, like, under five times. Before an exam or something.'

'You're very lucky.'

'I know. I'm an Olympic sleeper. When I was younger, I used to worry that I wouldn't develop a conscience, or whatever.'

'Because you were asleep?'

'Yeah. People always seemed to worry about things before they went to sleep. And I thought, if I don't worry about anything, perhaps I'm missing out on some, I don't know, some great insight.'

'I'm sure you have a very complex psyche, Michaela.'

'Is that why you asked me to stay the night?'

He laughed at that. An unflattering cackle that made my heart throb. I wanted to make his face break in half like that again.

Instead, I looked at the ceiling and smiled. I rolled over again, and thought that when I woke up, I would slip out of his life and into the morning, and message Eve: *I have a story to tell you.* We would spend weeks dissecting it.

Before I drifted off, however, he touched my shoulder with a gentle, index-finger poke.

'Michaela?'

'Mmm.'

'I think we should go for a swim.'

—

PAUL DROVE A red Subaru with a scratch across the back, like an omen.

I climbed into the front seat, put my chin on my knees, and immediately identified something to tease. His hand hovered over the gearstick, but only moved it between reverse and drive. 'Is this a manual?'

'I learned to drive on a manual.'

'You know, they've actually invented automatics. I think this might even be one of them.'

'I just like to be prepared.'

'To reverse at any moment?'

'Or park, or eject the passenger seat.'

We drove further along the peninsula, the harbour flat and dark on the horizon, and perfectly manicured gardens on either side. Ferns and palm trees overspilled, but within reason. Curated to look natural: the horticulturalist's answer to effortless cool.

He pulled up in a cul-de-sac lined with gates of prison proportions. He passed me a towel—a frayed brown bath sheet—and walked in front of me to the bottom of the street. There he turned and pushed a wooden gate, which gave way to a tiny gap between two buildings, not a metre wide.

'This isn't well signposted, is it?'

'Local secret,' he said, turning to me and tapping his nose.

'Are all of the locals underweight?' I asked, watching his shoulders brush either side of the narrow pass.

'Fat people don't live in Vaucluse.'

At the bottom was a little stone path, and on the other side a thin white shore. It was stacked with mansions: sloping green lawns, punctuated by tiny cabanas or outdoor showers.

In the morning light, the water was pale, and the silhouette of the city on the horizon was black.

Obviously, I didn't have swimmers, so I stripped to my underwear. The morning air was cool, like water.

'Do you do this often?' I asked.

'Not like this.' He took my hand.

'Will it be freezing?'

'The water gets warmer during the year. It's warmer now than at the start of summer.'

I must have looked nervous, because he laughed and touched my face. My cheek felt hot where his fingers brushed. 'Yes. It will be freezing.'

I gasped when the water reached my feet. I ran until it hit my thighs, then dived under, wanting the shock to be over as soon as possible.

I surfaced with an animal yell, my breath caught by the cold. Realising how pastel and still the morning was, I covered my mouth with my hand. On the shore, water lapping at his ankles, Paul laughed at me. It was a hooting laugh that skipped across the water like a stone.

I dived down and counted twelve dolphin kicks, resurfacing close to a moored boat. My body was warmer for the movement, but the morning froze on my face. It was cold enough to remind me, in every tingling pore, that I was, first and foremost, a physical thing. Before thought or feeling or reason, I was a stretch of skin, a bag of flesh, for the ocean to cradle or drown with indifference.

I watched the dawn ripple on the water, pink and creamy, and waited for Paul to surface next to me. When he did, I wrapped my legs around him, and he grabbed me, but in an awkward grasping motion, interrupted by twitching kicks that were keeping him afloat.

'It's fucking freezing.'

I laughed. 'You were the one who suggested a swim.'

I placed my hands on his shoulders and pushed. He sputtered as he went under, then, grabbing my ankle, pulled me down and used my shoulders to leverage himself up.

I surfaced my own sputtering mess, and splashed water in his face.

We continued like that for several minutes, in a coy pattern of bait and switch. I imagine that in each of the mansions that lined the shore, people were stirring: waking for Pilates or a spin class; pausing at their marble breakfast bar to take in their harbour view; perhaps scoffing at the splashing man and woman, who could only be described as *frolicking*.

I wonder if they thought we were drunk, or on drugs, or in love, or if they didn't give any thought to the distinction.

On the way back we stopped for petrol, and I went in for a snack, as if we were on a road trip. I bought a coffee and a Golden Gaytime. Paul laughed and bought a Maxibon. We ate them as the car flew through early morning green lights, and I savoured the moment like it was already a memory.

He played songs that I don't remember, hooking his phone up to a dongle. I looked out the window, his jumper stretched over my knees, my face stiff with salt, and saw myself as a worthy subject for a film with an indie soundtrack.

I had told him I lived in Newtown. As the university campus rose up, sandstone spires poking through the trees of Victoria Park, I gave more specific directions, until he pulled up outside the wrought-iron gates of Fairfax.

'You live here?'

'During semester, yeah.'

'You're a college student?' He looked at me, and I thought I caught him in the act of resizing.

'If you sleep with first years,' I said, holding his gaze tightly, 'you might find that some of them live on campus.'

'You raise a good point. Maybe I shouldn't sleep with first years.'

I stumbled as I stepped out of his car, not knowing whether his last comment was a joke. 'Well, I—I hope you have a good day,' I said.

'Thanks, you too.' His hands were limp on the wheel, and he was looking at the road.

I poked my head through the window, and with a conscious effort not to sound awkward, I added, 'That was fun, Paul. We should do that again.'

I turned, without waiting for a response, and took my fuzzy head and heavy limbs to bed. I did not wake up until dusk was stretching through my windows.

We should do that again. For the rest of the day Paul replayed those words to himself and smiled, feeling both conqueror and conquered. Or so he told me afterwards.

12

THE MUSIC WAS so loud that every statement, no matter how inane, had to be repeated until it lost all meaning or was replaced with: 'Don't worry.'

We were in the St Thomas' College bar on the first night of second semester. The bar itself was a windowless, stone-walled basement: a sweaty cell. The line was always long and bound to be cold, so Claudia insisted we get drunk first. I kneeled on her scratchy carpet and let her pour orange juice into my open mouth, and then vodka on top of that, and drank it, my face scrunched up against the taste.

What would Paul think, I wondered, if he saw me doing a juicy? The aftertaste was medicinal. I saw my college friends, my college self, through his darkly mocking eyes. This was not so much an exercise in self-reflection as self-bifurcation. The contrast between the girl kneeling on the floor and the woman I was around Paul rendered me a complex, unfathomable thing.

It was liberating to see myself as a cocktail of personalities. What were lives and habits for Claudia and Emily and Portia were for me experiments to be picked up and abandoned at will.

On the dance floor, Claudia, Emily, Portia and I held hands and mouthed the words of the songs to each other, like we were still in Claudia's bedroom and not performing for the boys who now gazed on. We can have fun without you—autonomous female fun—our little circle claimed, as if we hadn't just waited in line for an hour to have fun in this particular spot.

When I sobered up enough to measure time in the discrete increments of Top 40 singles, as opposed to one continuous sound, I suggested we go outside.

Claudia shook her head.

I ventured to the courtyard alone. Behind me I could hear the gravelly strains of 'Eagle Rock' by Daddy Cool. This, I knew, would be the boys' cue to drop their pants and waddle around the room. I could just imagine Portia's *Wait. What?* As if she didn't know from the first few bars that whisky dicks were limping her way. And I could practically hear Claudia's eyes rolling, like they were looking for a way out of her skull.

I quickened my pace. The push of bodies against mine was thick, and I registered each person as an obstacle to be navigated and shoved past, until I found, backed up against a wall, a wooden bench in a square of breathable air.

'Hey.'

Nick was beside me, rolling a cigarette with shaky hands.

The last time I'd seen him, it was across the crowded Jace, and we had avoided each other's gaze. What we shared—whatever it was—reared now in the space between us. Of course, for Nick, whose memories were not so hazy, it had always been there.

I moved a little closer up the bench, so he could hear me.

'I needed some air.'

'I know the feeling.'

We fell to silence. I scrounged for something to say. What I found was so strikingly formal and unoriginal, it did not so much break the awkward spell as intensify it. 'How was your break?'

'Fine.' Another pause. He licked the cigarette paper and sealed it. 'You want one?'

'Yeah, please.' I sounded famished.

He rolled in silence, while I watched. He had large hands with neat, trim fingernails. I thought that those hands had been on me, inside me. I took a deep drag and tried to focus on the act of smoking.

He exhaled. 'I'll probably head soon.'

'You're not feeling it tonight?'

'Not at all.' Nick looked at me, and I looked away. I blew a little cloud of smoke out over the heads of people in the bathroom line. 'Don't you get sick of it?' he asked.

'How do you mean?'

'You're smart, right?'

I was still looking out over the crowd. Ahead of us, a girl in the year above me at Fairfax decided she couldn't wait any longer. She was squatting in a pot plant, and her friend, on wobbly legs, attempted to drag her up. They fell on top of each other. The blind leading the blind. 'Smarter than some,' I said, gesturing to the drunken heap.

Nick laughed: a closed, single-syllable sound like *hm*. It was not much, but enough to reach around—past the conversation we were refusing to have—and prod me out of our stilted silence. My shoulders slackened as I exhaled, blowing smoke into the night.

'Whatever,' he said. 'Emily told me you're super smart.'

I looked at him. 'Well, if Emily says so.'

'And I can tell.' He leaned over, nudging me with his shoulder. 'You know what day it is. Which is why I think you'll be receptive to this chat.'

'Try me.'

He cleared his throat. 'Don't you think our lives are boring?'

'At one of the most prestigious colleges in the country?' I put on a posh teacher voice. 'Are we boring you, Nick?'

'But that's it, right? It makes it so much worse. We're some of the most privileged people, world at our feet and whatever, and all we can do is get hammered and tell each other about it. It's boring.'

'Of course it is. But the novelty will wear off soon. There has to be more to life, right?'

He looked at me, the ember on his cigarette glowing next to his face.

'Right?'

Our faces were very close. I could make out his pupils: wide and black; his brown irises like thin wooden picture frames.

'I'm not sure it's worth overthinking,' I said.

He smiled, without teeth. 'Good from you. I think a lot about what you said that time about St Thomas' boys having no inner life.'

'I'm very wise.'

'Seriously, though. You know, I would say that most of my friends aren't self-reflective. Like, at all. I don't think they're capable of it.'

'It's hard, I think. When you've always been told yes and more yes.'

'Exactly. It's as if nothing—nobody around them—has any . . . I don't know. Nothing they do ever has any consequence.'

I finished my cigarette and snuffed it out on the bench next to me. I thought about the last time we talked, just the two of us, in this courtyard, while music thumped and throbbed inside. What were the consequences of that night? I wondered. Didn't we exist for each other differently now? As traded bodies, as passion and pleasure and even pain. Yet I couldn't say I felt closer to Nick because of it. If anything, snatches of memory, like blotches of colour that precede a painful headache, obscured him as he sat before me, all bent brow and deep thought.

'My mum has an expression for those kinds of people,' I said. 'She got it from my dad. She used to say it about people at school who were, like, vapid and popularity-obsessed.'

'Oh yeah?'

'People who don't think about death enough.'

He laughed. 'I like that.' I hadn't seen that white-toothed laugh—the laugh that waved you over to whisper a secret in your ear—all night. And I was the one who had retrieved it. For a moment, it was as if this laughing Nick, this friend of mine, was the only version I'd ever known. I thought of the other Nick: those opaque memories—expressionistic flashes of skin on skin, and unfamiliar smells—and I wanted desperately to reconcile them.

I was so resolved to ask that, as I took a long, preparatory drag of my cigarette, I heard it in my own voice: *So what are the consequences for us?*

But before I could speak, a hand clapped my back so hard I coughed, and Sackers's face, scrunched with laughter, brutalised the space between us.

'Nick and Michaela! Looking very cosy. Reminiscing about old times, are we?'

'Get wrecked, Sackers.' Nick tossed his cigarette into the bushes and stood up. 'Can't a man have a dart?'

Sackers pointed inside. 'They're playing some bangers, mate.'

'Cool. We'll come in.'

With his arm around Nick, Sackers turned, almost thumping me with his broad shoulders. He looked back at me, as an afterthought. 'Coming?'

I followed them both into the throng—the choking smoke of the basement bar—where I lost them to a hundred other bodies, all bumping and sweating against mine.

—

EVE RETURNED FROM Europe a week into semester. I knew she had landed by the single-word text:

Brunch?!!

Eve and I had not spoken much while she was away, but her text dispelled any insecurities I'd been harbouring. That she could so easily pick it up again suggested our friendship had remained very much within reach. Also, I was desperate to tell her about Paul. I replied immediately.

Yes, can't wait to see you! Lots to talk about

Like what???

I'll tell you in person

The morning sped towards our meeting time, propelled by my excitement. Since our first kiss at the pub, secrecy had crept up on me in increments, one text at a time. And since I'd returned to Sydney, what Paul and I shared had grown richer, more complicated: irreducible to an anecdote.

If I was honest with myself, I would have noticed that there were, of course, other, less sentimental reasons for waiting to tell Eve about Paul in person. Namely, the opportunity to watch the news—that I had slept with him, several times now—play out across her face. Imagining her reaction, I saw, of course, its moral colour. *But he's your professor. There's a power dynamic.* But before she spoke, or even formed a thought, I was sure she would be shocked. And in her shock, I hoped I'd spot envy.

That Paul's desire had settled on me, in a lecture theatre that also contained Eve, suggested that, for whatever reason, I was *more* desirable. Of course I knew, and even told myself, that it was degrading to compete with another woman for male attention. Knowing this, however, did nothing to dull the feeling that I'd *won*. And it was this sister feeling that I couldn't wait to find in Eve: the sense of being, if not *beaten*, then at least passed over.

My other achievements—if they could be called that—were all dimmed, rather than sharpened, by comparisons with Eve. My results in the final exam especially, which owed so much to her. We had texted about them—one of the few conversations we had while she was away. When I told Eve mine, she qualified her 'wow' with a: *Really?!?!* The punctuation, in particular, picked at the scab of my guilt. She didn't need to be so emphatic about her incredulity.

So perhaps it was because I had resolved never again to borrow her voice—to pass off her ideas as my own—that I saw my relationship with Paul as an achievement. It was entirely independent of Eve, and for that reason a trophy I couldn't wait to show her.

We met for brunch at a cafe near Fairfax, opposite the hospital. I arrived before her, feeling uncharacteristically empowered. What a rare sensation it was: to have a surprise in store for Eve.

My first sight of her, however, reminded me how difficult it was—impossible, even—to beat her at her own game.

She was charging across the intersection towards me, wearing black flared jeans with joggers, which—as I assured her at the time of purchase—were right on the trendy/hideous fault line. Her pink jumper was so luxuriously thick-knitted, to look at it was to mentally reach out and touch it. And, crucially, she had shaved her head, revealing a perfectly round skull.

The effect was arresting. Like she was, by the simple fact of her naked-headed existence, reinventing what it meant to be beautiful. I felt the goalposts move. My own pixie cut seemed middle-aged in comparison.

As she picked her way through the tables and pulled up a chair at mine, she smiled down at me, her earlobes threaded with little gold hoops that only added to her elfin grace. In her smile, I detected the anticipation of a compliment.

'Fresh lid,' was all I allowed her.

She cupped her skull in her hand, like an afterthought. 'Thanks. I did it in a hostel in Budapest. I don't really know why.'

I knew why.

If the most privileged thing a rich young person can do is despise and disguise their wealth, then this was the aesthetic-lottery equivalent. I'm beautiful, this new look said, but I don't care for it.

We talked about her travels, and she told me how infuriating her schoolfriend had been, and how they'd parted ways in Bosnia.

The waiter came over with stylish, shallow glasses and a bottle of tap water. I hadn't read the menu so just ordered a bacon-and-egg roll. I was eager to wrest the conversation away from Eve's holiday and towards mine. I formulated the story in my mind while Eve ordered French toast and a cappuccino with one sugar, then smiled at the waiter like she was giving him a gift.

'Anyway'—she rested her chin on her hand, and gave me the same smile—'enough about me. I thought about you so much while I was away.'

'Really?'

'Yeah.' She leaned forward, placing her arms back in her lap. 'I couldn't stop thinking about what happened in O Week.'

'I can't believe you were thinking about my drunken escapades when you should have been thotting around Eastern Europe.'

Eve laughed, but wasn't deterred. 'I know I was encouraging you to talk to the college, but I don't think that's the right approach. I think college is the problem.'

'Not your vibe?'

'No, Michaela. Toxic cultures are not my vibe.' Her tone was dry: not quite sarcastic, but alluding to it. I said nothing, and she continued. 'Think about all the behaviours that seem totally normal to us: getting drunk and high all the time, filming each other debasing ourselves then sending it around the next day. Boys boasting about their sex lives, talking about women like conquests, making jokes about them publicly. It's not normal, Michaela.'

'Of course it's toxic. It's also, like, incredibly stratified in terms of class.'

'Of course.' She flicked her European-summer-tanned hand. It infuriated me that Eve's moral reasoning skills—her graceful intellectual sweeps of objectivity—were never more keenly applied than when she was in the category of oppressed rather than oppressor.

'I don't think you'll ever really cure or, like, make woke an institution that's so fundamentally based in reinforcing gender *and class* structures.'

My emphasis was combative, but Eve didn't hear it. She continued, in full flight: her hands expressive, like she was making a point in a tutorial. 'Exactly! This place won't change of its own accord. There needs to be some public scrutiny. Your story, Michaela, it could be a catalyst for change.'

The food arrived. I focused on my roll, relieved to have something to do with my hands and somewhere to look other than at Eve. We had come, at last, to Eve's intended destination.

I looked away, out across the street where pedestrians assembled at the crossing. A woman with green hair. A patient leaning on a drip, so thin their hospital gown hung as if from a wire hanger. A group of five boys, all wearing rugby shorts and thongs, walking with bedraggled steps towards the cafe where we sat.

It was becoming clear to me that I would not tell Eve about Paul today. Under her relentless gaze, which insisted I reveal myself to her, I had a vindictive need to withhold something. Viewed in light of the recent weeks with Paul, what happened between Nick and me might seem as relevant to my life as the events of a novel. I felt compelled to deny Eve this perspective.

At the table behind us, the group of boys piled in, with chair scrapes and gruff laughter. Stretching their arms across the backs of each other's chairs, their legs spread broadly, they seemed to fill the little cafe. They amplified our momentary silence, broken by me.

'Look, Eve,' I said, 'it didn't mean anything. I don't want to shoe-horn a meaningless experience, which I have—honestly—moved on from, just so it can fit some kind of trauma or victim narrative.'

She put her knife and fork down in an expression of exaspera-tion. Like I was being deliberately difficult. 'How can it not mean anything?'

'It was casual sex! Between adults!'

'You were too drunk to consent.'

'Sure, but sex is sex is sex. Who cares? We do it all the time. *You* love casual sex.' Eve's eyebrows, raised like a challenge, compelled me to substantiate my claim. I reached for an example. 'You had sex with Balthazar and it didn't revolutionise your friendship.'

'You know about that?'

'Eve, my room is next door. You weren't quiet.'

'Have you and Balth spoken about this?'

There was an urgency to her tone that disturbed me. I was conscious of our friendship as a physical, fragile thing. I had only known her for half a year, I reminded myself.

'No,' I lied.

'I don't know that any kind of sex, even casual sex, is ever meaningless. If that's what feminism has taught us, then we're deluding ourselves.'

The invocation of feminism was a relief. It marked a conversational retreat away from personal experience. Now we were dealing with theories, I felt less at risk of landing an accidental blow. I tried to continue in Eve's vein. 'But don't you also think that there's something archaic and problematic about insisting that sex is necessarily this incredibly meaningful act? Like, in theory, why is it so different from sticking your finger up someone's nose?'

'Okay, Germaine Greer.'

I wasn't familiar with that reference, which annoyed me. I knew Germaine Greer was out of favour with Eve, so I assumed it was an insult. 'Look . . .' I wiped my hands on a paper napkin, crumpled it and threw it on my empty plate. 'The bottom line is: what happened in O Week is in the past. I don't give a fuck, and you shouldn't either.'

'But don't you agree with me even a little bit? Like, even when it's casual, and *if* it's fully consensual, it's not, like, totally uncomplicated.'

I looked at the table behind her, where the boys were taking up so much space. I had no doubt that they were all nursing hangovers, and that the laughs that shot up like gunfire from their table came from telling each other stories of the night before. They were likely stories that involved girls: girls they'd kissed, touched, been inside. Girls who might have left their rooms earlier that morning, or who were perhaps still lying there. I didn't trust any of these men, with their dense muscular thighs, broad backs and thick eyebrows. I looked from them back to Eve.

'Sure.'

The waiter came with the bill. Seeing the group of boys, he turned to us and rolled his eyes. 'Fucking college kids.'

Eve and I both laughed.

——

I TEXTED PAUL to tell him that I was running late. My friend, I explained, was a talker. Although the real cause of my lateness was the time it took to walk back to Fairfax with Eve, sit in my room for long enough that she might think I was settled there for the afternoon, and then walk back out to the bus stop.

Paul displayed an unusual interest in 'this friend, this talker' as he called her. He wanted to know how long we'd been friends; how close we were; whether she was 'someone I trusted'.

I didn't answer. Instead I said, 'I didn't tell her about us.' Paul's face—slack with relief—was so uncomposed I found it endearing. The thought that he might owe me something, that I had the power to hurt him and instead chose to protect him, made me feel, suddenly, very close to him. I wrapped my arms around his neck.

When we had sex, he often declared, after only a few minutes, 'I am going to come.' He said this in the future tense, but by the time he spoke, it was already happening. Afterwards, he would apologise several times. 'Sorry.' 'I'm so sorry.'

'It's fine,' I told him. 'I like it when you lose control.' Although it was more the sense that I, watching him climax through less ecstatic eyes, *had* control.

I also liked that allowing him to come early was technically a selfless act, insofar as it truncated my pleasure. But I derived pleasure from it. I couldn't decide whether I was selfish or selfless. I luxuriated in the in-between.

That night, Paul asked if he could watch me touch myself. It was, I reflected later, the most intimate thing I had ever done. More intimate than masturbating. I asked Paul: 'How can masturbating in front of someone be more personal than doing it by yourself?'

He smiled illegibly, clutching his amusement to his chest. 'I think Sartre would have something to say about that.'

In the morning, we went for a swim and got coffee in a second-hand bookshop in Bondi. The coffee tasted harsh, but the shop smelled musty and safe, and the barista knew Paul. Walking back to his apartment, Paul put his hand, clammy from holding his warm keep cup, on the back of my neck. 'Now that uni has resumed'—his tone was full of the fake regret that often precipitates bad news—'we should see a bit less of each other.'

I said nothing. I bowed my neck, as if I could get out from under his hand.

'For example,' he continued, 'I don't think I should drop you back to Fairfax anymore.'

'That's fine,' I said. 'I can take the bus.'

'I just don't want to lose my job.'

'Of course not. How else will you meet nice girls?'

He laughed at that.

On the bus back to Fairfax, I stood, legs wide like I was surfing, and listened to a true crime podcast. A woman missing, presumed dead. A botched police report. Witnesses coming forward, decades too late, lamenting that they lacked the courage at the time to say there was something fishy about the husband. I kept rewinding, losing the narrative thread and listening, instead, to my thoughts. When, after forty minutes, I'd only digested ten, I pressed pause.

All I could hear was the idea that, when Paul laughed, it was not because what I said was absurd but because it was true. Perhaps his laugh was relief: that I didn't take him seriously; that I acknowledged *we* were not serious. And perhaps, by putting me on the bus, what he was really doing, was un-prising my grip on his life.

—

CLAUDIA AND I went for a walk one morning before class. She walked surprisingly quickly on her petite legs. I had to stretch my stride to keep up. When we arrived at the Glebe foreshore, we stopped so Claudia could take a picture of the Anzac Bridge—dewy and soft in the morning light—and watched rowboats pull through the still water.

I had thought about what Eve said as several days passed and I heard nothing from Paul. My stomach filled with wet cement whenever I thought about him. Perhaps, I thought, I was worth more than back-slapping remarks and crude jokes from the likes of Sackers. My body, my consent, my mistakes—these ought not to be for public consumption. And if I had to insist on my privacy, insist I be handled with care and dignity, then maybe I ought to start talking.

'Hey, I have a question.'

Claudia looked up from the photo she was editing.

'Do you think I should talk to Nick—you know, about what happened in O Week?'

'You've never spoken about it?'

'No. We just act like it didn't happen. And, I don't know . . . I wonder if it's more mature to just, like, bring it up and check that everyone is okay and it really was innocuous. Rather than letting, like, Sackers, decide that for us by joking about it.'

She slid her phone into the pocket of her running leggings and folded her arms against the breeze. 'I see your point. But Nick and Emily are together now. I mean, you don't want to be creating drama for the sake of it. Not that she would care, necessarily . . .'

'She'd never say if she did.'

'Well, exactly.'

'I'm conscious of that. Like, I don't want to go on and on about how I slept with her boyfriend months ago.'

Claudia looked out over the water, which was growing deeper and bluer as the sun rose, and spoke in a quiet voice that didn't seem to address me. At first, I thought perhaps she hadn't been listening. 'I had this boyfriend in high school—it wasn't a real relationship, very much a first boyfriend thing, like, we were just trying on intimacy for size. Anyway, one holidays his parents went away for the long weekend so I went and stayed at his house and, you know, lost my virginity and everything.' She waved her hand, as if to dismiss the memory. 'And every morning that weekend, I woke up to him fingering me.'

'Oh god, I'm so sorry.' My voice sounded too loud compared to hers.

'Yeah, it was awful. Every time I woke up his fingers would already be inside me. And I just . . . I didn't do anything. Like, I'd sort of roll over and have sex with him.' While she spoke, she was pulling her hair into a high ponytail, so tight I could see the skin on her forehead pulling back. 'And it wasn't until we read this Tim Winton short story in English class, about this woman who lived in a trailer park with an abusive husband, that I even realised that it was a totally fucked way to be treated.'

'That's funny.'

She looked at me, right in the eyes. 'Is it?'

'Sorry—of course it isn't. It's horrific. But, like, who would've thought Tim Winton would be the godfather of your bodily autonomy?'

Claudia laughed, her head tilted back to the sky. 'That is funny.'

We paused for a moment, letting dog walkers pass us.

'So what did you do?' I asked.

'Nothing. I just broke up with him. I said I needed to focus on my studies.'

I decided that in the next few days, when I felt up to it, I would message Nick and make a time, and we would talk about it. Like adults.

13

ON SUNDAY MORNING, cyclists sped past an horrific scene in Ku-ring-gai National Park. A motorcycle was shattered in pieces across the road, and what remained of it was wrapped—together with a young boy with no discernible features but a discernible shock of black hair—around a wilting gum tree.

Nick had gone for a drive, by himself, very late on Saturday night.

An autopsy later confirmed that he had taken MDMA.

He left no note, although going for a drive by yourself on drugs does not necessarily warrant a note. The spectre that he was not so much deliberate, but just deliberately reckless, haunted the scene. At least nobody else was hurt, everybody said, as if it were a run-of-the-mill traffic accident.

—

I WAS WITH Emily when she found out. It was awful timing. Not that there is ever a good time. But the place she happened to be when she took the call was so inappropriate, it gave us all the sense that we shouldn't have been there.

We were at St Thomas' College, at what the boys called a 'cellar lunch'.

A couple of times a year, the students who ran the basement bar at St Thomas' would descend into the stone cellars and hunt down cases of beer that were about to expire. From an establishment that thought drinking out of a shoe ('doing a shoey') was very debonair, this was not so much in pursuit of food safety as an excuse to throw a party. 'Lunch' was a misnomer, because food was never involved.

On one side of the St Thomas quadrangle trestle tables stood in a line, covered with white tablecloths. Dappled light cast golden pools in abundance.

We sat in old wooden chairs that had been dragged out from the dining hall, drinking beer and wine, with all the languor and blissful entitlement of a royal barge making its way up a river at dusk.

This particular day, the conversation was not frothy and free-flowing. There were frequent lulls, and I found myself laughing as a way of participating, not because anything was funny. Or perhaps the conversation was the same as it always was, but is tainted in my mind by what followed.

When the wine and the sun combined in a dull, dry-mouthed headache, Emily went to the bathroom. Because I was sitting next to her, and because that is what women do, I went to the bathroom with her.

The female bathroom in the all-male college was predictably tiny, like every cubic centimetre was a reluctant concession. There were only two stalls. One was nominally 'ambulant', with margin-ally more space, most of which was taken up by a silver bar. Emily and I, tipsy, went into the ambulant stall together. While I was peeing, her phone rang, and she answered. I rolled my eyes and waited until she was speaking, so that I could flush by way of interruption. I opened the cubicle door, and went to the sink to wash my hands.

I heard her phone hit the floor, and a guttural sound that I assumed at first must have come from outside, because—although it sounded close, and echoed off the tiles—it did not occur to me that it was human.

I opened the cubicle and found her crouched—not to vomit into the bowl, as I might have expected—but facing me. Her shoulders were heaving, and she was crying with deep, choking sobs.

I kneeled next to her and put a hand on her back, where I could feel her curved spine rising with her sobs.

'What's wrong?'

She tried to speak, but was bent over, her hands shaking.

So I stopped asking, and just said, 'It's okay,' over and over again, even though I didn't know what *it* was.

After several minutes, my concern was mingling with faint stirrings of irritation, and I texted Claudia to come and help.

Emily's in a bad way.

Claudia walked in, her black suede knee-high boots stark against the tiles, and said that she had expected to find vomit.

'I know, me too.'

'What's wrong with her?'

'She can't say.'

Eventually we got it out of her. When she told us, Claudia and I looked at each other, our expressions blank. I think, if I'm honest, my lips may have formed a smile.

'What do you mean *dead*?'

'He was riding his motorbike. They found him this morning.'

'Who told you?'

'His mum just called.'

She was calming down now, the constant questions leading her thoughts and breathing into a more regular pattern.

In the relative quiet, Claudia, ever practical, said in a voice that was only ever so slightly shrill: 'We should call her mum.'

I just looked at her.

'Her mum. She doesn't need to be here. She should go home.'

In another context, it might have sounded juvenile: to call her mother, as if parents were still escape hatches and not individual people with individual lives that didn't orbit ours. But it seemed the most obvious thing in the world, when Claudia said it.

The news was spreading. A small crowd gathered outside the bathroom, ready to give breathy condolences. These felt not so much like sympathy as performances of their own niceness. Or, at the very least, attempts to be included.

So Claudia and I took Emily to the car park, and sat with her in the gravel, one on each side, waiting for her mother. We didn't speak. Nothing was appropriate.

For the first time, I skipped my Sunday Chapel Choir performance.

When Emily had been picked up and we were alone, Claudia asked if I wanted to watch a movie with her, and I said that sounded ideal. She said it should be one we'd both already seen and loved, because it had to be a movie 'with cemented associations'. She didn't want to ruin a new one by having it remind her of this. So we watched *She's the Man* with Amanda Bynes and talked about her failed career, like lost youth and wasted potential were abstract ideas.

—

ALONE IN MY room, sharpened by its fluorescent light, it felt like the middle of the day. I had left the fan on and it whirred loudly, with intermittent clunks like the ticking of a clock.

I made a mental list of all the conversations Nick and I had shared, and reimagined them in light of the mangled motorbike, crushed glass, Emily's sobs. I wondered where I might have intervened.

It was almost midnight and I was still fully dressed, down to my mid-heeled black ankle boots and my mascara-tainted tears. I wasn't tired at all, and the thought of turning off the light and lying in that single bed, which would feel shadowy and cavernous in the dark, made me want to cry again.

I contemplated calling my mother, but decided it was too late. She would know exactly what to say, and it might break my heart.

I called Paul.

He didn't pick up the first time, so I tried again.

'Michaela?' His voice was surprised but clear. I hadn't woken him.

'Hi.'

'Are you okay?'

'Yeah, I'm fine. I just wanted to talk to you.'

'Are you drunk?'

'Do I sound drunk?'

'No, but it's so late. I just wondered.'

'This isn't a drunk call, Paul.'

'Should I be so lucky.' I tried to imagine where he was in his apartment. Probably his bedroom. 'So what kind of call is this?'

'My friend died today.'

He laughed. It wasn't a scoff of shock, but an actual laugh. I laughed too. It seemed the most sincere reaction.

'I'm sorry, I shouldn't be laughing, that's so terrible. It's just—that was so unexpected. I'm sorry. Are you okay?'

'Yeah, he wasn't like a close friend or anything. We had a lot of mutual friends, so everyone is pretty rocked by it. And it's just . . . in principle, you know?'

'How did he die?' He sounded like he was sitting down, relaxing into the conversation.

'Motorbike accident.'

'God, that's awful.'

'Yeah.'

Neither of us said anything. I became aware that I had been pacing my room and was now standing in the corner by the wardrobe, playing with the handle.

'Do you want to stay over?' Paul asked.

'Could I?'

'Of course. I'll come get you.'

—

THIS WAS THE first time that getting into Paul's car felt mundane. The previous times, there had been a sense of crossing a threshold, a thrill of penetrating another part of his life, of undertaking a journey together. This time, I just stepped in and kissed him on the lips without thinking.

'I'm so sorry I laughed before; I always do that when I hear really, really awful news. I can't tell terrible stories without smiling. It's such a bad quality.'

'I have that too,' I said.

'Really?' He looked at me and smiled. 'You did say it very abruptly.'

'Should I have eased you in? *I've been thinking about death . . .*'

He laughed, and moved his left hand from the gearstick to my knee. 'I'm glad you called me.'

When we were inside his apartment, he opened a bottle of red wine and, already pouring me a glass, asked whether I'd like a drink.

We sat on opposite ends of the couch, holding our wineglasses. I sat cross-legged so I could face him fully.

'Do you want to talk about it?' he asked.

I wanted to ask him why he hadn't contacted me all week. 'Not really. But it feels weird to talk about anything else.'

'I was going to tell you about this podcast I just listened to, but if that seems weird to you in light of the death . . .' He performed a mock shrug that said: *each to their own.*

I laughed. I liked how much effort he was putting into amusing me, with his playful commitment to the shrug. Perhaps, I thought, he'd had a busy week. I reached out a leg and poked him with my foot.

'It's very sad for a friend of mine,' I said. 'I think she was in love with him.'

'That's awful.' He was serious now, looking at me closely.

'I was with her when she found out.'

'Jesus.' He was giving me gentle prompts, not being glib, but not taking up too much space either, leaning back against the armrest while my words washed over him.

'She kept saying, *Why was he alone?* That's all she said, and I didn't know what to tell her. I said he must have felt like going for a drive.'

'So he was in a collision?'

'Sort of. With a tree.'

'Oh god.'

'They found him in the national park, apparently. He was riding a motorbike.'

'What? At night? By himself?'

'Well, exactly. I think that's the most awful part. Like, she didn't know whether it was an accident. So she just kept asking me why he was in that situation. Like, she really just wanted to know whether he'd *put* himself in that situation. We were standing in this group, and everyone kept saying things that they thought sounded soothing, like: *We loved him so much,* and, *They obviously found his body very quickly.* And I was just sitting there with this poor girl's head on my shoulder, like: Are you seriously trying to find a silver lining here?'

'People just want to ease the pain. It makes everyone more comfortable.'

'I guess.'

'I think it's a very natural response. But people don't realise sometimes that, by trying to lighten it, you're just proving that you haven't really *seen* the pain, if that makes sense?' This little interjection had the same intonation as his lecturing. *Does that make sense?* Like he was walking a few steps ahead and had stopped to look over his shoulder, to check that I was keeping up. 'Because if you really saw it, you would see it's too big, too heavy to relieve.'

'I see that.' I thought about the weeks after my father died: all the containers full of meals—fish pies and soups and casseroles— that neighbours and friends dropped around. I didn't like any of them. We froze a lot, and months later threw them out, thudding into the bin like bricks. *It's not about you,* my mother said at the time. *It's for them. They want to feel helpful.* I thought about telling Paul this anecdote, but I didn't want to seem self-pitying. Instead I said, 'You'd much rather have someone just tell you how awful and unbearable it all is, wouldn't you?'

Paul nodded.

I had finished my wine. I studied the brown flecks in the bottom of the glass. 'You know the last thing I said to him—the last conversation we had—I told him that I don't like people who don't think about death enough.'

'Oh, Michaela.' The way he said my name—with totally new meaning, like a word from another language—broke me. 'It's not your fault.'

The feelings I had hoarded all afternoon fixed themselves to his words. Shadows made solid: they acquired weight that threatened to crush me.

I put my head on his chest, letting him stroke my hair like a child, and cried.

'How do you know? How could you possibly know?'

He shushed me. 'I know. Trust me. I know.'

We were silent for a moment. I sat up from his embrace and looked through stinging eyes at a moth flapping against the ceiling light.

'It's very hard, I think'—Paul spoke cautiously—'to remember that it's not your fault. I think there's this instinct to make sense of things that happen to us. To put ourselves in the story. But things just happen, Michaela. There's no point to them. They just happen.'

I looked away from the moth and back at Paul, still conscious of the flapping sound its flailing wings made.

I kissed him then, holding his face with both hands. I wanted to hear my name said again in such tender tones, like a declaration.

He pulled back immediately. 'Are you sure?' he said. 'You've had a huge day. We can go to sleep, or watch something, or keep talking.'

I didn't say anything. I just kissed him harder, with my tongue on his. I thought I could melt into him, until I didn't exist anymore.

I put my hand on his erection and felt a destructive thrill. I was untethering from the day, from my mind. Skin on skin was all I needed to remind me that I was just a body—flesh and blood—and, for now, that was the point.

I climbed on top of him, and then we flipped once. He had one foot on the floor and the other leg kneeling on the couch. With every thrust I held his back and pulled him closer, hoping that if he went deep enough, I might break apart, like little pieces in his arms.

When he was finished, I relished the way he fell, panting, on top of me, like he was broken and I was the only thing holding him together.

I felt a bone-deep exhaustion, as if my body was being pulled underwater. I'd crossed an ocean since my hand on Emily's back, her spine curving under my fingers, bent over and unable to breathe.

'I was thinking about what you said before, about seeing other people's pain and about how seeing it for what it is—for how big it is—is more important than relieving it. Or not more important, but sometimes all you can do.'

'Well, sometimes just seeing it is a relief in itself.'

I felt his voice rumble where my ear was flush against his chest. I wriggled, trying to lie closer still.

'Exactly. Yes. I love that idea.'

'Some people think that that's what love is: being seen.'

'Do you think that's true?'

'I really do.'

'I love that idea,' I said again.

All this talk of love—talk but no declarations—hung in the room with our sweat and panting breaths. It was a shadow that slunk behind what we hadn't said. Love, the abstract idea, dragged with it, kicking and screaming, the action, the feeling: the leap of faith that was left un-leapt.

I started to cry, quietly at first so he didn't notice, until my tears trickled onto his chest. He stroked my hair and made soothing noises while the shadows expanded around us.

—

EVENTUALLY, WE MOVED to the bed, and I kissed him delicately, just brushing his lips with mine, in the tenderest way I could manage. He looked at me through half-closed eyes without really looking at me.

I floated into sleep, and when I woke he was sitting at his desk shrouded in the glow of his laptop. I told him to come back to bed.

Except I told him in a voice that wasn't mine: a child's whine— the same voice Eve used when she spoke French. My cringing embarrassment shocked me awake, and I rolled my face into my pillow, afraid of how he might respond.

'I was thinking about your friend,' he said.

'Which friend?' My voice was muffled through the pillow. As soon as I'd said it the night returned to me, with the curve of a spine, the crunch of a motorbike on gravel, and little brown flecks in red wine.

'It made me think about that Camus quote, about death being the one urgent philosophical question.'

'Do we need to have this conversation tonight?'

'Sorry, I didn't mean it as a conversation. It's just why I'm out of bed. Here: *There is only one really serious philosophical problem*, Camus says, *and that is suicide. Deciding whether or not life is worth living is to answer the fundamental question in philosophy. All other questions follow from that.*'

I sat up and crawled to the edge of his bed to see his screen. The heading at the top of his page read: '3.1. Suicide as a Response to Absurdity.'

'Are you reading *The Stanford Encyclopedia of Philosophy* entry on Camus?'

'Yes.'

'In the middle of the night?'

'Mmhmm.'

'You're a parody of yourself.'

I fell asleep in the foetal position, one arm stretched out on the cold side of the bed, which Paul had left vacant.

——

EVE TEXTED ME. I was sitting up in Paul's bed, the morning sun harsh on his white sheets. The sound of his shower hummed through the apartment.

> I'm so sorry about Nick

I imagined Eve in the Fairfax dining hall, where news of Nick's death would spread on whispers over breakfast. Were I there, I'd have to sit with Emily and Portia and Claudia, feeling eyes on my back, and know that my grief was considered greater, because— although everybody at college knew each other—not everybody was a *friend*. The friends of Nick's, the people who shared his drunken nights, and were therefore considered *close* to him: their grief took centre stage. In the comparative privacy of Paul's apartment, my loss was mercifully my own.

I went to the kitchen for a glass of water. It was cloudy with fluoride.

My phone buzzed with a follow-up text:

> I can't imagine how difficult and confusing
> it is for you. I hope you're okay.

Usually, Eve made fun of me, for considering myself a 'friend' of Nick's, or Sackers's or any of the boys Emily and Claudia and Portia chose to spend their time with. It was comforting, almost, to think that, to Eve, Nick was just another member of a group she considered beneath me (and, by extension, her). I was relieved that I hadn't told her his name, that day in the gallery, when she'd asked. These condolences, while exhausting in their sincerity, were at least uncomplicated.

I typed quickly and didn't reread before I pressed send, like we were talking in real life.

Thanks, I really appreciate it. It's such sad news.

Eve replied straight away.

You in your room?

Paul was out of the shower. I could hear him moving through his bedroom. I told Eve I'd be back later that day. I didn't say where I was.

Sleep seeped from my limbs as I moved around the kitchen. I unstacked the dishwasher, I made toast, I buttered and salted it. I ate a banana with yoghurt, muesli and honey. The day distilled in conquerable tasks, synchronised to the pitter-pat of Eve and I texting back and forth.

———

UNLIKE EVE, I WAITED after knocking until she gave me permission to enter.

When I swung the door open, she was still occupied. Her desk was full of books, clothes, even shoes, so she was sitting on her bed to write, cocooned in a pile of coats, her bald head bent over a dark green notebook.

'It's so good to see you.' She got up and held me, her grip surprisingly tight. I stood rigid for a moment before wrapping my arms around her. She did not let go but turned her head to whisper, deep down into my ear: 'I'm sorry.' Just when I felt weak and at ease, she let me go.

'Um, sorry to interrupt.' I spoke before I thought, wanting to fill the silence, which only amplified all the things I didn't want to talk about. I pointed to her green notebook. 'What were you working on?'

'Oh, you know.'

'No?'

'Just stray thoughts. Ideas for things I might write.'

'Those masturbation monologues don't write themselves!'

She hit me in the back of the head with the notebook. I smiled, and touched my head where it hurt.

'Where have you been? I haven't seen you for days.'

'I've been staying at Portia's.' It disturbed me a little, how fluently I lied to Eve, without any flavour of transgression.

'Right.' Eve tried not to grimace, her face resolute in concern. Normally when she heard the name Portia she would at least mime gagging, or launch into a hair-flicking impression, which was only funnier now Eve had no hair to flick.

She sat on the bed and picked at the mess around her. 'And how is everyone?'

'Okay. I mean, you can't be okay. They're rocked, obviously. But they're all supported, and whatever.'

'And you?'

'I'm fine.' My voice sounded strangely defiant.

Eve stood up again, her eyes level with mine. She was still drafting her face into an expression of concern, but for a little smile. 'I have an idea.'

—

WHEN EVE SUGGESTED she buy me ice cream, because I needed a treat, it was the use of the word *treat* that persuaded me. It underscored the futility. How childish, and how comforting, precisely because it was childish. Getting ice cream, as if it were a way of coping, made me feel like adulthood was still safely out of reach. As if all versions of me—other than the one that was feeble and selfish and had no responsibilities—were just pretend.

Wearing jeans and Birkenstocks, with the night tickling our toes, we crunched across the gravel car park and into her Honda Civic. It was a black cardboard box of a car, with jolting acceleration, and she drove it like a maniac. Her mother had owned it for years, and it had a leak problem, which she 'cured' by shoving cinnamon sticks in the aircon vents. These, of course, achieved nothing. I think Eve liked them as a talking point: a reason to list the car's defects. If this was a rare stirring of class-consciousness, it had the opposite effect. To have a car and think it was not good enough betrayed more about where she came from and what she valued than the intermittent dripping on my bare toes.

Eve got two scoops, so I did too. Inside the ice-cream shop, thumping techno music played, and the server called me 'babe'.

On the walk back to the car, Eve licked her ice cream like a cat. 'I had my first Aesthetics and Ethics lecture today. You're not taking it?'

That was Paul's subject. We had agreed that, to avoid 'complications', (which was our euphemism for *career ruin*) he should not teach me.

'No,' I said.

'Why not? You did so well in Paul's class last sem.' She pushed the ice cream further into the cone with her tongue.

'I'm taking History of Philosophy and Psychoanalysis.'

'Luke says that's a wank.'

Paul had said the same.

'Does Luke have to be the authority on everything?'

Eve shoved her cone, unfinished, in the drinks tray and turned the key in the ignition. 'What's wrong with Luke?'

'Don't you reckon he just loves to *look like* he's listening to you?' I took Eve's snort as encouragement. 'Like, he'll ask so many questions and touch you on the arm'—I touched Eve's arm in demonstration—'but glaze over when you start to answer.'

'I know what you mean. He does seem to see female attention as a way of buttressing his ego.'

'Exactly.'

'You know we're sort of . . .' Eve paused to focus on reversing, with a clunking gear change and a rapid, nausea-inducing swing. My cardboard tub of ice cream fell out of my lap, and a little creamy caramel flavour dribbled onto the floor. 'You know we're seeing each other?'

'How do you mean?' I tried to hide the spill by rubbing it in with my foot.

'We slept together the first time after his house party. And then, obviously, I didn't want to be exclusive while I was away. But now we're sort of picking things up where we left off.'

I looked out the window while I arranged my face. I could see Eve's profile reflected in the glass. I looked at her lips, sticky and sweet with ice cream. I thought about our kiss in the bathroom, how she had glanced off me and settled on Luke. 'Wow. I'm happy for you.' In the reflection, I saw my lips move like someone else's.

Eve laughed, and I turned back to her, checking that it was genuine. 'You're right, though,' she said. 'Luke can be a bit of a cunt.'

I laughed then too.

When we pulled up in the Fairfax car park, I was relieved that Eve sat back and started nibbling on her waffle cone rather than making a move to open the door.

'I'm actually going to stay at his for a couple of days,' she said.

'Moving in already?'

'No, just a sea change. It'll be good to get out of Fairfax for a bit.'

'Well,' I said, 'as long as you come back eventually.' I said *eventually* because I thought it wouldn't sound too sincere. My sense—too nascent for me to notice—that Eve and I were drifting must have been audible. Eve leaned over and placed her head on my shoulder. She had to stretch across the front console to do it. It was so forced, it felt like a consolation prize.

Back in my room, after we'd parted for the night, I heard Eve's door slam shut. I assumed she was leaving to go to Luke's. Not wanting to sound desperate, I didn't call out to say goodbye. Instead, I stood by my window and watched as the little lights and loud engine of her car confirmed my suspicion. Watching her retreat, with my room in darkness so she wouldn't see me at the window, I felt, already, that I was much, much more alone than if she had been asleep in the room beside me.

14

NICK'S FUNERAL WAS at a church in Turramurra which didn't look like a church at all—more like a conference hall. The sloping wood panelling on the ceiling was reminiscent of a school auditorium, and the light that streamed through huge windows was too abundant, too uniform, to convey a sense of divine intention.

The Chapel Choir sang, at the parents' request.

We hadn't rehearsed to sing at a funeral, so we just sung hymns we'd already learned. At the door, we were given funeral booklets that spelled out the order of service.

Nick's older brother, who looked just like him, couldn't finish his eulogy, and their mother—a small woman with an angular blonde bob and muscly Madonna arms—held his shoulders gently and read the last sentence for him. She was much smaller than him, perhaps half the width, yet he melted into her touch, and she seemed to hold him upright.

He was my best mate. A better, kinder, more generous person than I could ever hope to be. I'll miss you, Nick. We didn't have long enough.

Those were the words that she spoke on her eldest—now, her only—son's behalf, while he, weak-kneed and sobbing, clung to her.

When the eulogy was over, there was a long silence before Balth nudged me and waved the program.

We were scheduled to sing. We stood, eyeing each other, checking we were not the first to jump. I had to stifle a laugh. We sang, haltingly at first, and then stronger, as we forgot where we were and concentrated on how we sounded.

When the funeral was over, Nick's brother, father and two men I didn't recognise carried his coffin on their shoulders, and his mother walked behind. She was wearing sunglasses, which was a futile gesture, when her sobs were so loud, and her head bowed with loss.

In the third row, I saw Sackers's tuft of blond hair rising out of a suit. He was leaning forward, clinging to the pew in front. When the congregation stood to leave, he stayed seated. A gentle hand on his back went unacknowledged. His great, muscular shoulders shook.

Some of us stood to sing as the procession marched out, and others sat and cried. Nicola, proudly upholding the soprano part, shot the criers scathing looks when they failed to rise, as if they were cowards.

She sang with her face arranged in what I can only imagine she thought was an expression of grace. It struck me as slappable self-importance.

She sang as if she owed it to the mourners—as if it were a gift that she, being so copiously talented, was obligated to bestow. Like music might change people, might take them out of themselves, might touch them with a universal truth. Like we were all connected and God existed and Nick was going somewhere special, not just to a hole in the ground.

When the choir filed out last, Sackers had his arm around a friend's shoulder. His feet dragged behind him as he, weak with grief, stumbled out.

Eve was the only member of the choir, who didn't attend that day. She didn't say she couldn't make it, and when Nicola asked where she was, I snapped that it didn't matter, because we had enough altos.

As it transpired, it did matter, because I cried so much at the end that I couldn't sing. So we didn't have enough altos after all.

———

AT THE WAKE, Emily unnerved everybody with her politeness. At some point in her upbringing, an explanation of the distinction between manners and morals must have been omitted. Politeness, for Emily, meant a selfless regard for others—a putting of their interests before her own—that threatened to rub her out of existence.

Emily, Claudia, Portia, and I stood in the corner, our hands full of plastic plates and finger sandwiches. Nobody ate.

'Are you okay?' Emily asked each of us individually. And then proceeded to concern herself with anyone's wellbeing but her own—as if she could march the world back to order, away from cruelty and chaos, by sticking to rules she already knew.

'His poor mother.'

'His father looked devastated.'

'His brother is such a nice guy. He won't get over this.'

'Did you see Sackers? That poor boy . . .'

I started on the finger sandwiches, and tried to concentrate on the taste of egg and mayonnaise. Irritation swelled at Emily's high-pitched, gentle-toned commentary. I couldn't see her clearly.

Claudia, to her credit, was nodding and murmuring just enough to acknowledge Emily, without quite encouraging her.

Emily pressed on. 'His schoolfriends haven't seen much of him this year. That must be very hard for them.'

'Emily.' Portia's cup of milky tea rattled in its saucer. She placed it on a table. I swallowed and moved from sandwiches to biscuits.

With deliberate, uninterruptable movements, Portia eased Emily's plate from her hands and placed it by the lukewarm tea. Then she folded her into a hug. Emily leaned her head on Portia's shoulder, letting Portia's blonde hair enclose them both like a shroud. I was close enough to hear her whisper: 'We all loved him.'

Emily started to cry. Claudia and I relaxed, palpably. We patted her shaking back, while Portia held her in that graceful embrace and didn't let go. That Portia—from whom I expected no more than the usual *Wait. What?*—knew exactly when to reach out and when to let go, when to talk and when to touch, made me think she was perhaps the most perceptive of us all.

Nick's schoolfriends congregated near the door. Several of them had beers in hand. The sound, cruelly, was that of a party. So many young people in one room.

There was talk of the pub. Emily, Portia, and Claudia rallied at the prospect. I ached for a drink, but I knew only a smattering of these suited, slick-haired boys. They deserved to spend an evening undiluted by strangers, who knew Nick differently.

'I'm heading back to college now, if you want a lift?' Balthazar, car keys in hand, offered me escape.

On the multi-lane highway that stretched its arms out towards the Harbour Bridge, Balth asked why Eve hadn't come. I told him, honestly, that I didn't know.

'People grieve in different ways,' he said. He said it like he was playing the words back to himself and thought they sounded sophisticated.

—

PORTIA, CLAUDIA, AND Emily retreated to their family homes after the wake. I couldn't blame them, but I resented them the luxury. Balth and I went to a movie. I was subdued, and he was his best version of himself. He told me so many hilarious stories—most of them about people he'd offended—that I flattered myself he'd been saving them up for the occasion. Back at Fairfax, with Eve's room still vacant, my room felt both smaller and at the same time like it was my whole world.

I called Paul. He answered with a question: 'Do you want me to pick you up?'

At his apartment, Paul asked me about the funeral, I told him it was as sad as you would expect.

'It must have been devastating.'

When he said that—his face a mask of sincerity I hadn't seen before—I suddenly resented him.

How would you know? I wanted to ask. *You didn't know him at all.*

Instead, I said I just wanted a distraction. I kissed him.

'A distraction,' he repeated. His face was hollow and wounded, like a gently blossoming bruise.

—

THE WEATHER, THOSE days after Nick's death, was unseasonably, offensively warm. On Wednesday morning, the light fell on Paul's bed in theatrical shards, and my arm was hot where it caught the sun.

'We should go for a swim,' I said.

I expected Paul to say no, and to put me on the bus. But he didn't have class until eleven, and it was, after all, a glorious day.

We went to a beach Paul called Redleaf, even though the sign on the fence said something different. It was just off the main road, and the car park was framed by sandstone gates.

It had rained the night before, so every blade of grass was green and dripping, and every surface mirrored the sun with moisture. At the edge of the car park, stairs led down to a little harbour beach, cupped by a U-shaped wharf. The light reflected in such dense sparkles that the sea was a sheet of shimmering white. It was so bright and so beautiful, the whole scene hurt my eyes.

While rain had cleaned the city and its parks, it had turned the beach to mud. As we descended the stairs, I saw that the sand was damp and grey, and the water full of seaweed that floated to the top, coating the coast with grime.

I still think of Paul on rain-cleaned days, and think of their deceptive beauty. If I learned anything practical from him, who taught me so much that had no practical use at all, it is this: if you want to ruin a beautiful, perfect thing, go to a Sydney harbour beach in the aftermath of heavy rain.

We sat on the wharf away from the damp and grimy sand. From there we could jump straight into the water, and avoid the sludge at the bottom.

The first time I jumped, it took longer than I expected for my body to hit the water. In the freefall, I relished the irreversibility of my decision, which, for a moment, was free from consequence.

The water was crushing and cold. I climbed out quickly, the metal ladder digging uncomfortably into the soles of my feet. At the top, I spread out a towel and lay next to Paul.

We read in silence, me a novel and Paul flicking through student papers. I felt my skin crust under the sun. It wasn't quite spring yet, and the breeze snapped across my back in hair-raising breaths.

Paul pulled a Tupperware container from his bag, full of frozen mangoes. They were sticky and slippery, and the juice stuck to Paul's beard in a sheen.

As he sat cross-legged like Buddha, with mango sticking to his grey-flecked beard and a Fitness First backpack at his knees, I saw him through a stranger's eyes. He was robbed of the assertive thrust of the lectern, and seeing his cross-legged, hunched position, I found

202 | DIANA REID

a seed of pity—pity for an overweight man fading out of his prime, the slender trendy thing at his side not having the desired effect but, rather, accentuating the contrast.

I wondered whether this cruelty was normal in the rush and tumble of intimacy. Or whether it was some kind of thought crime: a crack that could only grow.

'I need to wash my hands,' I declared, and stood to jump in again.

Paul stood with me and grabbed me gently around the hips with mango-sticky hands. I stiffened, and wondered if he felt it.

He looked at me, the kind of look that sounds like swelling violins and precipitates a kiss. I shuffled my weight, leaning slightly back, which just pushed me further into his hands.

'Ouch.' I leaned forward, my head almost cracking his as he leaned down too.

'What's wrong?'

'Fuck me, sorry.' I looked at him and laughed. 'Splinter.' I showed him the underside of my foot, where a jagged needle of wood stuck out, framed by a thin trickle of blood.

'Ouch. Do you want me to get it out?'

He touched my cheek, and I brushed it away. 'No, I'll get it,' I said, more generously than my swatting hand implied.

Hobbling back to the towel on my heels did little to assert my independence. I pulled it out quickly, using the tips of my fingernails.

'I'll get you a bandaid,' he said.

'Don't be ridiculous. It's gone now.' I stood up again, and was irritated by the way his eyes crinkled with concern.

'It'll get infected.'

'It's covered in salt!'

'Salt's a preservative, not a disinfectant.'

'Paul, it's fine.'

'I'm just trying to hel—'

With a force that surprised me, and no doubt surprised him, I pushed him off the wharf. I waited for him to resurface, so he could hear me hoot with laughter, before I jumped in after him.

Back up on the wharf, we gathered our towels around us like blankets against the chilly breeze.

He put his sticky Tupperware back in his bag, where I imagined it would attract grains of fluff and sand.

'Michaela?'

I turned, the towel around my shoulders. 'Balth!'

His hair, usually floppy, was oddly voluminous on account of the salt. It made me smile.

'What are you doing here?' I asked.

'Well, Michaela, like many people, I enjoy going to the beach for a swim.'

'A swim in August? How brave.'

'Who could blame me?' His eyes, laughing, were suddenly alert as he took in Paul.

Paul's towel was wrapped high up his hips, near his belly button, perhaps in a deliberate effort to obscure the curve of his stomach. Balth, by contrast, in his sopping black board shorts, was so thin he was almost concave.

'Balth, this is Paul.'

Paul rested a hand on my shoulder. I saw the movement register on Balth's face in a flash of discomfort so strong, it almost looked like pain. I felt an urge to shrug Paul off, but willed my shoulder to stay still.

'Hi, mate.' Paul extended a hand. They shook quickly, before Balth put his hand to his forehead, shielding his eyes from the sun. His goosebumps glowed. Under the shadow of his hand, he looked at me. The discomfort I'd seen only a moment ago was gone. Instead, he was fighting a smile. I knew he was already savouring the experience of teasing me about this later.

'I've never been here before,' I offered. 'It's so nice.'

'A favourite haunt of yours, is it, Paul?' Balth offered, and I winced at his use of the word *haunt*.

'Um, I guess.' Paul was speaking loudly, in a deeper voice than I was used to.

'What about you?'

'What?' Balth's head snapped to me.

'Do you live around here?' I asked.

'Oh, yeah. Well, my parents do. You can see their place from here, actually.' He pointed to a huge slate-coloured house which was all straight lines and enormous single-paned windows, like glass in an aquarium. A green lawn sloped gently down to a jetty. Where the wood met the grass, a bronze sculpture twisted towards the sky.

I think my jaw actually dropped.

'That house? With the bronze . . .'

'With the insufferable sculpture? Yeah. Mum loves it, but she's deranged.'

'No, it's, um . . .'

From Balth's laugh I knew my attempts to be polite were transparent.

'It looks very expensive.'

'Oh, it is. Turns out money can't buy taste.'

'Must be tough,' Paul said, so curt that I found myself suddenly unable to look Balth in the eye.

Paul looked at his wrist, where, embarrassingly, he wasn't wearing a watch. He must have taken it off before he swam. 'We should go, Mick.'

'Yeah, well, nice to meet you, Paul,' Balth offered, as he continued past us on the wharf. Over his shoulder he called, 'See you soon,' and then—after a maddening pause in which I could hear his delight—he added: '*Mick*.'

'What a wanker,' Paul said, deliberately loudly, before we were out of earshot.

'You barely spoke to him.'

'Who was that guy? Some college friend?'

'He's one of the good ones, actually.'

'Jesus. He seemed like a simpering idiot.'

'I wonder what he'd say about you. You were pretty rude.'

We were back on the beach now, and started walking up the stairs. I took them two at the time and didn't turn around as I spoke to Paul.

'So, is he your friend?'

'I don't know, Paul, I'm not from Sydney.'

'What's that supposed to mean? *I'm not from Sydney*.'

'It means I don't know anyone. So anyone I sort of know is sort of a friend.'

'What's that? Some kind of catch-all excuse for having no taste?'

'I'm just saying beggars can't be choosers. We don't all have the luxury of disdain.'

We'd reached the top of the stairs. We'd scaled them quickly, following my angry pace. At the top, Paul paused. When he'd caught his breath, he ran a hand through his hair and said, 'I don't like it that that Balth kid saw us together.'

'Kid?' I was revelling in my irritation now. I heard myself from the other side of the car park, from the perspective of one of the people pulling their towels out of their boot and making their way down to the beach. I sounded shrill and, together with Paul, we looked like a bickering couple.

Paul spoke quietly, too quietly to be heard by passing strangers. 'He's a kid, Michaela.'

In the car, I looked out the window and watched the houses scroll past. 'I think . . . I think the problem is that you're not sure whether *I'm* too young.'

'Of course you're not too young. You're more mature than I am.'

'Nobody said anything about maturity.'

The car was heavy with silence. I imagined the regrets he might be having and hated him for them. 'Either you don't mind people seeing us in public together, Paul, or I'm too young to fuck.'

'Hey.' He put a hand on my thigh and squeezed gently. 'I'm sorry I was rude.'

I thought I had wanted an apology, but when it was so forthcoming, I resented the obligation it placed on me to accept it. I said nothing.

'I'm sorry.' He almost whined it.

Again the car was silent: an attempt at punishment on my part. For him, it seemed meditative. When he pulled up outside Fairfax and leaned in to kiss me, I turned my cheek. He laughed. And with his laugh he made me feel—for the first and only time—like a child. Powerless, stomping her little foot without making a sound.

—

I STARTED SLEEPING badly. When I was with Paul, I'd lie awake listening to him roll over, stand up, go to the bathroom, sit at his computer. I tried to keep my breathing regular, so he'd think I was asleep. And when I was alone at Fairfax, I'd stare at the ceiling and my thoughts would chase each other, like greyhounds around a track, snapping at the same incessant question.

What prompts a boy with the world at his feet to climb on a motorbike and ride into the darkness?

I couldn't shake the feeling that he was being chased.

The clunk of my fan marked the time, like a ticking clock or a bomb—the only reminder that the physical world progressed, while I followed Nick's voice, his inclusive smile, further into the past. Over and over, I replayed our final conversation in the St Thomas' College courtyard.

Nothing they do ever has any consequence.

As I lay there, binding myself in my sheets like rope, I listened for Eve in the adjacent room. I interpreted every tread in the corridor, every creak of a door, as a sign that she was returning. I pictured myself, bleary-eyed, knocking, demanding an audience.

Nick and Eve seemed, to me, connected. The thread linking them was thin—too thin to see—but in those quiet tired hours, there were moments when I heard it vibrate.

I thought about Eve's insistence that I report what happened with Nick a lifetime ago. Whatever happened in O Week happened to other people. A former self; a dead man. Yet it was that night, and the fragments of his touch, that I remembered when I thought about Nick, gazing out across his life and seeing a vast, consequenceless expanse.

Eve and Nick whispered to me: two voices conjoined in the same prayer. *Actions have consequences.*

I felt that I owed him one more conversation, and I played it out in my mind. We would take the event I could barely remember and sculpt it together, deciding what shape it took, before carefully placing it in the past. Without that conversation, the past took many haunting shapes. First was the fear that when Nick took to his motorbike that night, he wanted, at least in part, to die. And that, of all the complex ways he saw himself, there was a version—however indistinct—where he looked to his innermost reflections and saw a rapist.

I rubbed my eyes, as if to rub away these ugly possibilities. My imagination, I told myself, was my failure. My guilt—about what went unsaid; conversations I could never have—was not Nick's. No wonder it all seemed connected, when I sat up at night and viewed his life through the tiny slice he shared with me. There were other people, other relationships that were beyond my scope.

I reached into the back of my cupboard, where I hid my cigarettes. I still hid them, as if I were living with my mother.

I sat on the edge of my desk, one leg dangling out the window, and lit up.

With a start of recognition, like a flash of a remembered dream, I recalled the text Eve sent me the day after Nick died. I coughed, and climbed down from my perch to retrieve my phone.

There it was, not quite as I'd remembered.

I'm so sorry about Nick, she had written. *I can't imagine how difficult and confusing it is for you.*

Resuming my position—one leg out the window, phone in one hand, cigarette in the other—I read it several times.

How difficult and confusing it was *for me.*

For the first time, those last two words carried the weight of the sentence. *For me.*

I had been careful never to tell Eve who it was that first night in O Week. Once, in the gallery, I'd almost slipped.

You can tell me his name, she had said.

How difficult and confusing for me, in particular. Not for young people in general, when another young person dies.

Eve's absence at the funeral, her quick escape from Fairfax as soon as she'd heard the news—these solidified, in my mind, to a suspicion: a thought that came to me, first as a quickening of my heart. Then, it formulated in words.

Eve knew who had fucked me that first night in O Week. She knew it was Nick.

A knock on the door startled me. 'Jesus.' I had to clutch the desk to keep from toppling out the window. In doing so, I dropped my phone. It fell two flights and landed with a flat thud in the car park.

'Michaela?'

I opened the door.

Emily, looking apologetic. 'I'm so sorry.'

'What time is it?'

'Nine.'

I rubbed my eyes. In my mind it was much later. The halls were empty and silent.

'Are you okay?' she asked.

'I'm fine, I just . . .' I was going to say that I couldn't sleep. Except it was too early. I hadn't slept all week. When class finished at five that afternoon, I had drawn the orange curtains against the orange sunset and tried to have a nap. I obviously hadn't slept for as long as I thought.

'Sorry. You startled me. I dropped my phone.'

'What?'

'I was smoking out the window.'

Emily smiled. It was a smoke-free building.

'I missed dinner,' she said. 'I just came by to see if you wanted to get something on King Street? Thai should still be open.'

Hunger suddenly asserted itself. I could feel the edges of my stomach. 'Yeah. That'd be great, actually. I haven't eaten since breakfast.'

On our way out, we picked my phone up off the gravel.

'That's a relief,' Emily said, when I flipped it to reveal an unbroken screen.

It was only later, in the brighter lights of King Street, that I noticed a hairline fracture, severing the glass almost perfectly in half.

15

IF EVE'S ABSENCE were not so persistent, I would never have spied on her the way I did. But for days she didn't come home.

Although unrelated, her absence from my life—her empty bedroom; the mess on her floor undisturbed—only added to her absence from Nick's funeral. They carved a single, ever-deepening impression: that she was hiding.

I thought a lot about our last conversation, when she had urged me to tell my story. The first time, she'd suggested I report it to the college. But when we spoke after the holidays, her tone had changed.

Have you thought about reporting? became: *Your story, Michaela, it could be a catalyst for change.*

And her eyes, that second time, if I recalled correctly, were more manic. Wider, more purposeful. My drunken act—mine and Nick's—had become a cause for her to champion. And I could only imagine the righteousness with which she might have pursued it, once she'd set her sights on a perpetrator.

Whenever I imagined her like this—eyes wide, hands expressive, rapping on doors, firing questions like accusations—was when I most wanted to see her. If she just knocked on my door, I thought, knocked and entered without waiting for permission, then we could realign. She could tell me how she came to know, and we could, through conversation, see through the same eyes.

She might not know, I told myself. I could be misinterpreting her texts, and her absence. It was a leap indeed, to think that she had asked enough questions, and painted Nick's actions in such a light, that it might have caused a ripple, let alone propelled his motorbike on that night.

And yet the thought, like a mutating virus, returned repeatedly. The thought that she might have known, and that she might have presented this knowledge to Nick as a kind of threat: hunted him with it, even. In my seemingly continuous state of sleepless contemplation, I forgot Paul's advice—that there's no point. Instead, *Why did Nick die?* and *Did Eve know?* became different expressions for the same question. And that question became the point.

—

EVE'S DOOR WAS open. She always left it open. She'd even remarked that she thought it was self-important of me to lock mine. I walked past it every time I went to the bathroom. The little crack between the door and the frame tempted me, even though I knew, in an abstract rational way, that what it was beckoning me to do was wrong.

Her room was as messy as ever. The floor was uneven beneath my feet; the smell was of body odour and neglect. I opened a window and looked around, feeling stupid suddenly, as if I were the last one left playing an abandoned game of hide-and-seek.

On the wall opposite the window she had stuck several new polaroids. There were some sunny snaps of her Europe trip and, right at the edge, a photo of me at a bar taken that night we slept with the musicians.

My mouth pouted around my straw, my face angular. More harsh than seductive, such was the cut of my cheekbones. I looked, I thought, not unlike Eve.

On the bed below the photos were several books. Dog-eared, post-it-noted, highlighted. One of them was a forest green notebook, bending around a pen that had been shoved inside.

Still standing, I opened it. A daily journal, printed on thick creamy paper, with inspirational quotes at the top of each page, and an entry by Eve below. The first entry was from Eastern Europe. Eve evidently found the concept of travel journaling passé, because her entries were more various than recounts of her day. They were random explosions of insight and emotion, lacking any aesthetic care. Fundamentally un-bloggable. Except, perhaps, in the blackly comic juxtaposition between what Eve had scratched and what vapid quote the stationery brand had selected. I doubt the irony was lost on Eve.

Dream as if you'll live forever, live as if you'll die today.

—James Dean

Man in the hostel snored all night. Should be illegal, or at least taxed. Imagine being such a burden on the people around you. Is this the social contract I signed up for?!

I sat down, and read more deliberately. I skipped ahead several pages. The entries continued even after she'd returned home.

Life is ours to be spent, not saved.

—D.H. Lawrence

Studied with Luke in the library. Wondering what percentage of being smart is just being articulate. Ate some gum and three coffees all day. Will try to keep up tomorrow.

Each entry was dated. I flicked through, glancing up regularly to check the door. There was one date I was looking for.

If opening the journal were innocent (which it wasn't), then this was the real transgression.

I felt as if my chest was hollow and my heart floating to the top. My hands tingled with adrenaline. I stopped when I reached the date of Nick's funeral. It was a long entry.

> **A successful life is not a destination, but rather a journey.**
> **—Chinese proverb**

Nick's funeral today. Very confronting. I never think of mortality as a fact of my existence, or anyone else's really, unlike gender or race, for example. Ironic, perhaps, because it is the defining fact of existence? That it ends??

I couldn't bring myself to go. It's obviously tragic and terrifying. But I'm not a friend. I'm not really part of that milieu.

Here she had crossed out *milieu* and written *group*. As if she found her own vocabulary indulgent—expressing not the word itself, but something unsavoury about the person who used it.

I didn't know him. I only spoke to him in person once. It would be dishonest to grieve like I've lost something. And after O Week, it would be even more dishonest to sit there and listen to everyone say what a good guy he was. Such a good guy. Like that's the highest compliment?

So there it was: stolen confirmation. Eve knew.

The dead boy, the good guy, was, in Eve's view, a rapist. A night I couldn't remember had followed Nick, in the shape of Eve's ever-questioning belligerence. A wrong that refused to fade; a wound that wouldn't heal; consequences that sunk their dainty teeth in.

I closed the journal and placed it back at the exact angle I had found it. I felt smaller and more childish for my fussing: all the care I took not to be caught.

—

ON SUNDAY AFTERNOON, I arrived early to Chapel Choir. It was colder inside than out, and had the look of a common room rather than a place of worship. All the choir members lounged in the pews as if they were couches: lying down, feet up on the seat. I sat near the door and waited for Eve to arrive.

I hoped I might waylay her as she entered. I wanted to know what she had said to Nick, and when. I was primed to be cross-questioned. The fact that she didn't come to the funeral, I would say, aroused my suspicions. Nothing more.

From my vantage point near the door, I saw her walking across the oval. Her hair had grown into a light fuzz, which she had died bubble gum pink. Infuriatingly, this only made her more attractive. I was too busy registering this change to notice Balth approaching.

'*Mick*, hello.' Balth kissed me performatively on both cheeks. I swatted him away.

'Fuck off, Balthazar.'

'Did you have a nice time at the beach?'

'Oh, you saw each other at the beach?' Eve, now at the door, hugged me. She moved further inside and Balth followed, thrilled he was accumulating an audience.

'Yes, I saw Michaela at the beach with a lovely older gentleman.'

'And who were you at the beach with, Balthazar?' I said. 'You weren't swamped with friends.'

'I was there with a *plethora* of friends. And they were all my own age, thank you very much.'

'Who was it, Michaela?' Eve looked at me accusingly.

'He looked old enough to be her father.'

'He's just a friend.'

This was going exactly as Balth had planned. The small choir had congregated around me, those on the perimeter standing back against the pews, laughing at my discomfort, the closer ones firing questions. Only Nicola remained seated, her eyes wide.

'Who was he?'

'Are you seeing him?'

'How old is he?'

'Does he go to college?'

Balth laughed at that. 'He might have gone to college a few decades ago.'

'There are people in the world who don't go to college,' I snapped.

'How dare you.' Balth was energised by his pot-stirring. He clutched at his chest in mock outrage, like he'd been stabbed. The laughing choir grew louder. Balth almost had to shout, 'There's no shame in spending some quality time with your father.'

'My father is dead, Balthazar.'

Silence crashed in from all sides, filling our lungs like water. As if from far away, above the surface, Eve's voice sounded.

'It wasn't Paul, was it?'

Panicked, I pretended not to hear. I looked at Balth, whose expression was a version of my own—realising, too late, that amid his joking skirmish, something had shattered underfoot.

Eve grabbed my arm and forced me to look at her. Her eyes flicked between mine, the way actors' do in films. First left, then right, then back again.

'Michaela,' she said slowly, 'are you seeing Paul?'

The directness of the question, the fact that she leapt so smoothly from suspicion to confirmation, proved that, on some level, she must have already guessed. I didn't say anything. I just looked at her, mouth slightly open, and felt a bubbling urge to lie.

'Of course not.'

She looked like I had slapped her.

Two sharp taps on the music stand summoned our attention.

'When you're ready, ladies and gentlemen, I thought we might perform.'

I wish I could say that I stormed out piously, my head held high, or that I ran out in tears. But it was Eve who left. She did not look at me as she went.

—

'EVE.'

I pressed my ear to her bedroom door and knocked again.

'Eve, please. I'm sorry. I should have told you before.'

The door opened. The sun was setting through her orange curtains, flooding the room gold. She was backlit and blurred—a fiery silhouette.

'I'm sorry,' I said again.

She did not move but stood hands on hips, blocking the doorway. 'A professor sleeping with a first year student? Quite the cliché.'

'I'm not a student of his anymore.'

My voice was weak. Eve took over without effort. 'How long has it been going on?'

'A while.' I had to squint against the sun, but I could still make out her eyes: narrow and suspicious. 'We'd finished the course and everything.'

'Oh, well, that's fine then.' She turned, and I followed her in. The piles of clothes on every surface narrowed the room and soaked up the air.

I tried to cut through her sarcasm, to deal with the personal offence. 'I should have just told you,' I said.

'Well, yeah. I can imagine why you didn't.' Of course, knowing Eve as well as I did, I should have known that her morals were—as well as perfect and objective—deeply personal. That I might see the world differently, move through it making different choices, was an offence to who she was and the judgement she had exercised in choosing me as a friend.

'Obviously this isn't about you lying to me. But it's not irrelevant either. Like, this is exactly why this whole thing is so fucked up.' She threw up her hands, drawing violent, chaotic shapes. I had an urge to move further away from her, but given how small the room was, the gesture would have looked futile, like a caged animal stalking the perimeter. 'You obviously feel a real sense of shame about it, or you would have said something. He's trapping you in this twisted, secret—'

'I'm not trapped. I'm a consenting adult.'

'Hardly!' She took a step towards me. 'He's what? Double your age? Is there nobody his own age he could fuck?'

I balked at the confidence with which she reduced us—what we shared—to *fucking*. I couldn't use the word. 'It's not just sex.'

'Of course it's not. I'm sure the conversation sparkles.'

To my mind, the conversation always did. Perhaps it was because she had cut to the quick of my pride that my voice trembled when I replied: 'He's been there for me, Eve.' Sobs gathered, like a threat, in my throat. 'It's been a tough time.'

'Michaela—'

To my surprise, her arms were around me. I leaned my head against hers and clutched at her back. My words spilled out with tears. 'You didn't even come to the funeral.'

Eve pulled back, holding me by my shoulders, and studied my face, her eyebrows pulled together. Confusion usually registered on Eve's face as excitement, but this expression was new to me. She seemed genuinely at a loss. 'I didn't know you wanted me there. I just assumed . . . to be honest, I assumed you wouldn't want to go either.'

The accusations that had festered over the past few days swelled. Of course, it didn't occur to her that I might grieve him. Be upset, yes. Disturbed, naturally. But grieve the man who—in her eyes—was a monster? Her green notebook was still on her desk, assuming the exact place in her room's disarray that I'd assigned it. Ambivalence wasn't a feeling Eve could empathise with. And with Paul still in the room, stalking our embrace, I knew if I tried to tell her what I felt about Nick—how I thought she was wrong to judge so harshly—she would only despise me more. 'Well, you assumed wrong,' was all I could manage, through sobs.

Eve squeezed my shoulders, before letting me go. 'God, what a shit year you've had.'

I laughed, which Eve must have taken as encouragement. 'So when did Paul . . .'

'What?'

'When did he make advances on you?'

I laughed. A head-back cackle. 'It was the other way around. *I* kissed *him*.'

'When? In one of your academic meetings?' She said this like it was absurd.

'Outside the pub after that stupid Women in Philosophy event.'

Eve gaped at me as she reappraised her memory. Then her face split into a smile. She put a hand up to her mouth and covered a delicate little giggle. I laughed with her. The situation seemed suddenly so improbable, and at the same time so comically inevitable, it was hilarious that Eve had not known before.

We were still standing very close. The sun was at my back now, and Eve's eyes shone more green than blue in the dusk. She raised her hand and, with just her thumb, she wiped a tear from my cheek. The last time she had held my face like this—this close—it was in two hands, and we had both been drunk. 'Michaela,' she whispered. 'How are we going to help you?'

The thread between us, which a moment ago had felt so taut, snapped at her patronising tone. I crossed the room to stand by the door and, turning my face away, wiped my tears on my sleeve.

When I turned back, Eve was looking out the window, her face lit with a new idea. It was a familiar expression, one which usually thrilled me but now filled me with foreboding. 'No wonder you got such a good mark.'

'What?'

She looked at me, composed. 'No wonder you did so well in the exam.'

'Are you serious?'

'Well, you'd just kissed him.'

'Fucking hell.'

'Think about it from his perspective. You might have been less into him if he'd failed you.'

'Eve—'

She tried to talk over me, insisting that she was right.

Regardless of whether she was, I balked at her assertion that I should be forced to hear it, like it was a story about other people, and not my own life. I spoke louder, drowning her out. 'Don't you think—and I am aware how self-obsessed this sounds, and I really don't mean to upset you—but . . .' I took a deep breath. 'Don't you think there's a possibility that you might be . . . well, you were in Paul's class too, and you agreed he's attractive.'

'That was banter, Michaela. Young Stalin was notoriously attractive.'

'Sure. But you're telling me there's no world in which you're feeling, even in the smallest part of yourself'—she looked at me with such ferocity that finishing my sentence became a deliberate act of will—'jealous?'

Eve's reaction was dramatic enough to allow for the possibility—a kernel at least—of truth.

'Get out.'

She was calm; each word deliberate. When I stood, gaping, she repeated herself, in the exact same tone, without raising her voice.

'Get out.'

To my shame, I could not rise to the theatre of the situation. I turned, mumbling apologies, and closed her door gently, with a click not a slam.

———

I DID NOT go back to my room, but set out across the car park, desperate to salvage something.

The sun had set, and the evening was purple and grey. He called out my name across the dark.

'Michaela?'

Balth emerged from between two Volkswagen Golfs, their little white hatchbacks luminescent in the moonlight.

'What are you doing?'

'I'm coming to see you,' I said.

'Great minds think alike. I was coming to you.'

'Oh.' Now we were stranded in this liminal gravelly space, I wasn't sure I actually wanted to be the first to apologise. 'Shall we walk?' I said.

'Where?'

'Oval?'

So we headed to the oval, phone torches swinging, casting more shadow than light in the dark.

I started. 'I feel bad about what I said. It wasn't fair.'

'No, I should have never—'

I cut him off. 'No, it's fine. Really. You can't go through life not joking about people's parents for fear that they might be dead. At least, not at our age.'

'Well, for what it's worth, I'm very sorry.'

'No, I'm sorry.'

'This was meant to be my apology, not yours,' he said.

'Ah. I apologise for stealing your apology.'

He offered me a hand. 'Apology accepted.' We shook.

He said, 'I would have never said anything if I'd known—'

'I know.'

'—if I'd known it was a Freudian thing. You have to respect that shit.'

I laughed, relieved he was no longer attempting to be serious. He was so rarely sincere that he was no longer fluent in it. Or perhaps I was the insincere one. At the very least, sincerity was not the language of our friendship.

We'd reached the oval and were sitting down, me pulling at the grass, him hugging his knees.

'Eve did not seem pleased.'

'You have no idea.'

'Jealous, perhaps?'

His tone was so light, his voice so high and silly, that I had to laugh. It might have been trivialising, but I found him strangely soothing. I considered explaining our fight; articulating why her opinion meant so much, why her judgements—about Paul, about Nick—were torturing me. But these thoughts were thick and heavy, and I didn't want to break Balth's light spell.

'Can we not talk about it?'

'Of course. What do you want to talk about?'

'Nothing.'

So Balth—as only he could—talked about absolutely nothing, until my fingers grew cold and my stomach hurt with laughter.

—

OVER THE NEXT few days, I thought about my fight with Eve from a cooler, less cowering perspective. How dare she, I thought, hide in her room, conducting a performance of being hurt. Sure, I had lied to her about Paul. But she had been absent, and that absence had beckoned me into a labyrinth. I was not entirely sure that I had yet seen myself out.

That she hid in her room, resenting me for lying about Paul and accusing her of jealousy, seemed a cheap, trifling gripe in the scheme of life and death.

I was acutely aware of her next door: shifting weight, cupboards opening and closing, the indistinct hum of TV shows. But neither of us texted the other with overtures or apologies, or even starts of different conversations. Indeed, from the way I never bumped into her, even in the corridor or the bathroom, I had to assume we were avoiding each other.

When Eve did make contact, after several days of alert, ear-pricked silence, she managed to shock me. I should have expected that.

The email was not sent from her personal account, but from the student paper.

> *Dear Michaela,*
>
> *I am contacting you in my capacity as a reporter. I am hoping to write an article on the topic of the toxic culture at the residential colleges and the internalised misogyny it fosters. I was wondering if you would have any interest in being interviewed?*
>
> *Regards,*
> *Eve Herbert Shaw*

I read the email several times. I deleted it, and then moved it back into my inbox. She ignored the issue of Paul entirely. In so doing, as always, she articulated herself beautifully. If I failed to treat her with the respect, the honesty, of a confidante—if she was to be a stranger to my life—then I would be a stranger to her.

If only for the sense of outrage it gave me, I was glad she sent the email.

In my drafts folder, I kept a melodramatic reply.

> *I've read your journal. You need to get a grip. What happens to other people, what happened to me and Nick, is not about you.*

Leaving it there, unsent, empowered me. Like having my finger on a trigger.

16

PAUL AND I fell into a routine. One night a week, usually Tuesday, I would take the bus to his apartment after uni and we would cook a meal together. I helped, but only to chop and tidy, never to fry. He worked the wok or the pan with the same intuitive confidence as when he gestured from behind a lectern. But he was also possessive: he occupied the stove like his masculinity depended on it.

On Wednesday, which was the night Fairfax students went to the bar, I went to the bar. Thursdays were slow and painful, but they were like that for everyone who had been out the night before, so to suffer was to be included. I moped between the dining hall and my bedroom, wearing my nausea like a badge.

On Friday or Saturday night, or sometimes both, I stayed at Paul's. Perhaps because he was no longer my professor, or because, with our argument at Redleaf, we had survived our first fight, staying at Paul's had lost some of its thrill. It felt less recklessly erotic, and oozed instead into something more like comfort. Of course, I did not articulate this observation to Paul. I didn't want to admit to viewing our relationship in such a linear way. Like a story.

When I saw him on campus—walking through the Quad, or in the line at Reggio's—some of that first forbidden thrill returned. We would catch each other's eye and smile. This would make me suddenly, spine-tinglingly famished for him. Then we would text about how casually, how coolly, we'd ignored each other, before making plans to meet in private.

It was in these moments that I was most exhilarated. When I saw him like that in public, we could catch each other's eye as if looking at a stranger and think: *I know you.* It seemed to me that there were two worlds: my private world with Paul, and the wider world, wherein the smaller was a secret. This secret—this world of our own making—distracted me profoundly. For a few weeks, I forgot that there was also the world in my head and the world in his. And although we visited the same secret space, these were not, and never would be, the same.

WHEN I ENTERED Reggio's, I scanned the tables and coffee line for Paul. I took a corner table, and made sure I was facing out, so Balthazar would have to face the wall. I didn't think I could cope with another chance encounter between the two of them.

When Balth first suggested we meet at Reggio's, I hesitated.

'Can we go somewhere else?'

'Where else will I get the worst coffee on campus?'

'Exactly.'

'No, it has to be Reggio's. Eve won't be there.'

He had a point. Eve thought the place was full of 'college types', which was her way of saying she didn't like something. Law degrees, for example, were full of college types. As well as all corporate jobs, the suburb where she grew up, and the Australian government.

It was over three weeks since I'd last seen Eve. Three weeks, of course, is not long. But at college, where constant companionship was so often confused for friendship, time took a different shape. A few days ago, I had texted Balth to check that she was, in my words, 'alive'. He said he hadn't spoken to her, but he'd heard she was spending a lot of time at Luke's.

'Now, Michaela,' he said as he sat down, 'this tiff you're having with Eve—'

'Balth . . .'

He waved a sugar sachet at me. 'It's not good for the sisterhood and, more importantly, it's not good for me. Can you make your peace so I don't have to be a go-between?'

'A go-between? Has she asked you about me?'

'She just asked me the other day if I'd seen you around.'

'And what did you say?'

'I said that was a very personal question and how dare she and yes, of course I had seen you around.'

'Thanks.'

'Is this all about Paul?' He made the name sound sour. 'Very off-brand of you two to fight over a man.'

'No. I mean, yes. Partly. But it's more complicated.'

'More complicated?' His eyes were alight with mischief. He might as well have rubbed his hands together.

I hadn't come with the intent to confess. Indeed, for weeks, I'd kept my suspicions secret, assuming them like a burden. But Balth's levity was infectious. I felt suddenly that my secrets might be salacious: nothing more than titbits to be traded over coffee.

'Do you want to know?' It was a relief, already, to talk about it.

'You have to tell me now.'

'You can't tell anyone. Especially not Eve.'

'Michaela. You can trust me.'

'Remember I told you that I had sex with someone in O Week, and I didn't know who it was until Sackers brought it up?'

'Yeah.' Balth sounded wary.

'It was Nick.'

'What?'

'Nick. He was the boy I slept with.'

His spoon clattered on the saucer. 'Oh, Michaela.'

I knew from the way he said my name that he would refuse to take this lightly. I drank more coffee, for something to do with my hands. His voice washed over me. 'I'm sorry. I didn't realise . . . God, you poor thing. How complicated.'

'No, it's fine. I just . . .' I fixed my eyes on Balth; his face was taut. 'Eve was always on at me about reporting it.'

'What . . . as sexual assault?'

'Yeah. I mean, obviously I was too drunk to consent, so I see why she—'

'If you still wanted to report it, obviously I'd support you.'

'I don't.'

'Are you sure? I know it would be harrowing—don't speak ill of the dead and everything—but you're within your rights.'

'No, I really mean that.' I pushed my empty cup away. 'I wish I'd spoken about it with Nick. But, to be honest, I think we were both really drunk and keen at the time. It was just messy. I mean, I was so drunk I threw up in his bin. And he was so drunk he used his academic gown to wipe it up. I just think it was like your classic drunken one-night stand, with bad optics.'

'Bad optics.' Balth contemplated the expression aesthetically first, appreciating how it sounded. For a moment, he relaxed. 'I see what you mean. I suppose, if Nick were alive, it wouldn't acquire such significance.'

'Well, this is what I'm worried about.'

'What?'

The quickness of his question—the force of his curiosity—drove the conversation, at last, to a point of co-conspiracy. I leaned forward, and lowered my voice so it was almost a whisper.

'Eve knows somehow. She knew it was Nick. I wonder if she asked around and, like, found out it was him. I wonder if he knew that she was on to him. Or maybe she even talked to him about reporting it, like she did to me. Or in his case it would be more like confessing, I suppose.'

'So . . . what? You think that Eve, like, conducted an investigation?'

I winced at *conducted*. Its formality mocked me. I sat up straighter. 'I mean, how else could she know?'

'Michaela, we all live on top of each other. Sackers knew. Surely all your Fairfax friends knew. Eve wouldn't have had to investigate very thoroughly.' He didn't put air quotes around *investigate*, but his tone implied them.

'Sure. But that's not really the point. Sackers would've thought it was just a funny story about his friends being drunk idiots. Only Eve would have seen it as rape.'

'Yeah, but you know Eve. Everything is a moral issue. Isn't that her charm?' His smile seemed to minimise my concerns—not so much by putting them in perspective, but by trivialising them.

I wanted to physically take the words and show them to Balthazar. 'But what if she made Nick feel guilty about it? And what if he got on that motorbike . . .'

'Michaela.'

'What?'

'I'm sorry, but that's insane.'

'But—'

'Look, I don't know what else to tell you. It's crazy. I mean, first, we don't even know that what happened in the national park wasn't genuinely an accident.'

'He was alone! On caps!'

He reached across the table and put his hand on my wrist. I resisted the urge to yank it out from under him.

'We don't know,' he said. 'We just don't. Also, you don't know Nick. Trust me, I went to school with him. He's always struggled with . . .' He paused, visibly searching for the most delicate way to put it. 'His mental health hasn't always been robust.' Delicacy was not Balth's strong suit.

'But if he was already vulnerable'—my voice sounded high-pitched and weak—'surely having someone like Eve accuse him of rape . . .'

'Yes, but don't you see that it's just too complicated? It's never going to make sense. For every Eve factor, there will be others we don't know about. I'm not saying you're wrong—'

I scoffed audibly, because, of course, that was precisely what he was doing.

'I'm not!' he continued, more forcefully. 'I'm just saying that you shouldn't single out Eve as your villain.'

I felt physically exhausted by the number of times Balth had cut me off. His point of view rose up before me as a solid, impenetrable thing, and I resented him for the self-assurance on which it was constructed. To stand so firm and not be budged—what, then, was the point of conversation?

'So you don't see any world in which what happened between us, and Eve pursuing it, is relevant?'

He sighed and looked at me through new eyes, neither amused nor intrigued. His face was dull and grave.

'Look, Michaela. I don't know what else to tell you. A great guy died way too young. There's no narrative to it.'

———

EMILY, CLAUDIA, AND Portia didn't read the student newspaper. So when I woke on Monday morning to an article linked in our group chat, I knew it must directly concern them.

It wasn't until Balthazar texted me that I felt compelled to open the link.

> *Hey just checking in. Hope you're*
> *okay. Here if you need.*
>
> I'm fine! (I think???) Is something up?
>
> *Have you read Eve's article?!*

I opened the article on my phone, lying in bed. For a moment, another text from Balth obscured the screen.

> *I'm so sorry. I didn't think she had it in her.*

The first paragraph set the tone.

An unsolved murder, decades old. An eighteen-year-old girl, last seen leaving home to visit a St Thomas' boy, found dead on the St Thomas' oval. Her body beaten and bruised, discarded with a pile of stones.

Then there were more recent stories, told in an exacting, clinical style. No more deaths, but plenty of female bodies—mistreated and ill-used.

A girl sees her naked arse on someone else's phone screen. A photo of her, head obscured, bottom pale and spread before the camera. She is on all fours before a man, behind the jacaranda tree in the St Thomas' College quadrangle. They have been interrupted. And the photo evidence of that interruption will follow her, relentlessly, until she finds somewhere else to live.

A girl is caught in a ring of bodies. 'Eagle Rock' is playing, and pants and underpants have dropped together. She is alone—a circle of twenty boys or more flapping and jumping and taunting. They do not stop when they see her cry. They stop when the song ends.

A girl wakes up in a strange boy's bed, her face against the wall. As she wakes, searing pain creeps into her consciousness. She walks slowly, with her legs bent awkwardly apart, to the hospital emergency room, where, after several hours, a nurse finally removes her tampon.

And just when Eve's reporting started to numb the reader—a shopping list of degradations, enacted on a single, faceless victim—Eve switched to the first person.

'This author's story,' she wrote, 'is not so very different.'

There were parts I recognised with stomach-curdling clarity. The scratch of the academic gown; the metallic smell of the bin; the stomach-acid flavour of regret. Parts of it—the boy's aggression; how sore she felt the next day—were new. These details were not necessarily false. Rather, Eve's lucid, exacting prose rendered them more vivid than my memory ever could.

Reading the first-person paragraphs, I pictured Eve, not myself, enduring the ordeal. Her style was so bold and casually philosophical—her voice so perfectly encapsulating her confidence—it was not possible for the words to conjure another body, another face than hers.

While I was throwing up, he flung an academic gown at me. It hung open. It didn't cover me; it underlined my shame. He did nothing to help me secure it in place. Instead, he shouted at me.

In the following weeks, my sexual assault became the subject of campus jokes. People would raise their hands when I walked past and say the boy's name, expecting me to give them a high five. Like it was an achievement. A privilege.

All this time, his words resounded. *Stupid bitch*, he kept on saying. *Stupid bitch*. How did I end up weak and intoxicated in a stranger's bed? Why didn't I say no? Why didn't I fight him off? What a stupid bitch I was.

This author makes no claims to objectivity. If objectivity requires me to look upon those men and argue that they were drunk too, that young people don't know what they're doing, that everybody makes mistakes, that these mistakes are made everywhere and not just in residential colleges, then, quite frankly, fuck objectivity. You heard me. Fuck it. I'm not interested in journalistic commitments that require me to pretend I see the world through non-judgemental, depersonalised eyes.

I write from personal experience. I write from his bed. I write from underneath his thrusting weight. And when I write from that perspective, I also see with my own eyes, with my own moral perceptions.

So if you're going to write in the comments section that these events are unrelated, that the institution is not the problem, that institutions don't have their own morality, then please, go ahead. Free speech etc.

But this stupid bitch won't believe you.

When I finished the article, I read the parts about Eve again, and I felt for her again. Then I went to the bathroom and threw up. When I was finished, I put my fingers down my throat and dry-retched. I sat on the tiles, my hands cupping the cold porcelain, and marvelled at how much more affecting it was to read a story told about someone else than to piece together my own fractured memories and try to construct a picture of myself.

The group chat with Emily, Claudia, and Portia was relentless. The notifications nagged me all morning. They were getting coffee to discuss the article. From the tone of their texts, I could tell that the discussion would take place in the hushed tones reserved for scandal. They would dissect each story, indulging in the gorier details, and defending parts that didn't ring true—conducting a post-mortem to preserve their perspectives, their experience of what Fairfax was *really* like, as the truest of all possible narratives.

I said I wasn't feeling well, and locked myself in my room. I didn't reply to Balthazar. Instead, I lay in bed, wide awake, listening for any sound of Eve next door, flinching at the slightest movement.

The fears I'd harboured since I read Eve's journal—fears Balth had tried to dispel—returned with those precise details, fashioned into the first-person, but still, cruelly, true. I had never told her about the vomit, or the bin, or the gown. My suspicion—that Eve had spoken to Nick before he died—hardened to conviction, with none of the satisfaction of being proved correct. Rather, I felt sick and cold to see my worst fears so confirmed. I pulled my blankets tighter around me.

Although Eve's article did not name Nick, it dragged his person, his actions, dangerously close to the spotlight. With Nick gone, who was there to refute Eve's claims? *Fuck objectivity*, she had said. Objectivity, in this case, was long since dead.

I looked up the editorial board of the student newspaper. The only member I recognised was Luke, his face stern and self-important in the black-and-white photo on the website. I contemplated contacting one of the female editors and telling her that Eve was lying. As I played out this conversation in my mind, it faded quickly to absurdity.

'So what she's saying is true?'

'Yes, but it happened to me, not to her.'

'Oh. I'm so sorry.'

'It's okay.'

'And you're happy for us to report that?'

'I don't want to report it or anything. I just want you to know it didn't happen to Eve.'

'But it did happen?'

Swapping me for Eve didn't change the nature of the story, the dark-hearted thrust of it, especially because I was incapable of replacing any of her details with my own. I didn't remember Nick calling me a 'stupid bitch'. Indeed, I had never known him to display any kind of cruelty. Hadn't he sat and smoked and worried that his friends had no inner life? Who was that person—that Nick I knew—if not a man with a conscience? But I could hardly overlay Eve's story with my own anecdotal perceptions, accumulated over other, unrelated interactions, all of which would . . . what? Defend the man who had allegedly assaulted me? Even knowing that I could not correct her, I stared at the ceiling until my eyes drew shapes on it, and entertained the possibility.

———

THE DAYS WERE lengthening. When Paul called and asked what I was doing for dinner, I could have wept with relief. I thought that to see him would be, for a few hours at least, to live a different life—to go to a place where Eve's words were not the constant undercurrent of my thoughts.

We had finished eating dinner at the little table on his balcony. Sitting with one leg crossed over the other, I leaned my shoulder against the railing, and sipped a beer. It was a dark ale Paul had in the fridge. I didn't really like the taste.

There was a lull in our conversation, and I strained to hear the ocean.

'That article about Fairfax in the student paper was doing the rounds today.'

I took a large gulp. 'I didn't know you read the student paper.'

'I normally don't. But I normally don't have a vested interest in what's going on at Fairfax.'

I wanted to talk about anything, anything at all, except the contents of that article, and how they might or might not reflect my *interests*. I surprised myself with how breezily I replied. 'I know the girl who wrote it. I think you teach her, actually.'

'Eve Herbert Shaw? Shaved head with white stubble?' The pause between each question was forced—as if it were possible to know her without noticing what she looked like.

'Yes. She's allowed to take your class, seeing as she's not sleeping with you.'

He kicked my leg gently under the table.

'And her hair was pink last time I saw her, but that sounds about right.'

'Are you sure you're friends?'

'We had a fight,' I said. 'We're not really speaking to each other at the moment.'

'Oh yeah? What about?' Paul stood, and we went into the kitchen to wash the dishes.

I didn't look at him as I scraped my plate over the bin. I hadn't spoken to Paul about Nick for weeks. What happened between us—my hazy memory of it and Eve's visceral retelling; the mystery, that still suffocated me, of how she came to know; what Nick might have told her—I needed to keep these apart from Paul. So I said, 'About you, actually.'

I heard the plate crash into the sink. Perhaps it was louder in my head, because when I turned, Paul was rinsing it with a steady hand. 'She knows about us?'

'I didn't tell her, of course. It just sort of came out, after we bumped into my friend at the beach that day.'

'Right.' He put down the sponge and stood motionless, looking at the soapy water.

'I'm sorry.'

He wiped his hands on a tea towel, and I took it from him. He didn't look at me. 'It's okay,' he said. 'It's not your fault. It is what it is.'

What is it? I wanted to ask. But I said nothing. Instead, I dried the plates as he handed them to me.

'So this story she told in her article: pretty brave thing to do. I imagine it's caused quite a stir?' His voice was strained, teetering towards the upward inflexion. I said nothing, and he tried, again, to push the conversation along. 'People must be annoyed with her.'

'Yes. We are a bit.'

'We?' He looked at me, smiling. He'd caught the scent of a debate. 'I thought you didn't like Fairfax that much?'

'Well that's the thing. *I* thought I didn't. I mean, I always knew the culture was pretty appalling, but I guess I didn't sustain anything like her moral outrage.'

'It's where you live. You can't be outraged the whole time.'

'I could move out, I suppose.'

'Where to?'

I'd finished with the plates and watched as he wiped down the bench. His question contained no tremor of invitation—his apartment strictly the setting not the subject of our conversation. 'I don't know,' I said. 'I guess I don't have anywhere else to go.'

Later that night, when Paul's head moved down past my stomach, I took it in both hands and pulled him back up. I didn't explicitly say no, but he was pliant. He didn't ask why. I didn't really know why, except for an instinct that I didn't deserve that kind of pleasure. Lying there, helpless and writhing, while he buried his face in me and licked me with calculating strokes, seemed shameful and selfish.

Like stealing. That it might give him pleasure to give me pleasure wasn't an idea I entertained.

On a whim, I told him to choke me. He put a hand to my throat but didn't apply real pressure. I closed my eyes and did not ask again.

I lay awake for hours, trying to put a name to this incredible smallness; this feeling of being broken and fragile, and so totally in Paul's hands. When I eventually fell asleep, my dreams met me with whole conferences of age-appropriate, bookish women who might suit him better. They all had sumptuous hair and stylish substitute-for-a-personality spectacles. Their faces looked like Eve's.

17

PORTIA THOUGHT WE all needed a break. 'Especially Emily,' she said. Claudia and I agreed. I agreed emphatically when I realised that Portia's parents owned a beach house.

In the car on the way to Palm Beach, they spoke about Eve in tones that would have brought tears of frustration—hot and smarting—to her eyes. For weeks, the conversation had centred on the personal drama, as if she had made no political point. Claudia had decided, on the day the article was published, that Eve had something *against* Fairfax: that she had not had a good time. This was intuited not from the 'time' so graphically described in the article, but from the fact that she wrote it at all. Claudia sensed in Eve's article something deliberate—vindictive, even. It didn't read like an experience relived but one reshaped for a purpose. What this purpose was—who had pissed her off—was Claudia's favourite topic of speculation. To her credit, I couldn't fault her instinct for inauthenticity.

'She must have a problem with *someone*.' Claudia addressed the whole car.

As usual, I said nothing. My silence had become characteristic in these conversations. It was misinterpreted as loyalty, at least by Emily, who would usually press Claudia, with widened eyes, to *drop it.* This was difficult to execute today, with Claudia in the front seat, feet up on the dashboard, and Emily next to me in the back.

They assumed, incorrectly, that I had spoken to Eve since the article.

I had no intention of exposing her publicly. I couldn't reveal her story as mine without revealing that it was also Nick's. I thought about Emily's stilted politeness the morning after the ball, when she found out I'd slept with Nick: not allowing herself the indulgence of feeling hurt, but not yet over it either. My stomach ached, thinking of the pain she had felt then and the grief she had since endured. I knew—with gut-deep dread—that this pain would only breed and mutate if she saw the scene, as I now did, through the lens of Eve's disgust.

So whatever I might say to Eve could only be personal. There would be no threat, no intent on my part; no commitment to corrections. *How dare you?* might be a start. *How could you?* But when I imagined these kinds of conversations, I couldn't see past the opening line. All the qualities that first drew me to Eve were now keeping me from her. Her intelligence; her confidence; her eloquence: these were obstacles. Whatever I felt—however hurt—she would have rebuttals at the ready, justifications I couldn't surmount. If I saw her, I supposed, I would be compelled to speak. In the meantime, I assumed she was avoiding me, and I waited, paralysed, for circumstance to force a move.

In the front seat, Claudia continued, 'What happened to her was obviously awful and whatever, but the article was just so *much.*'

Portia nodded. 'The *stupid bitch* thing was a lot.'

I enjoyed their understatement.

'I did find that bit hard to believe. Like, the whole encounter was horrible'—Claudia spoke quickly, as she always did when working up to a *but*—'and they were obviously too drunk, but the yelling just seemed so cruel. He sounded like a real bully.'

'I think those boys can be cruel.' Emily spoke softly.

Claudia turned the radio down and asked her to repeat herself.

'I just don't think it's inconceivable that a St Thomas' boy might be cruel.'

Emily's words, unsure though they were, choked me. It was nauseating, hearing her discuss the boy in Eve's story—what he was capable of—as if he were not a boy she'd loved, but a faceless *type* she knew of.

I turned my face to the window. We were driving through the Harbour Tunnel. With dirty walls on all sides, I couldn't pretend to look at the view. I leaned my head against the glass and closed my eyes.

Claudia didn't turn to look at us, but spoke out, to the windscreen. 'I'm not saying it's inconceivable at all. I just reckon their behaviour is even more insidious than what Eve was getting at, because it's harder to call out.'

I texted Balth in an attempt to opt out of the conversation.

We're talking about Eve's article

Who's we?

Claudia, Portia, Emily

Must be nice to have something to talk about

Ha!

They're thanking her no doubt

Oh absolutely. Just grateful they've been liberated

Aren't we all

I could feel Emily looking at me. I put my phone away, holding it screen-down on my lap so I'd feel it vibrate if Balth texted again.

Claudia concluded from the passenger seat: 'I thought it was a bit much that she tried to draw a causal link between her experience in O Week and that murder decades ago.'

Portia's blonde ponytail swung as she turned to Claudia. I caught Emily's eye and resisted the urge to mouth along. 'Wait. What?'

'She spoke about them in the same breath!'

Portia kept her eyes on the road. 'That's a false equivalence, not a causal link.'

I stifled a smile.

Emily put her hand on my arm. 'Have you spoken to her, Michaela?'

'What?'

'Have you spoken to her? I know you're close.' This was so predictable: that Emily would be concerned for someone else's feelings. I didn't find it touching. 'Is she okay?'

'Yeah. She's fine.'

'So you've spoken to her?' Claudia's question, from the front seat, was more investigative than concerned.

'Not really.'

'I think she's already moved out.'

Claudia rounded on Portia. 'What?'

'Yeah, I saw her with all her stuff in the car park the other day. A boy was picking her up. It looked like a lot of stuff. Like, a moving-out amount of stuff.'

I tried to compose my face.

For the remainder of the drive, I stewed on the image of Eve's empty room. Despite spending most nights at Paul's, and despite making no attempts to contact Eve, I'd taken for granted that I'd have the opportunity to talk to her. If I thought she was avoiding me, I could have consoled myself that this move was evidence of cowardice. I felt, instead, that she had slipped away, out of my grasp. So quickly that my grasp could have only been very slight to begin with. Months ago, it would have been unthinkable that she could leave without saying goodbye. Yet here we were: a silent departure; an empty room. No traces of a friendship.

—

I'D ALWAYS THOUGHT that natural beauty, like a rose or a sunset, was edifying. Surely it taught us something about goodness, about the point of being alive, to lose ourselves in irrational, aesthetic pleasure.

That was until I saw the view of Palm Beach and Pittwater from Portia's parents' beach house high on the side of the hill. The water sparkled on either side of the peninsula; the sand was not white, but yellow, as if it had absorbed the sunshine. It was so beautiful that it was just indulgent.

'Yuck,' I said, and everybody laughed, without looking up from the photos they were taking on their phones.

The wind was tossing my short hair dry. At the beach earlier, only Emily and I got in the water. Up at the house, the two of us took turns showering under silver showerheads that were as big as plates, using the Aesop body wash lined up on the marble-tiled floor. We emerged smelling like a pair of freshly peeled mandarin segments, and joined Claudia and Portia on the balcony.

'It's so nice of your parents to let us stay here,' I said.

Portia was admiring the view through her phone screen. 'No worries. They're just happy it's getting some use.'

I knew she said this to make me feel more comfortable, but it seemed a spectacularly casual way to talk about a house. Like an item of clothing, going in and out of *use*, as opposed to property that could be rented out or mortgaged or inherited. I thought of my mother—the way she sometimes said *rich people,* with an amused, superior sort of smirk, like she was referring to a cult.

The boys were late, and they arrived to the dregs of sunset. The view faded to violet shadows, and the ocean grew louder with every passing wave.

The boys cooked sausages, and Portia made guacamole with pomegranate seeds, and a salad with eggplant and feta. Nobody mentioned Eve's article. We had agreed in the car that nothing would kill the vibe quite like inviting the boys to self-reflect. In this instance, I was only too happy to champion the vibe.

When they were halfway through their first case of beers, the boys started talking about Nick, as they always did: by toasting him, and drinking more. The night was cold, so we moved inside, and toasted Nick from deep linen couches in the living room.

Drugs were discussed, and a dealer summoned, and when Sackers headed out to meet him on the street, Emily slipped through the sliding glass doors onto the balcony. I followed.

We stood side by side, facing the view, although it was too dark to make out the horizon. There were just different shades of deep purple, lit by a pale moon.

'I wish they wouldn't,' Emily said.

Earlier that day, when we were on the wind-flattened beach, Emily was the first in the water. No sooner had the sea hit her ankles than she was diving headfirst into the white foam. She swam out past the break, until I thought I saw a rip and yelled at her to come back.

When we emerged, we were laughing, and I was panting, but Emily had that familiar, almost child-like look in her eye. The look that said: let's do it again. At odds with Emily's otherwise self-abasing politeness was her voracious, almost selfish, appetite for fun: for spontaneity as an end in itself. Thoughts became actions in the same intoxicating breath. *Let's get another drink. Let's go for a swim. Let's go to Macca's.*

And unlike so many people I knew—myself sometimes included—being *fun* wasn't a trait she consciously cultivated, like being beautiful or funny, to make her company more desirable. For Emily, it was a state of being, as natural and unconscious as being tired or hungry: an itch that needed to be scratched. The risks she took—downing another shot; swimming a few more strokes; climbing on the back of Nick's motorbike—were undertaken with instinctive urgency and an indifference to being watched.

All of which made me follow her, concerned, when she left the room. In the normal course, when drugs were on the table she'd lean in, smile, and say: 'Is there enough for me?' Knowing full well that, for her, there was no such thing as *enough*.

She was looking out across the water. 'I mean, I don't want to be that guy, but Nick was on drugs when he died.'

'They're all idiots,' I said.

'They are, aren't they?'

The ocean was hard to see. It looked solid, like darker-coloured sand.

'Nick would've loved this weekend,' I said.

'I keep thinking about that.' She put her head on the railing, her spine curved. Then she straightened up and turned, so the ocean was at her back, and faced me. 'But not in a nice way. Any time I start to have fun, even today, down at the beach with you, I just think: why do I deserve this? How can I walk around, in the sunshine—how can a day be so beautiful—and he doesn't get to enjoy any of it?'

My mouth felt dry. 'I'm sorry.'

'I should have helped him more. He used to get so quiet; sometimes he couldn't talk, not properly, not really, for whole days. And

I'd assume he wanted to break up with me or something. I just assumed it was about me.'

'We all do that.'

'Anyway . . .' She crossed her arms and looked out over the peninsula once more. The wind petted her hair. 'Let's talk about you. How are you?'

'Oh, you know me. Nothing to report.'

'Please.' She looked at me again, and I thought I'd never seen her look so sad. Like she couldn't be bothered to cry. 'Please, tell me a story.'

'Well, I'm sort of seeing someone.'

'Ugh!' She stretched out past the railing. 'This is what I wanted to hear. Who?'

For weeks, I'd felt that what Paul and I shared was as fragile as my imagination. As if telling someone else would only confirm I had made it up. But when I told Emily, it seemed so real—more real than this curve-cornered house with its otherworldly vistas.

When I told her how Paul and I had met—on opposite sides of a lecture theatre—I braced for her reaction. A shocked gasp. Perhaps a squeal of delight, as she imagined how the story might sound when regaled later.

Instead she narrowed her eyes and leaned a little closer. 'Do you like him?'

'I do.' As soon as I'd said it, I realised how totally it was true. And even truer now, for having been said aloud.

She smiled. 'That's great, Michaela. I'm happy for you.'

Through the glass sliding doors, I could see Sackers removing a plate from the microwave. The others were leaning over the marble kitchen island like it was a watering hole.

Emily touched my hand, which was resting on the railing. 'You know what we should do?'

I shook my head.

'Let's go for another swim.'

'Now? Isn't that dangerous?'

But she had already taken her towel off the railing and was walking down the stone steps, across the road and then the sand, and then into the great rumbling blackness, with or without me.

—

THE WEEKEND AT Palm Beach was the first all semester that I hadn't stayed at least one night at Paul's. When I'd told him I was going away, he'd teased me.

Palm Beach? What are you? A socialite?

Haha. It's my friend's house

I wish my friends had beach houses.

You're that friend Mr Bondi Apartment

Harsh but fair. So when will I see you next?

Sometime next week?

We've got a guest lecturer this week,
actually, so I'm freer in the days. We
could meet for lunch on Tuesday?

Sounds good! Where?

Meet at my office? 1?

We had never met on campus. I assumed that this was the natural escalation in our relationship which, for weeks now, had felt less like a sequence of dates and more a consistent thread: a part of my life. If anything, I was disappointed that we were creeping out of secrecy and into the sunlight. It felt like the end of a chapter I'd devoured too quickly—one I should have savoured.

We followed the familiar narrow staircase up to his office. He placed his Diet Coke on his desk, where it sweated and left a ring in the wood.

Like a student, I sat in the chair in front of his desk. Paul stood on the other side. For a mad, panicked moment, I thought I might have imagined the months between us, and that he really was just my professor. 'What's this about?'

He looked out the leadlight window and scratched at his beard. 'Paul?'

He placed both hands on the desk. 'I think we need to stop seeing each other.'

My response was so immediate, it was as if I had, in some hateful place, seen this coming. 'Are you kidding?'

'It was rash in the first place, and it's gone on too long.'

'You're kidding.'

'Michaela, I wouldn't joke about this.'

'And you called me into your *office* to tell me this?'

'I thought I owed it to you to do this in person. And I figured it was a bit counterintuitive to organise an off-campus meeting in order to make this less unprofessional.'

I stood and walked to the other side of the office. I wanted as much space between us as possible. I steadied myself on his bookshelf, my hand on a thick, dusty volume. In the corner of my vision, the charcoal drawing of a nude female torso taunted me.

'Because this is *very* professional,' I said. 'Breaking up with a student in your office.'

'I'm sorry.'

I looked at him. His hands were at his sides, and he stood, limply, behind the desk. He looked so useless.

'Is this because of what I told you about Eve? About her knowing about us?'

'Obviously not.'

'Is that obvious? You seemed pretty concerned about it.'

'Of course I was concerned. But not for the reason you think. When you told me about your friend, it just confronted me—'

'Confronted *you*?'

His hands, now firm and expressive, were no longer at his sides. It was strangely vindicating to see him so worked up. It made me feel that at least this was hard for him too.

'Confronted me with how much I'm asking of you—to have any kind of relationship with someone so much older. Of course it's affecting your friendships.'

'Right. So you're worried about my friendship with Eve, not her enthusiasm for journalism. Bravery, I think you called it.'

'It's not just Eve, obviously.'

I was annoyed by the fluency with which he spoke her name, like it was familiar to him and thick with associations. I wondered how well he knew her, whether he thought she was brilliant. There were over one hundred students in his course. He wouldn't know each of them by name.

He continued, 'You're eighteen, Michaela. You're still in first year, for fuck's sake. You should be going out every weekend, making mistakes . . .'

I moved closer and put my hands on the back of the chair—the chair I'd sat in as his student. 'Wow that's really big of you. What a good guy.' My sarcasm was shrill—I didn't recognise myself. 'I'm sure the fact that you're seriously professionally compromised by having slept with a teenage student hasn't even crossed your mind. You've been too busy thinking about me.'

'Of course that's crossed my mind. I've always accepted those risks. I just . . . I think if we were to have a serious relationship, going further than what we have now, you would have to sacrifice a lot. You don't even realise what sacrifices you'd be making, because you're so young. But believe me, the kind of life you would have as my partner, and the kind of life a normal twenty-something would have, are very different.'

'Wow.'

'What?'

'That's pretty fucking patronising. I don't know what I'm sacrificing, because I'm so young.'

'You don't! It's a statement of fact, it's not patronising.'

'Well, I feel patronised. It seems you think of me as very immature, all of a sudden.'

Paul was leaning on the desk now with both hands, as if to steady himself. 'I've never, ever thought of you as immature. I've always admired you. You know that. I think you're brilliant and . . .' He stumbled. I ached, ravenously, for the next word. 'And beautiful and you've obviously got a lot of potential, but this was a big mistake. I'm sorry. It was wildly inappropriate. I don't know what I was thinking.'

With this, he sat at his desk, his head in his hands. Posing for a portrait of regret.

'It doesn't cure the inappropriateness, you realise.' I hated the clipped, clinical way he'd said *inappropriate*. Like he was objectively assessing someone else's behaviour. There was no guilt to it, only absolution. He knew what he'd done wrong. Like self-knowledge was consequence enough. What more could you ask of a man than to acknowledge his faults?

But I didn't want him to wear *inappropriate* with such detached comfort. I wanted to force it on him, like a straitjacket, as he writhed and kicked until he was forced into submission.

'We have to put a stop to it, Michaela.'

'Stopping it isn't an erasure. It doesn't mean you've done the right thing.'

'At least it means I've stopped doing the wrong thing.'

'Not at all. Now you've just fucked a teenager *and* fucked her over.' I spoke the words in violent little jabs, like I could bruise them into his mind. Let them flower, showing him that I had been misused, and throb, making him feel that he was the one who had misused me.

'You're not a teenager.'

'I'm eighteen.'

'That's an adult.'

'I thought you hated arguments about semantics.'

Paul couldn't look at me. He hung his head. In the silence, adrenaline coursed through me. I realised that our conversation had acquired an impersonal, combatant rhythm. I was finding a sick pleasure in my own replies.

Paul looked up at me. His face was hollow, his eyes empty.

'I—' He looked down and swallowed audibly. For a moment, I thought he was going to cry. But he continued, dry-eyed. 'I really don't want you to hate me.'

My exhilaration dissipated. He was pleading. I sensed that if he moved, he would have shook. I was still standing and, looking down at him slumped over the desk, I had an urge to reach out and comfort him. 'I won't hate you, Paul,' I said. And then, no longer intending to hurt him, but because I thought I owed him the truth, I added, 'I'll almost certainly resent you.'

'Ah.' This was a gasp, as if at a physical blow.

'It's asking a lot to demand I look back on this whole saga with *fondness*.'

This time, when he looked up at me, he was crying. 'I will.'

My throat felt strangled. 'I don't think there's anything else to say.'

I left before he could respond, passing for the last time under the thick, generous curves of that charcoal portrait.

—

I RAN DOWN the stairs, and relished the stream of tears that attested to my pain. At a furious pace, I walked down through Glebe until I hit the foreshore.

Looking out over the water—the Harbour Bridge seated under the Anzac Bridge like a child—I let my feet dangle and saw myself as a damaged, broken thing.

I considered calling my mother.

An emaciated man, his shaven and bumpy bald head poking out of a garbage bag, his mouth wide and wet, shouted as he passed, 'You're beautiful. God loves you.'

I laughed. Concerned, perhaps, that I was flattered, a woman walking a Shih tzu called out to me, 'He says that to everyone.'

The west side of the city was burnished with gold where it reflected the afternoon sun. I regretted my conduct: how I'd scratched at him with detached retorts, like we were just conversation partners, adopting opposite viewpoints for the verbal sport. It wasn't raw enough. All my composure had done, I now realised, was show him how much I still cared. In attempting to adopt an analytical position, to stand above and apart from my break-up and sneer, I had performed—debased myself even—for his approval. Crying, door-slamming, perhaps hitting him in the chest with my balled-up fists, like a scorned woman might in a foreign movie—all these options had been overlooked. These might have been hysterical avenues, but they would at least have expressed my emotion. I could have owned it then, authored it, and he would have been a trespasser. Instead I'd spoken as if we were fencing, and he was my respected opponent.

I called my mother. I didn't tell her about Paul. The cornerstone of my burgeoning sense of adulthood was a little box labelled: Things My Mother Doesn't Need to Know.

I told her it was nice to hear her voice, and she, presumably already knowing the answer, asked how I was. I told her I was on a walk and described how stunning the city was from here, and she said that when she visited I should take her there.

Our conversation was like a hug, and with no particular prompting I started to tear up. Because mothers always do, I'm sure she intuited that it was about a boy. She didn't ask explicitly, but right before I hung up, she told me I was beautiful, and that she loved me.

—

THE NEWS THAT Paul and I had broken up put Balthazar in a particularly gleeful mood. So gleeful, in fact, that it seemed to overwhelm his capacity for empathy, while also rendering my sulking blacker and more indulgent in comparison. So I told him I was studying a lot, and we agreed to see each other again when exams were over.

I did not have any exams that semester, only essays, with submission dates later than any of my friends'. I spent most days in the library. At about four in the afternoon, self-hatred and boredom would culminate in two or three hours of study. Until then, I would roam the internet and feel sorry for myself. I pored over old message threads with Eve, and Paul, with a more critical eye than any of my prescribed readings. While I initially read Eve's texts with a vindictive enthusiasm—looking for early signs of betrayal—after several days, I realised I was feeling something more like longing.

I contemplated texting her.

Paul broke up with me

I knew that if we undertook the activity together, then hating Paul could prove potent and seductive. It could even be the restoration of our friendship. First, we would need to address her article. I would have to accept Eve's use of my story as, if not a good thing, then at the very least, something done for the right reasons. This did not seem impossible. But what did seem unbearable was adding to this indignity her pity. She would rush to condemn Paul; to protect me; to enclose me in her angular embrace. But her platitudes would be laced with smugness—a whiff of *I told you so.*

I imagined telling her that Paul ended things on account of our relationship being *inappropriate.* A look of horror would express her sympathy. But the twitch of her mouth, fighting off a smile would reveal her pity to be at least in part self-serving.

Eve was the one who knew Paul as our professor. Emily and Balthazar, and likely many others, knew this as an anecdotal fact, but only Eve *knew* him, had been lectured by him. So it was precisely because I needed not only pity but also moral outrage that, even after all she'd done, I found myself mourning her as well as Paul.

When I recounted our relationship—when I told Emily, for example, that the man I'd spoken about at Palm Beach was just 'a false alarm'—it was with Eve's tongue: to position my audience to confirm, as Eve would, that I had been misused. Not inconvenienced, or even hurt, but *wronged.* Men were pigs and I, being a woman, was yet another entry in the vast database of female suffering—ever-connected; ever-growing; a universe of its own, bigger than the internet.

In all subsequent retellings, the fact that he was older and, crucially, my teacher was what I rendered salient. It went like this:

ME:	I slept with my philosophy professor. *(With emphasis)* My first year professor.
FRIEND:	How old was he?
ME:	Like, forty.
FRIEND:	*(Aghast)* Wow, what a creep.
ME:	Yeah, and then do you know how he ended it?
FRIEND:	How?
ME:	By telling me what we were doing was 'totally inappropriate'.
FRIEND:	That's fucked.

That concluding line, or variations of it (*You poor thing; Jesus Christ; What a cunt*), soothed and smoothed the Paul Saga until it formed a clean geometric shape. With the story so packaged, I could stand on our shared history like a pedestal and look down on Paul, and ignore the fact that he was a man, frail as all men are, who, for a brief brutal moment, confused wanting me with loving me.

———

ON MY LAST day in Sydney, I went to Claudia's house for a swim. Fairfax was already emptying, with Portia and Emily flown off on family holidays and Eve's room abandoned beside mine.

We drove together in Claudia's white Volkswagen Golf, ascending a long windy hill with the harbour on our left. Claudia's voice filled the car with ambient noise, like a radio on low volume. I noticed she had stopped speaking, and I felt my mouth move, but I didn't say anything. My body was out of reach.

'Did you hear what I said?'

'Yeah.' I laughed, and that seemed to satisfy her.

Nobody was home. The ground floor was one large room with a marble kitchen island and floor-to-ceiling windows bathed in smooth grey sunlight.

My footsteps sounded clunky, and when I said, 'Wow, your house is so nice,' my words echoed like we were in a bathroom.

Out the window there was a pool, which seemed gratuitous, given that just beyond the pool was a strip of sand and then the whole harbour. It was the kind of garden where models would pose in unwearable clothes, or slender people would wave away canapés at cocktail parties. There was no pool fence: just green lawn folding into light blue water on light blue tiles. Council laws, I was sure, required people to fence their pools. Drowning children, like parking fines, must be middle-class concerns. I had been at Fairfax long enough to recognise this kind of rule-flouting as class performance. Because rules only apply to certain *kinds* of people.

'The view is amazing,' I said, realising I was staring.

Claudia was standing at the marble counter, opening a packet of biscuits. 'Isn't it? You'd never know the beach is here from the street.'

I looked at the beach, which was smaller seen from this distance. The water was flat beneath the low-lying clouds. On the far side was a stone path with narrow steps—barely shoulder-width—leading up to the road.

I responded, but only after I noticed she was looking at me expectantly. 'Totally, it's beautiful.'

'It's so fun to show people who aren't from here. It's such a local secret.'

I lied and said, 'I've never been here before.'

Later, the sun came out and we went for a swim, and I felt Paul's hands all over my body, everywhere the water touched me.

Spring was sweating slowly into summer. When we emerged from the sea, our hair stuck slick to our scalps, and beads of water dripped down our necks without urgency. My head rang with the sound of splashing and laughter from a paler peachier morning, when I was in this same spot, feeling like a different person.

That night I was so paralysingly sad that I crawled into bed after dinner and closed my eyes around eight o'clock: as soon as the sun stopped gilding the edges of my curtains. When I wake, I thought, I might feel happier.

18

SUMMER WAS INSIGNIFICANT, and not just in light of what followed. The days and nights seemed to flow over me, without my participation. I went back to Canberra and, for the first time in my life, found my mother's interest in me oppressive. That she wanted to know whether I'd be home for dinner seemed to me as patronising as it was reasonable. My movements were subject to, and therefore restricted by, her convenience, which I knew was normal for two people living in the same household, but because she was my mother—the fact of which automatically made me feel like a child—I resented her.

A schoolfriend got me a trial shift at the restaurant where she worked. It was fancy, and politicians ate there often, I was told, although I didn't know any of their faces let alone their portfolios. I got the job, and was surprised how much I liked it. Every task was equally unimportant: bring dessert spoons, offer bread, remove empty glasses, unfurl napkins, replenish water jugs. I developed a mental bureaucracy—a hierarchy of tasks—and ran through a list to check they were done in order, scanning the high-ceilinged room with my mantra: *Beverages, cutlery, food.*

I saw some friends from school. We went for hikes and to the pool. At a New Year's party, I ate watermelon slices and drank red wine from a goon bag, and almost exactly on the stroke of midnight I vomited reddish pink to bring in the New Year. It looked, as my friends observed with laughing horror, like period blood.

I spoke to Emily, Portia, and Claudia, but only occasionally. They were all on holidays with their parents. Claudia and Portia were skiing in Europe, and Emily was in New York. I did not want to speak to Eve.

All the while, between dry lips, and sunburned skin that peeled and flaked my foundation at work, between the taste of goon and cigarettes, between hikes and swims and text messages, I felt empty. On sunny days my schoolfriends would drive to Kambah Pool, and I'd swim out to the middle, where it was deep enough to float, and I'd look at the sky and listen to my breathing, and think of Eve. In the afternoon, before work, I'd shower and lie on my bed, wet hair dampening my pillow, and touch myself until I came, thinking of Paul.

Unfortunately, I had already formed a picture of my summer, which included him. I'd seen myself catching the bus up to Sydney to visit him and staying in his apartment. I'd seen us at the beach during the day, and going to a movie at night, or cooking for each other, learning each other all the time. Home was a poor substitute to this imagined, loving summer.

Three months passed. I turned nineteen. I was a little older and perhaps a little wiser for having nursed my hurt, but all I remember feeling, when my mother drove me back to Fairfax, was pride in how tanned my legs looked with my feet up on the dashboard. I imagined Claudia and Portia complimenting me—which, of course, they did, lamenting how difficult it was to tan while skiing in the Alps.

—

I'D CONTEMPLATED NOT returning to Fairfax for my second year. But my scholarship—or, more to the point, my mother's face if I told her I was forgoing it—rooted me there. For Eve, the scholarship had always been an accessory. At one time, it expressed her intellect. Now, she threw it away like she'd outgrown it. For me, it was too *useful* to acquire symbolic status. I needed money and a place to live. Fairfax gave me money and a place to live.

So, for the second time, I arrived at college for the start of O Week. This time, I arrived to a larger room, the day before the new crop of first years were due. During the holidays, Emily and I had signed up to be student representatives, which meant shadowing the first years as they moved through the O Week festivities and shepherding them home—ideally before they were so drunk they were throwing up, but definitely once it had got to that point. Of course, with two student representatives for one hundred first years, our effectiveness was limited. There would be girls who would go unnoticed—just as I had.

The third year students chose Emily and me because 'they knew we could handle it', which meant they'd seen us in similarly compromised situations ourselves. I felt that, if I were to stay at Fairfax, which I intended to do, then I should at least participate in a constructive way.

But the opportunity to participate constructively did not arise. By the time the cars (from dusty Toyota Corollas, to P-plated Range Rovers) were rolling into the car park, and girls in sandals and white sneakers were piling out, maintaining a studied distance from their parents, everybody was talking about Eve.

The Fairfax staff were worried. A speech was being prepared. It was a tragedy, the master was reported to have said. At first, we thought she meant: the contents of the story. But, when she gave her speech, it became apparent that the real tragedy was the number of parents who had pulled their girls out of Fairfax.

—

THE MORNING OF Orientation Week, the local newspaper ran an exposé about Fairfax and St Thomas'. Each of the stories listed in Eve's original article was quoted, along with several others that had been unearthed in the intervening months.

Sins piled up like bodies in a mass grave. Female first years had been lined up and ranked according to their attractiveness. Teenagers had been plied with alcohol and driven hundreds of kilometres into the country, where they were handed fifty dollars and told to hitchhike home. Others had had their heads shaved. Girls had been invited to parties where 'big tits' was a publicised condition of entry. Broken property and soiled beds and ravaged bodies. It was a gory, unruly, consequenceless mess of human behaviour, and the consequences, it seemed, were finally catching up, in the form of Eve, so angular and articulate, knocking at the door and claiming a debt.

Her comments formed a large part of the article. She made sweeping statements—about structural failures, about intersections of privilege, about how the colleges ought to close—but her prose truly soared wherever it was armed with personal details. On occasion, she even articulated thoughts I didn't know I'd had until I saw them there, on the page.

The hardest part was the alienation. I had no one to talk to. I felt sure that if I did, no one would believe me.

And then, most brazenly of all, she added:

I can't tell you what that feels like.

In these lines, her betrayal had a particularly serrated edge. It was cruel to think she *could* have understood me.

While I was still in bed, curtains drawn, my mother called. Eve's story had made its way into national newspapers, where my mother had read all the allegations second-hand. She then looked up Eve's original article and, because that was her nature, read all the comments as well.

'Isn't Eve Herbert Shaw a friend of yours?'

I placed a hand over my stomach, which felt like it was writhing. 'Yeah.'

'It's a fantastic article. Appalling if it's true.'

'Yeah.'

'Are you okay?'

I spoke louder. 'I'm fine.'

'You sound sick.'

'I'm really fine.'

'Is it true? Is that what it's like?'

I pulled the phone away from my face and covered my mouth with my free hand. I did not want her to hear me cry.

'Michaela?'

'Yeah, it's true.'

—

EMILY AND I sat on Sackers's flesh-coloured couch. Because Sackers represented the college in several sport teams, he had been rewarded with an even larger room than the previous year. The couch, for some reason, came with him.

He'd positioned it in front of the fireplace, together with two green armchairs, creating a little sitting room. Behind us was a double bed, and a desk beneath a great bay window. On the desk, Sackers had placed two framed photos: one taken at his high school graduation with his parents; the other at last year's St Thomas' College ball, where he was almost indistinguishable in a row of dinner suits. I looked closer. Sackers was mid-speech, his eyes mischievous and his mouth open in a strangely flattering O, which accentuated his square jaw. On his left, Nick was looking at him and laughing, like he'd said something truly outrageous.

'These are nice,' I commented, and Sackers grunted, as if to prove he wasn't capable of any more sentimentality.

He had invited us to a meeting with the St Thomas' College senior student, who was responsible for organising their O Week. When he messaged Emily and me, I thought the word *meeting* was officious, but when the senior student arrived and shook our hands, and Sackers pulled out a notepad and pen, I realised that a meeting was just what they had in mind.

For the first few minutes, Emily and I were not given the opportunity to speak. In light of the media attention, Fairfax and St Thomas' College had made the decision to cancel all O Week events involving alcohol. Sackers and the senior student dismissed this as 'outrageous'. This was not offered as an opinion, but as a statement of fact—so obvious it scarcely need be said aloud, like: *sexism is bad.*

My legs were slick with sweat against the couch, and I stood to open one of the bay windows.

Social media calls to name the perpetrators probably accounted for the urgency of the meeting. Sackers was defending St Thomas', the institution, as a way of defending himself. His behaviour, his drunken gropes and 'jokes', now looked less like anecdotes and more like mistakes. For Sackers, of course, I doubted they would ever acquire the colour of crimes.

The general consensus was that bright young women like Eve shouldn't be forced to protect the men who had abused them. Of course, in the abstract, this sounded like a perfectly reasonable proposition. Still, the thought that Eve might name Nick tortured me. In light of this concern, the O Week social calendar seemed so trite an issue, I could not look at Sackers without wanting to shake him.

He pointed at me with his pen. 'Michaela will speak for us.'

'What?'

He sighed irritably and spoke louder and slower, as if I were stupid. 'We can handle the St Thomas' administration, but we need someone over at Fairfax arguing our case. We need to present a united front if we're going to get them to reinstate the O Week activities.'

'Why me?'

'You're, you know, argumentative and opinionated and whatever.'

I contemplated lying, and saying I'd help out, so I could leave the oppressive heat and leather-stick of his room. But I couldn't help myself.

'Just to clarify'—I pursed my lips, the way Portia often did when she was confused—'why are we so concerned that the drinking events are cancelled?'

They looked at me in stunned silence. I could make out Emily at my side, hiding a smile.

'Just like, in light of the, you know, rape allegations and whatever?'

Sackers's neck grew red. He matched my mocking, high-pitched voice by lowering his. 'It's tradition!' The word *tradition* was laden with value, like it was a synonym for *good* or *essential*.

The senior student leaned forward. 'Michaela, right?' His tone was patronising—indulging my little tantrum—and his hand gestures were forced, like they'd been learned. I could tell that somebody had told him, perhaps from a young age, that he had good leadership skills.

'Yep.'

'Michaela. Of course we all agree that St Thomas', like the rest of society, isn't perfect, and that there is room for improvement. But for the first years, who have come here to make friends—at great cost to their parents, I might add—it's totally unfair to deprive them of the opportunity to bond with each other and enjoy the good aspects of college.'

'I just think the college needs to take this seriously,' I said. 'Or at least be seen to be taking it seriously. I don't think we should be fighting them while they're trying to prioritise really urgent cultural changes.'

Sackers broke in, his arms across his chest. 'So you think that Eve girl is right, then?'

'I do.' Emily hadn't spoken for several minutes. There was a moment of stunned silence, before Sackers erupted.

'That's bullshit.'

'I do!' Emily sat up straighter.

'You love it here.'

'I've had fun and everything. But that doesn't mean this place isn't flawed, or that you guys aren't influenced by it.'

The senior student stopped gesturing deliberately. His hands stayed on his knees, clenched into fists. 'But you know that's not true. You have friends here. We can't all suddenly be chauvinistic pigs just because of a few articles.'

Emily looked like she was about to cry.

'You're not listening to her,' I said. 'She's not saying you're bad people.' Sackers raised his eyebrows like a challenge, and opened his mouth to cut me off, but I barrelled through, speeding up. 'It just makes sense. When you take so many privileged people and you insulate them from outside influences, it's no surprise they end up in this bubble that's super sexist and racist and classist. It makes total sense that you're a bit, I don't know, morally impoverished.'

'It's not like it's this total bubble,' Sackers said. 'You're on a scholarship. Nick was on a scholarship.'

'Fuck right off.' Emily's voice was so loud I jumped a little. 'Don't start making claims to diversity. How many non-white friends have you got, Sackers?'

He started to smile, and Emily interrupted, with a raised index finger. 'And don't you dare say: *me*.'

With his eyebrows pushed up, and his mouth hanging slack in an expression of offence, Sackers looked like a baby with a hulking, cumbersome body. 'I'm not going to reel off a list for you. My whole rugby team isn't white, not that it matters. It's a stupid point. St Thomas' is no different to private school. If I wasn't here, I'd be hanging out with the exact same people anyway.'

'But you wouldn't be doing it with such an aura of self-importance,' I said.

'If it's so unimportant, then why are you here?' The senior student sat with his legs wide. He tilted his chair back on two legs, leaning against the wall.

'You know what?' I stood. I pictured myself pushing the chair, and him toppling out of it. I wanted to reveal to him his true nature—a meagre, irrelevant creature, capable of shame and embarrassment. 'That's the first intelligent thing you've said.'

I left the room, leaving the door open behind me, because Emily stood with me, and followed close behind. She did the honours and slammed it, hard.

'I should've slapped Sackers,' she said.

'It's okay, I'm sure he'll get slapped one day.'

We emerged into the St Thomas' quadrangle, which was washed white while my eyes adjusted to the sun. 'I could go back and do it?' Emily said.

I laughed.

'I'm only twenty per cent kidding.'

'Don't. You can't do anything without affirming them. If you slapped him, they'd say it proves you're crazy. I should have just walked out at the start. They're never going to change their minds.'

Emily looked at the ground. '*Morally impoverished* was nice, though.'

'Thanks.'

The sandstone walls of St Thomas' College were reflecting the sun, and the heat in the quadrangle was like an assault. Emily raised a hand to her face and swatted away a fly.

'I know what to do,' she said.

'Yeah?'

'I've got tequila and limes in my room.' She looked at me expectantly.

'Okay?'

With none of her usual enthusiasm, but with a grave urgency, she said, 'We should go to the beach and get drunk.'

We did. On the beach, we severed the limes with her car keys and licked salt water from our hands before taking a shot. The sun and the alcohol dried my thoughts to a slog, and the ocean absorbed me, and allowed me to forget, for a moment, everything Eve had done—to me, to Nick—and everything she might do yet.

———

I LEFT THE dining hall for the first day of classes alone, with two minutes to go until my lecture started. It was for a second year philosophy subject and I had been thinking all morning about what I would say to Eve. I had chosen a short dress for the occasion, to flex my tanned legs. It was petty, but I have come to accept (now at least, if not then) that I am a petty person. She might have taken my story—made more of it than I ever could—but at least my lithe, thriving body was my own.

And what a lot she had made of my story. An in-depth report was set to air on national TV in the coming days. I had no doubt Eve would be interviewed. Television seemed inevitable. She had a face that cried out for cameras. I dreaded our confrontation but also felt resigned to it. I was determined that she not drag Nick, the memory of him, into this storm she had started.

The St Thomas' Facebook page had taken to posting long, puffed-up pieces, using words like *besieged* and *attacked* and *crisis*. Balth sent me screenshots and we joked about how militaristic it all sounded.

> *This is what happens when you go to a school that makes you do cadets*
>
> Did your school make you do cadets?
>
> *Oh you bet. I hated it*
>
> Because you weren't good at it?
>
> *Because school is already oppressive enough*
> *(Also I was dreadful at it)*

The security door at the back of Fairfax beeped as it locked behind me. At the bottom of the driveway, a crowd had assembled. I had to walk through them to get to class. Over one hundred people, a mix of students and staff, some with signs and posters, all emblazoned with variations of DOWN WITH THE COLLEGES.

A pair of St Thomas' boys walking ahead of me, wearing chinos and Patagonia tees and with identical haircuts, sighed. 'For fuck's sake.'

With my head down, I pushed past them and into the crowd.

I saw her hair first: dark and slick. She was the best-dressed person in the throng, with a black linen dress that would have made a less slim, model-proportioned woman look like a medieval pig farmer. She was shouting with the rest, but stopped mid-sentence when she caught my eye.

'Michaela?'

'Violet, hi.' I smiled and gave a breathy sort of laugh, attempting to acknowledge the awkward reality that she was, in a way, protesting me.

'Hi.' She walked back a few paces to where the crowd was thinner. I followed her. 'Are you still living here?'

'Yeah.'

'Oh.' She paused and looked at her feet: sleek leather slides. 'How was your summer?'

'It was fine. Worked a lot.' I felt compelled to tell her that I worked. I didn't want a picture to crystallise—a picture that fitted so many of my friends: of champagne on European ski slopes, and Christmas lunches with three-hundred-dollar hams.

'Are you still doing philosophy?' she asked.

'Yep, I'm actually on my way to a lecture right now.'

'Oh, I shouldn't hold you—'

'Violet!' It was not his lecture voice, but the softer, fonder tones I knew intimately. As soon as I heard it, my blood seemed to expand, threatening to burst my veins. I stood motionless, and saw his bearded face emerge at Violet's shoulder.

'Paul, you know Michaela, right? You taught her last year.'

It was admirable—alarming, even—how quickly Paul masked his shock with blank politeness.

'Michaela, yes, of course I remember.' His smile was detached: just an empty muscle movement.

'So *you're* protesting the colleges?' I asked, crossing my arms over my chest, with what was probably an obviously confrontational tilt of my chin towards him.

'Yes,' he said.

'So Michaela, you know Eve, obviously.' Violet was trying, valiantly, to keep the conversational portions to small-talk-sized chunks.

'Yeah, we're friends.'

'Isn't she fantastic? It's amazing what she's been able to achieve. So brave.'

'Yeah, she's great.' I scanned the crowd for her delicate features. 'Is she here?'

'I think so.'

Violet looked over her shoulder, while Paul continued to look anywhere but at me.

'I can't see her,' Violet said.

Paul's refusal to meet my gaze, coupled with Eve's apparent transcendence, made my thoughts rear, jaws snapping. He held a flimsy cardboard sign limply in one hand. How tubby and soft he looked, I thought.

'Don't you think all this protesting, all this media scrutiny . . .' I paused, waiting for Paul to look at me. His eyes met mine. 'Doesn't it in some ways just confirm for the colleges that they matter?'

'But they do matter. They've caused a lot of harm to a lot of people.' Violet was holding her own cardboard poster flat against the top of her head, using it like a hat. Beneath it, she looked at me through narrowed eyes.

'Of course they have,' I agreed. 'But every article starts with some variation on "home of our future leaders". I just don't think they need to be told over and over again that they represent something larger than themselves.'

'Of course they represent something larger than themselves. They represent privilege and power. Do you realise what percentage of our CEOs and cabinet members went to these colleges?' She pulled her sign down to her side with a quick, frustrated movement.

'I'm just saying that while protesting is very noble and whatever, the boys I know, who live up there'—I pointed over my shoulder, up the drive, where sandstone spires were visible above the tree line—'don't feel at all subdued by it. It just confirms their lifelong belief that they're all big fucking deals.'

'What do you suggest we do?' Violet's arms were crossed over her chest, mirroring my own.

'I see her point.' Paul touched Violet lightly on the arm. A placating touch that was intended to come to my aid. But there was a fluidness to it that gutted me. The lightness of his brush against her; the way she relaxed upon it—not tensing—like she'd been told, unfairly, to calm down. Instead she sighed into it. I felt light-headed and the pounding sun stung my eyes. I never wanted to see either of them again.

'Thank you, Paul.' I said his name with the perfect amount of vitriol: just enough for him to taste it, but not quite enough to make Violet suspicious. 'Anyway, I'm late, but it was great to see you . . . Violet.' Again, I imbued *Violet* with an acerbic thrust: I did not so much mean *Violet* as *not-Paul*.

I thought I caught a wounded flinch in his eyes, and was surprised at how it stabbed my gut—not with triumph, but with something closer to guilt.

Violet called, 'Bye,' behind me, while Paul remained silent. I hoped he was watching me walk away.

I slipped into the back row in the lecture theatre and immediately scanned the room. No Eve.

My phone buzzed with a text. Paul.

It was nice to see you. Sorry the circumstances
were so . . . weird (for want of a better word!).
I hope you've been well. No pressure at all,
but would you like to catch up for a coffee?

I spent the lecture with an insect for a brain, droning and vibrating, bashing its wings again and again against my phone screen.

In the break, while others peeled out for coffee, I noticed that the Word document I had opened was empty, but for a title. When the lecture resumed, I replied.

Sure

The rest of the day was just ambient noise beneath my palpitating heart.

19

THE NEXT DAY, Paul and I met for coffee on the steps outside the library, overlooking Victoria Park, at Paul's suggestion. That we meet in such a public place was a clear sign we were strictly friends. He was daring people we knew to run into us: declaring our relationship above board.

I had spent the day unproductively, anticipating our three pm coffee, and when the time arrived I made sure to be six minutes late. Five might have seemed calculated.

He was waiting for me on the steps, and there was some initial fumbling about whether we'd both go and get coffee, or whether one of us would save the spot. Eventually, he wandered off with my order and some coins I'd shoved, perhaps too insistently, into his hand. I looked at my phone and then, worrying that it might make me seem too young and distractable, I put it in my bag, and looked out over the park. The trees were rustling in the afternoon breeze, dappled light dancing on the grass like ripples in a river. Watching them was not a distraction. It made me more nervous, and when Paul eventually sat down beside me, I jumped a little.

The mood of our meeting was taut, and showed no signs of slackening, so I decided, looking at him through frowning eyes, that

I would be more aggressive than usual. Perhaps if I were patently irritable, he would conclude that I no longer cared about his feelings.

'So you and Violet are seeing each other now?' I said.

'Yes. Who told you?'

'I could just tell.'

'From the other day? How?'

'I guess I know you well.'

He laughed, and took a sip from his keep cup. 'Well, we have similar interests, I suppose.'

'Are you philosophical about everything? Is all your bickering just you two acting out some kind of Hegelian dialectic?'

'We don't talk about work much, actually. I'm too insecure.'

He'd never referred to himself as insecure before, certainly not intellectually. I didn't like how serious he seemed, the way he placed the words carefully: narrowing his eyes like they were coming into view. Was this the confessional, softer Paul that Violet revealed?

We talked about other things for a while—what we'd done over summer, what films we'd seen, what courses I was taking. Then, pretending to people-watch, but unable to focus on anything except his tiny, shuffling movements next to me as he sipped at his coffee and ran his finger around the lid, I asked, 'Was there any crossover? Between Violet and me?'

'No.'

'But you must have known you liked her.'

'We were just colleagues. It didn't start until summer. When I broke up with you it was because . . .' He paused, and his eyes flicked from me to the park. He addressed the rest of his sentence out to the trees. 'It was for all the reasons I said at the time.'

'And she didn't inform any of those *reasons*?'

'Would you prefer it if I'd slept with both of you at the same time?' He looked at me again.

'Of course not.' I hated his perceptiveness. When we were sleeping together, he'd always made me feel like an older, wiser version of myself. Now, in hindsight, and when he spoke to me like this, in a cool tone, devoid of promise or suspense, he made me feel wretchedly young. A pathetic, girlish creature who didn't understand herself, much less other people.

'It must be a tense time at the colleges,' he said, in what was clearly a concerted effort to push the conversation into new territory.

I took his comment personally, as if he were trying to tell me that *I* was tense and needed to calm down.

I said, 'Yeah, it's tense. You would think we were being invaded. A lot of closing in of ranks; a lot of discussion about how we shouldn't talk to the media.'

'What would you say if you spoke to the media?'

'I really don't know. The whole thing has been quite confronting.' He looked at me, expectant. 'Remember when Eve's article came out?'

He nodded.

'And I said I didn't want to talk about it?'

A murmur this time. He sensed a confession.

I don't remember being cognisant of a crossroads. But looking back, it seems obvious that I chose, in that moment, to hurt him. Or, if not to hurt him, then to console myself, by taking my smallest, weakest fragment and presenting it to him. *See?* this private part of me would say. *You didn't know me at all.* How could it be intimacy—what we shared—if we'd kept so much to ourselves?

'The story she told in that article, about what happened in O Week . . . well, it actually happened to me.'

'What?'

'I mean, she may have embellished it. But the broad strokes are me. Inspired by.'

His response was so immediate, it left no room for the slow, deliberate rationalisation he so prided himself on. 'You need to tell people.'

'To achieve what?'

'I don't know, some kind of retribution, or restoration.' He fumbled; academic terms seemed to fail him. 'She's lying. You've been wronged.'

I laughed. He must have intuited the irony: that he was lecturing me on how I had been *wronged*, like Eve was the only person to wrong me.

When he continued, his voice was much gentler. 'It's just so unfair.'

'Look, she's taken my story, but she's probably put it to better use than I was going to.'

He leaned back, both hands against the step he was sitting on. 'That's a very utilitarian outlook. The fact that other people might benefit from your hurt doesn't erase it.'

We were back into our old rhythm, this dance between conceptual and personal, which had been the language of our relationship. It was often whispered, with our heads on the pillow, or mine on his chest. Here, with his feet up on the steps, his hands gesticulating, I saw that we could keep talking like this forever.

'The problem is,' I said, 'the boy who was with me that night, he's'—I couldn't hold Paul's gaze; I looked at my hands—'he's that friend of mine who died.'

He opened his mouth, but made no sound.

'She hasn't said yet who did it, but I'm worried she will. I know it's silly—'

'No.'

I could tell this interjection was meant to be supportive, but I spoke faster, desperate to finish the thought, which, until now, I hadn't fully formulated. 'She's doing all these interviews, and there's all this talk about naming the perpetrators. I don't think I could bear it if she did.'

He nodded, but didn't speak, as if he sensed I had more to say.

'I know it's silly to fret about a dead man's reputation, in the scheme of things. But I just don't have her conviction. I don't know how she could do it.'

'Michaela, I really think you should talk to her about this.'

'But I don't even know what happened. I don't know.' Tears escaped me. To my horror, he patted me on the back.

'God, you're a good person,' he said.

A sob broke from me at the absurd confidence with which he could just declare that, and at how much it meant to hear it.

I waved his patting hand away. 'How can you say that?'

'You're still thinking of others.'

'Isn't that what Eve's trying to do?'

'It's not the same.'

I wiped my eyes and laughed in what I hoped was a self-deprecating way. 'I'm sorry. I shouldn't have brought it up.'

'Are you okay?' He watched me closely. The tremor in his voice suggested he was not asking whether I had stopped crying—whether I was okay now—but whether I was generally, spiritually, *okay*.

This concern for my wellbeing irritated me, as if my mental health were an abstract, detached concept, not something he held in the palm of his hand.

'Of course I'm okay. I'm fine.'

'You know, there are a lot of counselling services available on campus if you need to talk to someone.'

'You want me to see a university counsellor? About my sexual experiences?'

'If you need to.' He was nodding.

'Oh, the stories I could tell.'

That shut him up.

'I'm sorry,' I said, perhaps too quickly.

He looked at me, holding my gaze. 'You know, I still feel very, very guilty.'

'Well, I'm very, very glad to hear that,' I said. 'I'm kidding. Not fully kidding, though. I do feel a bit vindicated to hear that you're suffering.'

He snorted.

'But I do see the distinction between being hurt and being wronged.'

'That's very mature of you,' he said.

'I don't feel very mature.' I rubbed my eyes. 'I don't think I see things clearly.'

He must have thought I was rubbing my eyes because I was about to cry again, or maybe my voice sounded less sure than I thought, because he reached out and touched my face. It felt like the most natural, and at the same time the most significant, thing in the world—a touch so tender it tickled with memories.

'It's not clear at all,' he said. 'It's wrong to lie, it's wrong to steal, it's wrong to hurt. But at the end of every class, people are less sure about what's right and wrong than when they started. That's when I know I've done my job.'

My throat felt tight. I hated him for being so wise. I hated, too, that we were embarking on what appeared to be a friendship, where we could discuss deeply personal matters, and he could touch my cheek and set me on fire, and then go back to Violet. It seemed crucial to my structural integrity—to prevent me from breaking into thousands of irretrievable pieces—that I withhold something from him.

'I think I should go,' I said.

'Of course,' he said, picking up his keep cup and standing. 'It was so nice to see you. I'd love to see you again.'

I stood too. 'I don't know. I'm not sure we should be friends.' I had one foot on the step I had been sitting on and one on the step above it, which made me feel, ever so slightly, like I was leaning over him.

'Right.'

'I'm sorry, it's too . . .'

'No, I get it.'

'Well, I'll see you around.'

He stepped towards me and, not sure whether it was for a hug or a kiss, I brushed my cheek against his beard noncommittally. I marvelled that I could be so clumsy with a body that used to pour like water into mine.

I wanted to say one more thing before we parted, so I might cover the space between us. 'Maybe I'll take one of your courses,' I said.

'Maybe. You might learn something.'

—

HAVING SEEN SO much of Eve in the paper and online, it was strange to see her in class. It was inevitable that we would take some of the same courses. In my Aesthetics class, she sat at the front of the lecture theatre. I spied her head from the back row—her hair longer now, with a little sweep across her forehead: the colour back to her darker, natural blonde.

At first, I watched her with the dispassionate eyes of a stranger. Gradually, over the course of the lecture, her appearance receded, sinking below a thousand other perceptions and impressions of the Eve I knew. If I knew her at all.

The lecture was all introductory materials—nothing substantive. I did not bother taking notes. Instead, I went online and read every

article and follow-up article that had been written since the year
started. I looked at her tagged photos on Instagram, to see which
radio and news programs she'd been invited on to, and I read her
Twitter feed, to see what new praise she was being humbled by.

When class was almost over, I put my backpack on and waited
in the aisle, ready to run after her.

She was halfway across the Quad by the time I surfaced on
the other side of the crowd. She was wearing a white cotton dress
with little puff sleeves and colourful Nikes with ankle socks. As I
came up behind her, the sun bore down on the thin cotton, and
I could make out the shape of her legs all the way up to her hips,
and the line of her underpants. The backs of her arms and legs
were summer-honeyed.

'Eve.'

She turned, raising a hand to shield her eyes from the glare.
I had expected to startle her, but beneath her hand, and the shadow
that obscured her eyes, her face broke into a broad smile.

'Michaela! It's so good to see you.'

She hugged me. I did not put my arms around her but stood
rigid in the embrace. She didn't smell like anything.

She pulled back and flicked her fringe from her eyes. 'Hold on,
let's get out of the sun.'

She took me to the shade of the cloister, from where we looked
out at the Quad: fluorescent green framed by sandstone arches.
The university, in this bold summer light, looked like it did in ads.

Eve leaned against the cool stone, and smiled again. 'How was
your summer?'

'It was fine. Worked a bit.' I was mumbling. The confrontation
I'd imagined was fading under the strangely oppressive glare of
this polite chitchat.

'Yeah, same here. Nothing much to report. The holidays feel like a long time ago.' She smiled the way she always did when she was bragging—a sort of laugh that acknowledged the lack of humility without apologising for it.

'Yeah,' I said. 'You've been busy.'

'It's been crazy.'

I couldn't believe the casual boldness with which she alluded to the articles. I studied her face for any flicker of discomfort, any acknowledgement of awkwardness. There was none. She was totally relaxed, as if I were not the person she spoke about so publicly but just any other person—anyone in the world, interested as all people ought to be, in the marvellous work she'd been doing.

'Violet said she bumped into you coming out of Fairfax.'

Eve's smug smile persuaded me that she knew about Violet and Paul.

'Yes,' was all I managed.

'So you're back at college?'

'Yes.'

Eve looked at me, maddeningly, with satisfaction, as if she'd made some kind of bet and my answer was proof that she'd won. 'Of course you are.'

'I'm still on a scholarship, Eve.' I stated this as a fact, but my gaze, I hoped, was assertive. 'There's nowhere else in Sydney where I can live for free.'

'Sure. But at what price?'

It inflamed me: the smug way she turned money to metaphor, like *price* wasn't material.

She shifted the bag-strap at her shoulder. 'Hey, I have to go. I've actually got an interview in a few hours.' That faux-humble laugh again. 'But let's get coffee?'

As she started to turn, I snatched at her arm. 'Hey, about your interview . . .'

She crossed her arms and looked at me, her chin tilted up, her eyes proud and defiant atop those sharp cheekbones. It surprised me: how my heart thudded and sweat slid beneath the weight of my backpack. As if I were the one transgressing, by attempting to comment on *her* story. The severity of her gaze—no flicker of apology—was sufficient to shift the burden. *Prove me wrong*, it said.

'You've got to stop, Eve. You can't tell people it was Nick.'

'Oh, so you can say his name now.'

'What?'

'You've always protected him. Relentlessly. All the times we talked about it—around it—you never said his name.'

My backpack suddenly felt cumbersome and childish, so I took it off and rested it on the sandstone. Playing out this conversation for months opposite an imagined Eve was by no means prepara-tion. It made the real Eve, who now stood before me, all the more formidable.

'It's not fair to him,' I said. 'He's a real person. You can't just take something that happened to other people and embellish it, twist it, until it proves your point.'

'Embellish?'

'Well, it's not hard for you, is it? You wrote the St Thomas' boys off right from the start. You didn't see any of them as real people.'

'That's rich. You were just as disdainful as me. Just because I made a rational assessment about that environment breeding problematic individuals—and had the integrity to *act* on that assess-ment—doesn't mean I'm suffering some kind of failure of empathy.' She was infuriatingly articulate: repackaging my argument in more eloquent ways before knocking it to the ground.

'And how did you go about making this *rational assessment*? You certainly didn't speak to me about it—'

'I tried! You wouldn't talk!'

'—and I don't know what you said to Nick, or who told you about the yelling, or whether you made it up.'

'Michaela—'

'I don't know if you told him your version and that's why he felt so guilty . . .'

'Michaela, what are you talking about?'

I took a deep breath. 'You obviously knew what happened between me and Nick, and I never spoke to anyone about it.' My voice quivered, as the thought followed the words. I swallowed. 'I never even spoke to Nick. But I'm sure he felt very guilty, especially with people like you interrogating him. He wasn't stupid. He would've known what kind of a threat the whole situation was to his reputation and—'

'Don't you dare say *career.*'

'Well, I'm not wrong, am I? You could've got him expelled from college for taking my virginity without my consent. That's a threatening thing for a man.'

Her voice, for once, was very quiet. 'I didn't know he took your virginity.'

'That wasn't really my point. I was just being hyperbolic. You get the gist. He would've been terrified. And trapped.'

'Michaela, stop. I . . .' She raised her hands as if to pull at her hair but, finding it too short, she stroked the fluff instead. It looked as soft as a newborn's. 'I can't believe this. Do you think I have something to do with his death?'

'No.'

'That's an awful thing to level at someone.'

I looked at her. The sun was behind her, and in the shadow of the cloisters, her face was hard to make out. 'So is rape, to be honest.'

'You really don't remember, do you?'

Dread thickened my blood and made my voice sound distant. 'What?'

'I didn't speak to Nick about it. Or anyone else.'

'What?'

'I didn't need to.' Armed with a taunting smile, she looked almost like she was enjoying herself. Her nostrils might have flared. 'I was there.'

I looked right at her, blinking stupidly.

'I was there that night. In Nick's room. I was the one who found you and took you home.'

I shook my head while Eve went on. 'You were naked. I mean, you were wearing his academic gown, but it wasn't covering you properly. Your limbs were so floppy. Your head was practically lolling into your own vomit. And Nick did *nothing*.'

'Why didn't you say anything? Why didn't you check in with me the next day?'

'I did.' Eve took a step closer and I shifted back, my shoulder bumping against the sandstone. 'I came to your room, don't you remember? I asked how your night was, and you just said it was fine. We didn't know each other yet. I didn't want to press the point. I thought . . . I thought it would be humiliating.'

I laughed and, despite myself, the laughter conveyed pain rather than amusement. 'Because that article, all those interviews—they're not humiliating?'

'Do you know how I ended up in his room?' Her tone was retaliatory. 'I was in the corridor and I heard him yelling, so I went to see what was going on. That's when I saw you vomiting. I had a conversation with him, Michaela. He wasn't nearly as drunk as you. I've never seen someone as drunk as you.'

I dug my nails into my palms. I wanted her to stop. 'Okay,' I said, hoping that would be the end of it.

'He was yelling at you.' Eve walked towards me. 'Properly yelling.'

All I could see was her face, her head a taunting cut-out. 'Eve, stop.'

'He kept calling you a *stupid bitch.*'

I thought I saw a twitch of triumph pass across her otherwise beautiful features.

'I said stop.'

'But it's true! I'm sorry, Michaela, but that's what happened.'

It was the apology—the *sorry*—that empowered me. Her face was sickly sweet with sympathy. Like she genuinely believed that she cared.

'Stop.' I turned from the cool cloister and stepped out into the Quad, the sun brilliant at my back. Over my shoulder, I called out to her. 'You have to stop.'

—

WITH EVE'S REVELATION, our friendship was unwritten, conversation by remembered conversation, as I became an object to pity; to observe; to contain in words. Never a subject worthy of her love or admiration.

Shame, wet and clammy, clung to me. I felt as if Eve had watched me through a peephole in the wall; as if my thoughts were written in a journal by someone other than me, and read aloud by Eve. The version of myself I had always tried to be around her—self-assured, opinionated—mocked me. *Stupid bitch.* When Eve spoke those words, it was with such force, such a sense of ownership, that it seemed she was not quoting Nick at all but speaking them directly.

Before Eve took my story, she had been my witness. I grappled with this new authority. I tried to picture the scene through her eyes. Not as she wrote it, or spoke about it, but as she *saw* it at the time. When she was there. Though it turned my stomach, and brought tears to my eyes, I could see myself, head *lolling* as Eve had put it, fragile and debased. I could even see Nick, face not wide with concern, but selfish and narrow in horror. But I could not—would not—hear him shout. I pictured his mouth moving, but the voice that emerged was always Eve's.

That night, she was interviewed on national television. Emily, Claudia, Portia, and I watched her on the common room TV. Squeezed four across, we filled the couch. The more extroverted first years ventured from their rooms and sat on the floor around us.

They gasped in horror as Eve relayed her story. When the interviewer asked how she'd felt the next morning, and Eve said, in a choked voice, 'Ashamed,' one of them sighed: 'That poor girl.'

I watched Eve as if she were a stranger. With her hair slicked into a pixie cut she looked, I thought, a bit like me.

The interviewer announced that their time was almost up. I realised my hands were clasped together. I unfurled them, slowly, my knuckles fading from white to pink.

'Finally, I have to ask'—the interviewer looked up from her notes and stared straight at Eve—'did you ever consider reporting this to the police?'

Eve smiled. Not a polite smile of attention, but a victorious little tremor. 'That would require naming the perpetrator.'

I inhaled sharply and looked at Emily. She was transfixed, oblivious to my panic.

'Do you know who he is?' the interviewer asked.

'Yes.' Eve paused. I heard myself breathing. 'But I won't name him.'

'Why not?'

Eve took a deep breath. She was so consistently articulate, even off the cuff, that you would have to know her intimately, as I did, to recognise that this short speech had been prepared.

'I really believe he is a product of the institution. And when I say I want justice, I don't mean that I want him personally to suffer. I want institutional change. As long as I don't name him, my perpetrator is a stand-in for all of them—for all the people institutions like this create and enable.'

Masterstroke.

The first years thought so too. 'She's amazing,' one of them said, then, to the four of us: 'Did you guys know her?'

The others looked to me to answer first. I did not speak.

Claudia answered for me. 'They're really good friends.'

'Wow.' The first year nodded, like she understood. 'You must be very proud.'

—

WHEN THE SHOW finished, my phone vibrated with a text from Paul.

> *Just saw Eve on TV. You must be relieved.*

I opened it, so he would see the read receipt, but I didn't reply. After several minutes, my phone buzzed again.

> *I know you said the other day that you don't want to be friends, and I totally respect that. But I just wanted to let you know: I'm here for you if you need.*

I left him on *seen*. He did not text again.

20
———

'I THINK I was in love with him,' I told Balth. We were in his bedroom at St Thomas'. He was sitting on the windowsill, a cigarette hanging out the window, and I was on his desk, my feet dangling just above the floor.

'Really?'

'Yeah. It's a really shitty thing to realise.'

A cup of tea, which Balth had poured me, was steaming untouched at my side. My thigh was warm where it almost touched the cup.

'Isn't love, you know, all you need?' Balth hung further out the window, tapping the ash off his cigarette. 'What makes the world go round? Or was that money?'

I wasn't in the mood. I was determined to make him be serious, which was to require him to defy his nature.

'I feel like I was holding off,' I said, 'and then it was just when I put my trust in him—just when I allowed myself to imagine what we might be like together, how the future might look—that he decided he wasn't into it anymore. And I kind of hate myself for that.'

Balth spoke quietly, rolling his cigarette back and forth between his slender thumb and forefinger. 'You shouldn't hate yourself for liking him. Or for being vulnerable to someone. It's actually sort of humanising.'

'But I was so much happier before. I was like this island.'

'Yeah, you were pretty far out in the ocean.'

'So you think I should've been more vulnerable—that Paul just wanted me to need him?' I said *need* in a mocking tone, like it was ridiculous that people might need each other.

'You can be a bit scary.' He took one last drag of his cigarette then threw the stub into the bin. From where I was perched on the desk, I could see the embers fading.

'Ugh. Eve and I used to have this joke that men—boys we knew—weren't interested in us because we were too intimidating. We used to be like: obviously if everyone is driving the other way, you're in the wrong lane, but also, everyone must be driving the other way because I'm *such* a catch, you know?'

He lay on the bed with his hands behind his head and spoke to the ceiling. 'To be honest, you might have been on to something.'

'That was a joke. Probably not for Eve—she's pretty deranged.'

'I don't agree. I mean, obviously I agree Eve is deranged. But I just mean'—he paused here, choosing his next words—'if Paul did love you, I don't know that he would've said so.' He rolled his head towards me, as if to check that I wasn't upset. He continued, 'You're not the kind of person who seems receptive to being loved.'

'Are you saying I'm cold?'

'Sort of. I don't imagine you were frigid, of course.' He gave me a sly, sliding look. I threw a pen at him, which he tried to catch, but fumbled with. He left it where it fell between the sheets.

'Unlovable then?' I asked.

'You're anything but unlovable, Michaela. I think it's easier for you to think that . . . to characterise yourself as perpetually unattached. It lowers the stakes on all your relationships.'

'I don't think it would be healthy to walk around thinking that everybody is in love with me.'

'No, but I think it's a bit self-indulgent, frankly, not to even entertain the possibility.' He was talking to the ceiling again. I wished he'd face me.

'Wow.' I tried to inject my tone with hurt. It worked.

Balth sat up, swinging his feet onto the floor, and leaned forward, his elbows on his knees. 'Like, we spend so much time talking about how beautiful other women are. Even tonight, you wanted to know how beautiful I thought the woman in the movie was. You talk about it in this abstract way, like it's not a power that you have.'

'Well, it's not as if I'm an oil painting. Like, I suppose I'm as good-looking as any young, privileged, not-overweight person is. I have nice teeth and clear skin and—'

'It's astonishing to me that you seem to genuinely believe that.' He was standing now, and paced to the window, before turning back to me. 'Like, it isn't totally obvious to you that you're . . .' He paused. When he did speak, his voice trembled with significance. 'You're very beautiful.'

'Oh, Balth.'

'Don't look at me like that.' He was framed by the window, the light from the car park casting a glow around his head, in which that floppy black hair danced.

'I had no idea,' I said.

'Of course you knew.'

Of course I did. I thought about the ball—the way he'd extended the invitation as a joke and then, on the night, reached out to touch my arm, inviting me to take him seriously. And I, laughing, had pretended not to notice. I thought of our many conversations—the way he listened to me intently, with nodding, vocal focus, never just formulating the next thing he'd say. Even when he cut me off,

I saw now, he was not drowning me out, suppressing my thoughts with his; he was only ever calling me back, guiding me down another path, to a place of greater clarity. And sometimes, in our brief silences, I caught him looking at me as if I were some kind of artwork and just looking was a pleasure, and an education in itself.

I started to cry. 'I'm so sorry,' I said, wiping the tears from my eyes, luxuriating in the movement, which was a truer expression of how awful I felt than the few words I could manage.

'No, don't be silly,' he said. 'I'm very much over it. Look at you: you're a mess!'

I laughed, wiping my eyes with quicker movements. 'Why didn't you say?'

'Because you obviously didn't feel the same way.'

'I'm so sorry,' I said again. 'So, are you . . . are we . . . are we okay now?'

'You mean: am I still in love with you?'

'I guess.'

He paused a long time before answering. I sniffed delicately, wanting his hurt, not mine, to make the louder sound.

'No,' Balth said. 'Not in the same way. I relished it at the time. I felt so *abject*, like a poet. Now I just feel a bit less immature and greedy on account of our friendship.'

'How do you mean?'

'I think I really want the best for you, as much as I do for myself.'

'I feel that about my close friends, I think. Only a select few.'

'It's edifying, isn't it?'

'I suppose so. It's nice to feel a tiny bit less selfish.'

'I fucking hope I'm on the list—of people you want the best for.'

I laughed. 'You are. When I think about it, though, Eve never was. Maybe that friendship was doomed from the beginning. She certainly didn't want the best for me, as it turns out.'

'It makes me so angry, what she did to you.' He sat back down on the bed with his back against the wall and his knees drawn up to his chest. He fiddled with the sheets, clenching them in his fist, and then smoothing them out.

'I don't know,' I said. 'Nick wasn't hurt, I guess. Not in the way I'd feared. So I suppose she hasn't done that much harm.'

'Except to you.'

'Sure, but she's probably still done a good thing. Like, for society.'

'Do you think so?'

'Yeah, I do. This place—this kind of institution—it wasn't built to last. I think it was always trying to be something it's not.'

'The brochures would say that's aspirational.'

'Sure. But I'd say it's delusional.'

'Still, I hate that it was your life that got appropriated, just so she could make her point,' he said. 'It's like, she gets to be the martyr, but you had to do all the suffering. Even if there is some broader social benefit, she's still wronged you. It's still unforgivable.'

'That's what Paul thought.'

He stood up and went to the window, leaning out into the night. 'I never understood the expression: *those who can't do, teach.* Until Paul the professor of ethics.'

I laughed, and he turned to catch it. I saw how happy it made him, to make me smile.

'I just think,' he said, 'if someone had to be hurt, it should have been someone less remarkable than you.'

I was crying again, and he crossed the room, and leaned against the desk, putting his arm around me. I let my head fall on his shoulder, and felt that of all the choices I'd made, this one, at least, was right.

'I love you, Balth.'

'God.' He laughed, patting my arm. 'You're in love with every-body tonight.'

———

FOR DAYS AFTER Eve's television interview, our encounter lingered, her white cotton dress blowing in and out of my vision, like bedsheets drying on a clothes line.

One question hounded me. *Why didn't she make it up?*

She had spoken to so many women, compiled so many stories, she didn't need mine. And even if she did need a story to tell in the first person, then why not invent one? After all, it seemed she'd never had any intention of naming a perpetrator.

I consoled myself briefly with the idea that Eve's actions were personal. She chose my story to hurt me because, in whatever way, I had hurt her. Perhaps because I'd lied to her about Paul. Or perhaps she'd found out that I had read her journal or copied her in that first semester exam—the one in which I had done so well. I took each of these guilty episodes—beads threaded on a rosary of regret—and used them, like a backstory, to buttress my role in Eve's narrative. I had hurt her, so she hurt me.

But when I tried to articulate to Balth the peculiar hurt she instilled, my view of the scene grew indistinct.

'She's nuts,' he said. 'I always said she was nuts.'

'Don't you think that's particularly nuts, even for her? To, like, pretend that nothing has happened? She was so unfazed when she first saw me. Like, it didn't even occur to her that I'd still be mad.'

'It's not that surprising, to be honest. She's brilliant, obviously, but she lives in her own reality.'

'But if she lives in her own reality, isn't that all the more reason to just make something up?'

'You should ask her.' He said this with a steady, deadpan stare.

'Are you kidding?'

'If it's causing you so much grief, why not?'

Of course it troubled me to think that Eve took my story when she could have just imagined one. But what was troubling me more, what had always troubled me since I first read her article, was: *how much* of this one was true?

Parts of her story were exactly as I remembered them, which only made the other parts—the parts that hurt the most—impossible to dismiss. The *grief*, as Balthazar put it, was for my own version of events. It seemed an irreparable indignity: to have to take Eve's word for it.

—

AS SOON AS I saw Luke approaching, I knew why Balthazar had invited me.

'Eve's probably here.'

'I haven't seen her.' Balth couldn't disguise the cheek in his eyes.

'You knew she'd be here.'

'She could be anywhere at any time, Michaela. It's good for you to stay on your toes.'

Luke was making his way through the front door, picking through the people who had spilled into the corridor and were leaning against the walls, nursing plastic cups of spirits or room-temperature beers. The music was difficult to make out. Even the bass barely pulsed. Just a rumble of voices, reverberating off narrow walls.

Luke caught my eye as he passed. He nodded. 'Michaela.'

I could make out beads of sweat on his forehead. Instinctively, I wiped my own. He passed me without further comment.

Balthazar had invited me to a schoolfriend's house party. We ate dinner in Newtown first, and by the time we walked to the party, the sun had set, and my steps were exuberantly light. 'Did you tell your friend that you're bringing a plus one?'

'It's not that kind of party.'

Now, standing in the sweaty corridor, at least a bottle of wine deep, watching Luke shuffle past me, I couldn't think of anything to say. I took his frosty greeting as confirmation that, for Luke, I'd only ever been a means to access Eve. I was more amused than offended to see my dislike reciprocated. If Luke and I were only ever pleasant to each other for Eve's benefit, then that, at least, was something we had in common.

I followed him a few steps deeper into the house. I stood on my toes and saw him join the throng in the living room. He leaned down to accept a kiss on the cheek, and his hand stretched—out of my view—presumably settling around a slender waist.

I heard her, then. Or I heard the laughter she started. An elegant hand danced into view, illustrating a point.

I retreated and found Balthazar, still chatting in the corridor. I grabbed his arm and headed up the carpeted stairs.

He prattled behind me. 'Michaela, thank god. I was trapped talking to this honours student. His thesis topic is whether numbers are real.'

'Balth.'

'I asked him if the word count was flexible, and he didn't even flinch.'

I'd reached the top of the stairs and turned around so abruptly he almost toppled backwards. 'Balthazar!'

'What?'

'Eve's here.'

His eyes widened. 'You're sure?'

'Yes. I just saw her.'

He bowed as low as he could in the narrow staircase and gestured with his arm, letting me pass. 'After you.'

I didn't move.

'Good luck.'

———

SHE DIDN'T FACE me until I tapped her on the shoulder. 'Eve. I need to speak to you.' I thought I'd never sounded so formal.

Not wanting to be interrupted, I led her outside to the front of the house. On the other side of the street, Camperdown Park was floodlit. A wall of graffiti overlooked us. The bright lights, obviously installed for safety, cast sharp shadows with the trees, only rendering them more sinister.

Eve and I stood on the road. She smoked. I clutched at a red plastic cup, regretting that she'd scored the better prop. She spoke first.

'Michaela, is this about Nick again? I'm not going to tell anyone.'

'I know.'

She exhaled with so much frustration, she might as well have tapped her foot. Like I was taking up valuable time.

'I just want to know—'

'I don't have anything else to tell you.'

The wine loosened the link between thought and words. I spoke quickly. 'I have to know: why didn't you ask me?'

'What?'

'If you were never going to use our real names anyway, you could have just asked me. Before you used my story.'

She straightened up and flicked the end of her cigarette. With a toss of her head that settled in a posture of defiance—chin up, cheekbones to the light—she said, 'You never replied to my email.'

The email was still in my inbox and my unsent reply still in drafts.

I am hoping to write an article on the topic of the toxic culture
at the residential colleges . . . I was wondering if you would have
any interest in being interviewed . . .

I shook my head and expressed myself with an exasperated little gasp. For a moment, I wasn't capable of words, only these frustrated, strangled sounds. To suggest that the email sent, in her own words, in her *capacity as a reporter* was her only line of communication with me, when all we did, for months, was talk and talk: in person; online; on the phone . . . I couldn't speak. And when I did, I ignored the email, as I had done ever since I first received it.

'Then you could have made it up,' I said. 'Why didn't you just, like, use your imagination?'

At last, the reaction I'd been seeking, for weeks now, appeared. Her face formed a wounded scowl, and for the first time, I saw that she was capable of ugliness. There was something about the contrast between her natural beauty and the expression she was contorting, that thrilled me.

Encouraged, I pushed on. 'Or did you? Did you make parts of it up?'

She was faltering, her mouth moving, unable to articulate herself in words.

My laugh was manic, but I couldn't stop. 'Is that all you could come up with? It's a pretty poor effort.'

She shrank, like she knew what was coming. The shame I had felt for months—at being someone she used, not someone she loved—the shame that reached a crescendo with that mocking revelation: *I was there*—the shame that had so suffocated me, now spoke for me.

I looked her right in the eyes and said, without venom, just like it was a statement of fact: 'Stupid bitch.'

I turned, and headed back to the house before I could see her reaction.

I found Balthazar in the backyard, smoking on a crate and telling a girl he'd just met that he knew, from the moment he clapped eyes on her, that she was a Taurus.

He stood when he saw me, knocking over the crate.

'I called her a stupid bitch.'

With strength I didn't know he had, he picked me up and swung me in a hug.

I felt, I think, a little proud.

———

MY FRIENDSHIP WITH Eve, I was slowly understanding, had never been a friendship at all. I tried to approach my memories like Paul, or even Eve, would.

What is a friendship? I asked myself. If I were to write an essay about it, I thought, then this would be the thesis statement:

Companionship and all that it entails (sharing the other person's company; having things in common; liking the other person) is a necessary but not sufficient condition for friendship. Love, however, and all that it entails (trust; being seen) is. In this essay I will . . .

I told this to Balthazar, who said I was such a wanker, he queried whether I deserved friendship. But he said it in such an affectionate way—as sympathetic to my pain as he was intolerant of my self-indulgence—he made me feel loved, rather than undermined.

So I came to think, and I still think, that Eve took my story because it was a good story. That was reason enough. There was enough specificity, enough quirky detail—kernels of truth—to make it real for her audience. Which is why, of all the accusations

I levelled at her in all the arguments we ever had, the one that hurt the most—or, at least, produced that peculiar ugliness—was the claim that she lacked imagination.

Thinking about friendship, in this abstract, methodical way, I found myself, many times, back in Balthazar's room. *Pretty far out in the ocean*, he had called me. Because I resolved to be less distant—more immediate, more expressive, more whatever the opposite of distant was—I emailed Paul. I thought I would try, for once, to let him see me: fully, vulnerably. And I thought I might see myself differently, which, it seemed, could only be a good thing.

> Hi Paul,
> I know this is totally inappropriate, and selfish even, but I wanted you to know that while we were together, I was in love with you a bit.
> I've never been in love before, so I'll just explain the way this feeling manifested, and you can decide for yourself whether the term is descriptively accurate.
> I wanted to be around you all the time. My appetite for your company was insatiable. One time, when you were in the shower, I folded your underwear for you and put it on the bed. Then I decided I was crazy, and put it on the floor again. When I was alone, I would list all the nice things you'd ever said to me, and smile to myself like an idiot.
> I don't know why I'm sending you this, and I really don't want you showing it to Violet. I know that's a big ask, when this is obviously a transgression on your relationship, and can only be cured by letting her in on it. But I would just hate it more than anything if I became a personal joke between you and her. Please, let this be ours.
> I hope this email explains why our coffee the other day was so tense.
> I'll see you around.
>
> Michaela

I did not read over my draft until after I had sent it. The words came naturally, and reading it back, I was struck by their clarity. It was fitting, I thought, to say goodbye to Paul in a long, fluid email rather than the frigid silence of a read-receipt on a text. Because all Paul and I ever did, really, was talk. Indeed, the talking, as I have reflected many times since, was always better than the sex. It was more sensual, more spiritual, more like the touching of soul to soul, the giving of the self, that transcendent sex is supposed to be. When Paul and I talked we were like dancers, keeping time with each other, moving through muscle memory and instinct and, above all, trust—trust in each other's abilities.

Email was also a more fitting medium than text. At the time, I liked the symmetry: that our first mode of contact might be our last. I sent it via my university account, to his. A therapist, or any first year psychology student, might have told me that I did this to punish him. While we were sleeping together, we had been meticulous about ensuring that no communication between us was visible to the university. By sending him an email—by putting our relationship in writing, and on the university server—I was exposing him.

I do not remember if this was my intention at the time, or if I was conscious of the possibility, but afterwards, I would always recall the email, and describe the particular thrill of pressing send, with a giddy sense of victory.

—

I DID NOT see or hear from Paul after that. Not until I attended my graduation ceremony, and even then I only saw him from across a crowded hall, robed almost to anonymity.

That was also, incidentally, the next time I saw Eve. After that first lecture, and our conversation in the Quad, I considered dropping the course. But she did not come back. It was an aesthetics subject, about the intersection of art and ethics. As someone who told stories that sparked sweeping cultural changes in notoriously conservative institutions, perhaps she considered herself an expert on the topic.

So it was not until I graduated from my philosophy degree, with my mother by my side, that I realised Eve had dropped out of philosophy entirely. Several arts degrees were graduating in the same ceremony. When Eve's name was announced, and she ascended the stage to shake the chancellor's hand, she was awarded a degree in cultural studies.

Eve had always been snobby about philosophy. In our first year, she had told me it was the most 'legitimate' of the humanities. I asked her how she measured legitimacy. *Social utility*, she said.

So I repeated past mistakes, and I interpreted her degree change as part of a larger narrative: one involving me. Perhaps, I thought, she was trying to avoid me. At the very least, I might have been a factor. The thought that I might make her uncomfortable—that I might make her feel anything at all—warmed me.

On that day, when we were both awarded our degrees, I was careful to avoid her gaze. The Great Hall was cavernous, and awash with black robes, so the venue lent itself to blanking as much as it did to congregating.

Holding my piece of paper, with my cap and gown, my happiness rose until it matched my mother's. She took many photos, and gave me a card congratulating me on my success.

'It's not enough to succeed. Others must fail,' I told her. She laughed. I said it as a joke, but if it was funny, it was only because we knew it to be true.

EPILOGUE

PLACES, LIKE PEOPLE, change even while they stay the same. Returning to Fairfax all these years later, my younger self stalks me, like a shadow. No longer a residential college, it now operates as a kind of function centre. Professionals attending conferences sleep off their jetlag in the main building, and the dining hall tables are covered in gift bags and nametags.

Today, I am here for a book launch, and the faces that congregate in the entrance hall are foreign to me. But the wood-panelled walls and high white ceilings are so achingly familiar, so laced with associations, that I cannot help but look at the building through eighteen-year-old eyes. There the courtyard, where we stretched out our lunch breaks, intermittently talking and scrolling on our phones, jacaranda flowers browning in the grass at our feet. There the gap between two high-backed chairs—the distance Eve leaned to whisper in my ear. There the windows where I sat and sighed clouds of smoke into the early morning, sobered by the mistaken thought that these might be the best days of my life.

In the main hall, we take our seats. The crowd is mostly women—devotees of an in-vogue female author. With their upturned, expectant faces, they look just like the students who used to populate these halls.

I still see those students every now and then. But when we moved out of Fairfax and the boys out of St Thomas', it became clear that for many of them all we had in common was coincidence of time and place. That coincidence dragged out for a few years—into share houses and drunken weekend nights. For some of them, the boys in particular, it will drag on and on, all the way up into boardrooms and private school parents' associations. For me, I found I slipped out of their circle so naturally that I didn't even notice. Not until I went to the pub on the fifth anniversary of Nick's death and realised that—with the exception of Claudia and Emily—I had not one single thing to say to anybody present.

I listened to Sackers tell me about how long the hours were at his investment banking job and reflected that he was tracking well for the affairs and mid-life crises I'd predicted all those years ago. At one time, I might have thought this with a superior sort of smirk. Sipping my beer, listening to him drone on, his fluffy hair conforming to a short-sided, long-topped cut, I just found the thought depressing.

—

SPEECHES BEGIN, AND the crowd is quiet. The interviewer's dress style is self-consciously literary, or (which is to say the same thing) inoffensively quirky: long necklace; a bold, expensive print. The author, she says, 'needs no introduction'. The author laughs to acknowledge the compliment—her head lowered, fringe obscuring her eyes, suggesting the compliment makes her uncomfortable, but only because she is humble, not because it is untrue. The audience laughs with her, and when she speaks, the silence is one of reverent awe.

Eve is as articulate as ever—her hands and her face eloquent; her words beautiful. I notice her nails are manicured and painted a dark forest green. She is wearing a blood orange silk top, which ripples, underlining her points. The crowd laughs, and then, suddenly serious, nods. Then gasps. I watch these undulations with detached fascination. Eve cannot perform to me the way she does to them. I hover beyond time, somewhere behind the veil that separates strangers—on the side that shares history and memories. And Eve on stage is not just the graceful, billowy-sleeved creature she is for them. She is also the Eve of her past: the girl who sat on that very same stage, before a crowd of strangers, and writhed and moaned and declared proudly: *I just came.*

And now she has come back, in a new state of ecstasy—not of challenge, but of triumph. When the interviewer asks her, 'What's it like to be back in Fairfax and see it so changed?', she replies, with a laugh that echoes throughout the audience: 'It's about fucking time.'

She is here—we are here—to discuss her memoir of her time at Fairfax. That her name is larger than the title on the book's cover says everything about her success in the intervening years. Much has been made of the memoir in the media. Of course, I read everything. For example, I know already that it opens at the beginning, with the story that made her famous—my story. I know, therefore, that I am unwritten.

Balth, who has only ever given me excellent advice, told me not to come today. I told him I derived a sick, self-flagellating pleasure from watching Eve succeed. 'It's my kink,' I said.

No matter how hard I try, I cannot unstitch myself from Eve— any more than I can unstitch Eve, who sits on the stage as if on a throne, from the girl who sat there at twenty. Her successes seem to illuminate my failures; her career; her fame. The very fact of my obsession is an exercise in failure—to care so much, when Eve doesn't care at all; to centre her in my life, while I remain a closed chapter in hers. 'What does it say about me,' I asked Balth, 'that the person I cannot forgive, whose success I most resent, is another woman?'

He told me, as he often does, that I was being indulgently analytical. 'Women are people too, Michaela. And some people are cows.'

—

THE INTERVIEW CONCLUDES with loud applause, and excited whispers about how Eve has either met or exceeded the crowd's high expectations. The admiration is universal. Even I admire her. Indeed, my admiration is a complicating factor. She has, objectively, done good in the world. That this fact can coexist with my hurt—the *use* of me, not as a person, an end in herself, but as a *tool* for Eve's goodness—only hurts me more.

Which is why, when I join the line for a book signing, it is with a sense of purpose. The line moves slowly. The women in front of me flick through their fresh copies. I read the endorsements on the back cover; words I've read several times online, and could probably recite from memory.

When I approach the front of the line, my mouth is dry, and the voice inside my head louder than Eve's. Pen in hand, not looking up, she has to repeat the question.

'Whom should I address it to?'

'Michaela.'

'Michaela . . . ?'

Our eyes meet. In the moment before Eve locates a smile, I see panic flick across her eyes and lips.

I don't say anything. I hold her gaze, demanding that she look at me—a person who exists; who is real; just as real as she is.

Then, under my unbroken gaze, she picks up a pen, bows her head, and writes my name. *For Michaela,* she writes. And nothing else.

What happens next is better than an apology. She takes the book—the book that contains my story, and now also my name—and she gives it back to me.

ACKNOWLEDGEMENTS

MY THANKS FIRST to my family for their endless support: to Karen Reid, Peter Reid, and Maureen Ryan.

To my publisher Robert Watkins, for championing me, and to James Kellow and the whole team at Ultimo for your tireless work, and for allowing me to play a part in the beginning of your new press. It has been a privilege. To Ali Lavau and Rebecca Hamilton for your wise comments—the text is much better for both of you.

To my agent, Fiona Inglis, and everyone at Curtis Brown—especially Benjamin Paz—for believing in me from the outset, and for all your work every step of the way.

To my very first readers, Tom Davidson McLeod, Rex Dupain and Patrick Hall, without whose encouragement, comments, and faith, this book would still be a Word document on my desktop.

To Kate Dennis and Ruth Ritchie, for your generosity and enthusiasm; for seeing the potential in me and in this book, and to Ruth, in particular, for your faultless advice.

And finally, in addition to the friends mentioned above, to all my friends for all the conversations over the years. Whether they were about *Love & Virtue* or had nothing to do with it, they have shaped me and how I see the world, and they are all somewhere in this novel. In particular, I am very grateful to: Maddy Connolly, Luca Moretti, Laura Parmegiani, William Ryan, and, most of all, Patrick Still.